the Confessions of X

A NOVEL

SUZANNE M. WOLFE

THOMAS NELSON
Since 1798

© 2016 Suzanne M. Wolfe

All rights reserved. No portion of this book may be reproduced, stored in a retrieval system, or transmitted in any form or by any means—electronic, mechanical, photocopy, recording, scanning, or other—except for brief quotations in critical reviews or articles, without the prior written permission of the publisher.

Published in Nashville, Tennessee, by Thomas Nelson. Thomas Nelson is a registered trademark of HarperCollins Christian Publishing, Inc.

Thomas Nelson titles may be purchased in bulk for educational, business, fund-raising, or sales promotional use. For information, please e-mail SpecialMarkets@ThomasNelson.com.

Publisher's Note: This novel is a work of fiction. Names, characters, places, and incidents are either products of the author's imagination or used fictitiously. All characters are fictional, and any similarity to people living or dead is purely coincidental.

Library of Congress Cataloging-in-Publication Data

Wolfe, Suzanne M.
The confessions of X : a novel / Suzanne M. Wolfe.
pages ; cm
Summary: "Before he became a father of the Christian Church, Augustine of Hippo loved a woman whose name has been lost to history. This is her story. She met Augustine in Carthage when she was seventeen. She was the poor daughter of a mosaic-layer; he was a promising student and with a great career in the Roman Empire ahead of him. His brilliance and passion intoxicated her, but his social class would be forever beyond her reach. She became his concubine, and by the time he was forced to leave her, she was thirty years old and the mother of his son. And his *Confessions* show us that he never forgot her. She was the only woman he ever loved. In a society in which classes rarely mingled on equal terms, and an unwed mother could lose her son to the burgeoning career of her ambitious lover, this anonymous woman was a first-hand witness to Augustine of Hippo's anguished spiritual journey from religious cultist to the celebrated Christian saint and thinker. A reflection of what it means to love and lose, this novel paints a gripping and raw portrait of ancient culture, appealing to historical fiction fans while deftly exploring one woman's search for identity and happiness within very limited circumstances"-- Provided by publisher.
ISBN 978-0-7180-3961-5 (paperback)
1. Augustine, Saint, Bishop of Hippo--Fiction. 2. Christian saints--Fiction. I. Title.
PS3573.O5266C66 2016
813'.54--dc23
2015029203

Printed in the United States of America

15 16 17 18 19 20 RRD 6 5 4 3 2 1

STOUGHTON PUBLIC LIBRARY
STOUGHTON, MA 02072

Acclaim for *The Confessions of X*

"Suzanne Wolfe gives us, in *The Confessions of X*, the absolutely compelling story of the mysterious unnamed woman with whom Augustine spent so many formative years of his life. This is a beautiful and worthy book."

—Brett Lott, *New York Times* bestselling author of *Jewel* and *A Song I Knew by Heart*

"I hope your whole afternoon is free: you are likely to read this absorbing—truly *engrossing*—novel in a single sitting. And after you close *The Confessions of X*, you are likely to pick up Augustine's *Confessions*, whether for a first or fifteenth read."

—Lauren Winner, author of *Girl Meets God* and *Still*

"Saying I love Suzanne Wolfe's new novel is like saying there are waves in the ocean. It totally transported me. I have lived a complete life as the concubine of a Saint."

—River Jordan, author of *Saints in Limbo* and *The Miracle of Mercy Land*

STOUGHTON PUBLIC LIBRARY
DISCARDED

"A gorgeous, poignant story—a journey both in time and to the soul. Wolfe's writing is evocative, her research immaculate. I am a fan."

—Tosca Lee, *New York Times* bestselling author of *Sheba*, *Iscariot*, *Demon*, and *Havah: The Story of Eve*

"Writing in glorious detail, Wolfe brings to life a woman 'lost to history,' and in so doing animates the full, profound, thrilling world she inhabited, and the aching knot of love and faith that sustains, undoes, and ultimately uplifts her."

—Erin McGraw, author of *The Seamstress of Hollywood Boulevard*

"*The Confessions of X* propels this story into a fresh understanding of the conflicts warring in the life of the saint and Bishop of Hippo."

—Luci Shaw, author of *The Thumbprint in the Clay* and *The Generosity—New and Selected Poems*

"*The Confessions of X* is a masterpiece of historical fiction. With beautiful descriptions, well defined characters and thorough research, Suzanne M. Wolfe makes the ancient city of Carthage rise up from the pages. Wolfe transforms a sliver of history into a remarkable story of forbidden love, unfathomable sacrifice and redemption of the human spirit. *The Confessions of X* is one of my favorite novels of the year."

—MichaelMorris,awardwinningauthor of *Man in the Blue Moon, Slow Way Home*, and *A Place Called Wiregrass*

For Greg

"There is no saint without a past . . ."

—St. Augustine of Hippo

CHAPTER 1

There is a well in the courtyard where I sit that is not yet dry and at daybreak a young man in a dark tunic comes to draw water. One by one he fills earthen pots with the bucket he hauls again and again and again until the ground blooms dark beneath the well and water runs along the gullies between the stones where thirsty dogs lap it up. When he stoops his neck shows white below the hairline, tender like the milky stems of new grass in spring, his eyes brown and liquid like a doe's. He sets the smallest vessel brimful beside me with a piece of flatbread he takes from a sack.

"Here, Mother," he says. "May your prayers be heard."

I do not speak to him with my tongue but my eyes speak. They say: "I thank you, you who could be the son of my son's son. As for my prayers, there is no one left to hear."

Long ago in Rome I saw a woman so ancient of flesh that she was kneaded and furrowed like God making the world. She was earth, root, and stone, and the shadows of the buildings of men fell across the square in silent homage. I have become that woman, and the people in the courtyard do not jostle me, although it is crowded, but leave a circle around me as if I were charmed or cursed. They think I am wise because I am old past counting and all those who knew me are dead or dying. I would tell them that if it is wise to have lived so long, to have borne so much desolation and not to have died of it, then I am wise indeed.

When the people in the courtyard ask me what they must do in such times, I am silent; when they ask where God has gone, I am silent; when they show me the bloated bellies of their children, I look away. They think endurance is wisdom and perhaps that is so, but it is not the wisdom of men but of women, for though we live longer, history does not remember us and so we are a mystery to each generation.

Now that the city of Hippo Regius is besieged, the people whisper that the world is ending, that the clouds will part, and the Christos will descend to scourge the city of men and lead the blessed to the city of God. But first the barbarians from across the sea, the Vandal hordes, a plague of locusts swarming the land, consume our orchards, our crops, our vines, our livestock, all growing things under the sun until there is nothing but the barren husk rattling in the wind and the emptiness of children's eyes. They smote our bishop and he will die and his flock will be scattered. His death will be the beginning of the end of all things.

On the long journey of my life I have seen many beginnings and many endings. I have seen many deaths, and sometimes the living die and sometimes the dead live on and it is difficult to tell the difference. My son died young and I died with him, yet I breathe. His father lives, yet he also died forty years ago on that day in spring when the air was filled with blood and the world tilting forever beneath my feet.

I have come to this place to sit beneath the pear tree he planted to remind him who he is. My garments against the trunk are blackness upon blackness and perhaps, if he looked, he would see the shadow of his heart and would know, irrevocably and for all time, he is that same man though more than sixty years have passed. And so I have come, to rest here against this tree, the tree he planted against the day of his judgment, to see if what he said was true when he wrote, "It was not the pears my unhappy soul desired. For no sooner had I picked them than I threw them down and tasted nothing in them but my own sin."

Each day we gather in the courtyard of the church outside his window. Many come and the sound of their prayers is sometimes like the thrumming of bees deep within the hive in winter and sometimes like the cry of an animal in the dark. Its ebb and flow sets the leaves shaking and the shadows dancing until it is hard to know what is sorrow and what is joy, what is greeting, what is farewell. Such has been the sound of my life as it has passed along the wide corridors of time to this moment, here in this place, where I will once more look upon his face.

Now the church bell is ringing and soon the chanting of the faithful will rise like smoke from the campfires of the enemy outside the city walls and hope and fear will again contend in the souls of men. Their prayers for him and for their own deliverance are spoken in the same breath and none can tell which is which, save God. Thus the desires of our hearts knot and twist until we cannot discern the one from the other, neither seek to know, and so we weave the tapestry of our lives and wonder at the pictures we make.

An old dog makes his home in the courtyard and lies beside me when the shadows shrink to knives against the walls. He is the only one who does not fear me, his breath ragged, intermittent, his ribs fretted with want, abandoned by his master in the exodus as I myself was abandoned. My hand rests on his head like a blessing as I feed him bread, piece by piece, for he has few teeth and those carious; the crusts he mumbles wetly in my palm. He reminds me of Torch, too old now to be much use on the farm except to lie in the sun and dream.

Once I had my fill of touch, skin smooth and languid against my flesh, my body falling, falling, the smash of it, then darkness and a slow returning. Later, my arms drawing him down once more, the rush of our meeting a vortex and a roar.

Then the sweetness of my son's limbs, brown, creased, firm as figs ripe for eating, his body slippery as I bathed him, then sheeny with oil as he lay kicking before the fire, his hands clutching the air as if to catch up the stars. Never have I loved with such rapture, that tiny body bequeathed me out of blood, a long laboring through the night and then the day coming and with it, you, my son.

Memory for the old is not solace but a terror and those with clouded minds are God's favorites. I remember your hair springing strong and silky as young wheat between my fingers as I kissed your forehead on the day I left. My little son whose hands I still feel fisting my skirts in the marketplace, shy of the skitter of mules, the bully of legs crowding the stalls, the shouts of sellers, hands now blunted and veined as your grandfather's, my father's, a laborer's hands wearing an iron citizen's ring as you lead me through the street, I your child, you the parent. I have it still, this ring that once encircled your finger, that once was warmed by your flesh, and have worn it on a chain against my heart these forty years.

And afterwards, after the parting, your letters so brave, your pain ducking and peering behind the lists of days, books, hymns, lessons like a child playing hide-and-go-seek, until the sudden finding, the wail, "Oh, Mama, I miss you!" Then that last perfect summer we spent together as if the world and you in it would be forever golden and ripe with promise even as the vines and orchards grew heavy, the grain swelled on its stalk, all things living delighting in plenitude.

Then the news that you were gone. I never saw you dead but the picture of you upon your bier plays ceaselessly before my eyes.

Oh, my son.

Once he said that memory is a longing, that the pictures we make in our minds are the soul's remembrance of the place where God dwells in immutable light. I have found that place and it is a lonely house, a place for kites and jackals, a fit dwelling for the God who stayed the knife of Abraham but would not spare my son.

Many and many are the times I have watched you sleep, my son, and never was sleep so still, so absolute, as this your long last dreaming. The goneness of you is an ache in my bones on a winter's night with the wind blowing cold and desolate off the mountains, my heart a hovel fallen in upon itself, the sky a mocking eye.

Gift we named you, so blindly bestowed. Adeodatus. Given by God. Iatanbaal in my mother's Punic tongue. And I a month short of my seventeenth year. My body was a woman's, my heart a girl's, and my womb was stunned by its swelling, its stirring a burden that would not let me rest. When, after all that anguish, I reached down and touched the rounded orb of you, a new world crowning and crowned, it was another birth entire, my own, this strange anointing above the lintel of my soul.

Long ago he said that when something is lost to us, its image is retained within us until we find it again. Crippled by the loss of it, the memory demands that the missing part should be restored. This I believe.

We are, he and I, as if never parted yet we have been as distant as the stars that roll in darkness and never meet.

CHAPTER 2

My mother died birthing me and when the wise-woman showed me to my father saying, "A girl-child"—eyes averted, voice ashamed—he took me in his arms and held me tight to still my wailing, for he loved my mother and I was her remnant. She was Punic, from the tribe of the Imazighen, the free people, ancestors of the Phoenicians who crossed the seas to Africa and settled on these northern shores, and from her I got my light skin and green eyes. He was a poor man, my father, an itinerant mosaic-layer, often drunk but never violent or unkind, his love for me a lame and faithful dog that followed upon the roads we trod from job to job and curled beside me when I slept, the heavens a spangled canopy, the ground, oftentimes, our bed.

I was wet-nursed and weaned in Carthage at my father's sister's house. My father began to take me with him on his travels when I turned four, curled like a mouse in a nest of cloaks he made for me in the cart when I was weary, skipping at his feet or, best of all, riding on his shoulders, for he was a young man then, his back not yet bowed from bending to his craft.

I first remember colors though I could not name them. The

clip and clink of tiles gritting my fingers, these my first playthings tumbled in gaudy heaps in the marketplace of Carthage or piled on the ground at work sites. Slate, basalt, marble, veined with blue and red and green as if lapidary spiders had spun fantastic webs within—these I sorted when I got older and laid in baskets my father heaved onto the cart pulled by our patient mule, tramping the countryside, a shabby legion of three.

I was his apprentice, he often boasted, as good if not better than any lad. He would wink at me when he said this and the other craftsmen would laugh. Many of them had daughters at home, and I could tell by the way they would look at me that they missed them sorely. Some had sons with them, learning the craft, much older than I, gangly youths who teased but tolerated me, for one of my tasks was to fetch water from the well when they were thirsty or needed it to mix mortar. Sometimes they gave me things, a necklace plaited out of flowers, a bird crudely carved from wood, to carry to a kitchen-girl or one of the lady's maids. I soon learned that if the girl accepted, I would receive pieces of honeycomb or perhaps an apple for my mule, but if the girl rejected the gift, the boy would be sullen and bad-tempered for the rest of the day and I knew to keep away.

They were given the heavy work, carrying baskets of fine rubble to be laid as the base of the mosaic, mixing mortar and then shoveling it over the stones as the second layer, the men smoothing it down with long trowels until it was even, checking constantly with a lead plumb line suspended from the apex of a triangular wooden frame laid flat. This was followed by another layer of mortar mixed with terra-cotta. Above this, the final layer of pure mortar was applied only by the craftsmen themselves when it came time to lay the tiles, and only in small areas, for the mortar had to be wet, the tiles laid swiftly and precisely before it dried. Each son would stand near his father, ready to supply him with fresh mortar, and tempers grew short if the mortar dried too fast and the next batch was not yet ready. I would scurry about with my bucket and dipper so that setting mortar could be dampened and made pliable again. My father had no boy to do this for him and did it himself. It made him slower than the rest but he was an artist of figures rather than of geometrical designs used in bordering—a much rarer skill—and the client never complained.

He called me Little Bird because my eyes were always bright and watchful, he said, my head cocked to one side as I squatted next to him. When he placed the first tile I would hold my breath, for this, to me, was the beginning of the magic.

"What is it going to be, Papa?" I would ask.

"Wait and see," he would say.

He would lay another tile beside the first and then another and another until, suddenly, as if sprung from the very earth itself, there appeared the delicate curve of a stem bending under the weight of its bell-like flower or the jagged points of a tiger's teeth or the rounded scales of a golden carp barely glimpsed beneath a gauzy, azure pool. I see him still, stooped, intent, laying whorls and lines until an image grew—bird, fish, tracery of frond or vine, worlds flowering piece by piece before my eyes, a miracle of making, the motion of his fingers deft, continuous.

"How do you do that?" I would ask.

"Ah, Little Bird," he would say. "It is the art of broken things."

I thought, then, that he was remembering my mother, and perhaps he was. But now that I have lived more than twice his lifespan, have picked through the shards of a broken life, fitting them to a pattern that, once set in time, I cannot change, I know that he was speaking of himself. Most rarely blessed by the gods with an eye for beauty and the gift of making, he had taken to drink in grief over my mother's death, and slowly, inexorably, his gift began to fail. Once held to be one of the finest mosaic makers in all of Africa Province, sought after by senators and noblemen to adorn their villas or the churches and temples they endowed, his fame dwindled, and before he died his hands trembled so he could barely lay a tile and the only work he found was in adorning the tombs of farmers and freed slaves. I know now that he kept me by him not only because he loved me but also because he knew he would not live to see me grown.

As I grew older, I was given more important tasks than fetching water. I would sit cross-legged before heaps of tiles and sort them into piles of similar colors, terra-cotta at first as these were cheaper than stone and it did not matter if I broke a few. Next I was entrusted with stone, slave-quarried from living rock and brought in ships from distant parts of the empire or in mule-trains from the southern mines. Sometimes, using a tiny hammer and chisel, I was allowed to chip little squares of tile from rods of terra-cotta, for it seemed that however big the heaps of tesserae awaiting the day's work, by noon each was gone and the workmen were shouting for more, the tic, tic, tic of the chisel's edge the sound of summer and my childhood passing.

When I was ten, my biggest and most important job was when

the mosaic was finished and had been allowed to dry, only a few hours in the fierce, dry heat of our African summer. Under the direction of my father who worked by my side, we scrubbed the tesserae with brushes dipped in sand and oil and then rubbed them with leather cloths, smoothing and burnishing until the whole floor shone, my father explaining that any roughness in the surface would catch on sandals, dislodge the tiles, and destroy the mosaic over time. Such polishing we do to our memories so they will not snag on our souls and cause us to stumble.

Thus in spring and summer my childhood was spent outdoors going from place to place, my father kneeling in bathhouses, churches, the atria of Romans to make pictures they would tread upon. And after the day's long labor, a settling round the fire, bats stitching the moon's white cloth above my head, the *chuck-chuck* of sleepy birds, the uplifted wineskin against the firelight, my father's swallow my lullaby.

"Sleep, Little Bird," he would say. "Sleep."

At the large estates of the wealthy we would turn from the road, toiling with weary hope up paths sentineled with poplars. Slaves in belted tunics bent in the fields, their children crouched doglike in the ruts, a shy wave or greeting called and we would know the master kind. Mute stares told us otherwise, the overseer's brute vigilance, his whip coiled snakelike at his belt. I'd take my father's hand and watch my feet lift up, set down, until we passed that grove of human shapes, my liberty a pain that made me gasp, the wings of a trapped bird beating in my chest.

Sometimes I glimpsed the *domina* on a balcony or terrace, stretched out upon a couch under a fringed canopy, pleated, draped, sandals tipped with gems, her bracelets clashing as she moved, jewels jouncing in her ears like Minerva come to earth, her maids reverent acolytes of grace. It seemed to me an Elysium unparalleled.

Slaves' and laborers' children were my playfellows on those summer days, a hooting rabble let loose in field and vineyard or squatting sphinxlike on muddied banks, braiding the current with nets we wove from reeds, the fish we sought silver-coined and lithe, some river god's teeming progeny. We vied with crows at harvest-time, arms aloft, flapping parodies of flight, mouths empurpled with the juice of grapes. Tearfully I fed the ducks and chickens outside the kitchen door and told them of their deaths, then watched with longing as the spits were turned before the fire.

CHAPTER 3

One house I remember in particular for there I made a friend, a boy a year older than I and the eldest son who did not scorn to play with laborers' brats. I did not know this dark-haired, barefoot boy, who first showed me a book and how to say the symbols figured there, an alphabet my mother's ancestors, the Phoenicians, had bequeathed to us, how to snare rabbits, and which berries were good to eat and which gave us a bellyache, would return to me when I was a woman to succor me when the world turned to night.

We arrived at an estate just as the rising sun cut through the poplars edging the road, striping the ground with shadow so it seemed we trod on steps. Slaves dressed in white were watering plants set in urns under the long, cool colonnade that fronted the house, the floor tiles winking in the sunlight like a thousand jewels, the trickle of water a reminder that my throat was dry from the parching dust of high summer, my feet gritty from the roads.

A dog was barking at the back of the house. When a foreman approached my father and they fell into conversation about the work he was to do, I set off in search of a well. I did not fear losing him, for he had told me that the job was large and would take many weeks, and I was used to shifting for myself in strange places while he worked.

The kitchen well I sought lay at the back of the house within a small courtyard surrounded on three sides by walls against which plum trees had been trained to grow, their branches wide like candelabra with tapers of heavy purple fruit. The scent of thyme and lavender thickened the air, and from within an open doorway came the sound of voices chatting, clattering pots, and someone's cheerful whistle.

The dog I had heard stuck a shaggy head out of the doorway and growled, his lips curling above yellow teeth, brindled fur erect along his back. I stopped dead in my tracks and looked down, knowing not to challenge him but keeping a wary eye on the door. A face appeared, saw me, and spoke sharply to the dog. He shook his head as if puzzled and then lay down with a great sigh, his chin resting on his paws, his eyes still fixed on me as if to say: I am not allowed to eat you . . . yet.

A bucket rested beside the well and in it floated a gourd for drinking. As I dipped and raised it to my lips, a boy darted from the kitchen and clipped my shoulder, sending icy water down my tunic. Furious, I picked up the bucket and dashed its contents in his face. He stood blinking through tendrils of hair that clung to his face like the seaweed my father fashioned in his pictures.

"I was going to the river," he said, "but it seems it's come to me." Then he spun on his heels and took off running. "Come, Naiad," he called over his shoulder. I followed, my thirst forgotten.

I found the boy wading in a stream, which to our childish eyes seemed as wide as a river. A small bird suddenly rose squawking and flapping from a hollow under the bank and the boy jumped. We looked at each other and laughed. In that moment we were friends.

"Look," he said, pointing to silver slivers flashing along the current wriggling around his toes like pondweed. "Minnows."

The water was cool, the mud at the bottom clouding our toes until we stood motionless, holding hands, to let it settle. I felt a tickling like when my father stroked a blade of grass over my feet when I was drowsing and did not want to wake. I wiggled my toes and the fish darted away.

"My name is Nebridius," he said, when we were sitting on the bank warming our numbed feet in the sun. "I will call you Naiad."

Naiad. Spirit of the river, the fountain, the stream. My first word in Greek, a language other than the Punic my father spoke or the Latin of the Roman landowners, my first word in that literature of bards and philosophers I would grow to love and would give me solace in the years to come. I repeated it carefully as if I held an unknown food in my mouth. It was Nebridius's first gift to me.

How could we know, he and I, in that faraway of our innocence, that water and the crossing of it would become an emblem of our devotion to another, the one who would take our love and then discard it when he found a greater? But that was far in the future, and those days of high summer passed as if each were a year, each moment an hour, so wholly did we live inside our bodies whose only pain was thirst or hunger or weariness and those soon mended. Like rocks in a riverbed we stood in time, heedless of its flow, and did not dream that one day we would be swept into a current and carried to the shores of an unknown place.

For the first time I was invited as playfellow into the home of a rich landowner, Nebridius's father. At first his mother looked askance at my tunic with the braid coming loose around the hem, my tangled hair and dirty face and feet, until she discovered that she and her maids could spend endless hours cleaning me up and dressing me in the softest and most brightly hued clothes I had ever worn. Nebridius would lie on his stomach on the rugs at his mother's feet in her boudoir, his chin cupped in his hands, and watch this transformation with a mock adoring face that made me giggle until I was bade hold still.

I think his mother longed to have a daughter and I was her substitute for a time, a doll to dress and bathe and adorn with trinkets from her jewel box. I gave myself up to her ministrations with a tiny inward swoon, for her hands were gentle, her voice soft, and I had never before been mothered.

The luxury of that house dazzled me and made my senses quiver: couches piled with cushions so that to lie on them was to drown, the softness of the rugs beneath my feet, which before had trod only earth and stone. She kept perfumes in tiny glass vials, which she let me smell one by one—spikenard, myrrh, balsam, sandalwood, cinnamon, oil of crocus—if I was careful and replaced the stoppers tightly, for each cost more than an Arabian stallion, she told me, saddled with Spanish leather tooled in gold. All my life since, a fugitive waft from the perfume-maker's stall in the market or the drifting veils of senators' wives carried in their litters by ebony slaves would transport me back to that room where I first learned what beauty was and why sculptors give it female form.

Best of all, there was a burnished silver mirror that showed me for the first time what I looked like. I stared transfixed at the bleary image of a girl whom I had only glimpsed before in water that scattered into a thousand shimmers when I bent to see more closely. Now I saw that my nose was small, my eyes large, and my hair a dark cloud about my head.

In the mornings Nebridius was closeted with a tutor, an elderly Greek with mild, watery eyes and a wispy beard, who made him memorize and recite aloud endless reams of what Nebridius later told me were Greek authors—Homer, Aeschylus, Euripides—and the Roman lawyer and rhetorician, Cicero. Later in life I would read all these authors for myself, but then the names sounded strange and exotic except for Cicero's name, which made me giggle. It meant "chickpea," a nickname he had been given because of the shape of his nose, Nebridius told me with much hilarity. In honor of our first meeting, he dubbed himself "Nereus" meaning "wet one"—Greek for god of the sea. For the rest of our lives, when we wrote to one another or talked in private, I would call him "Nereus" and he would call me "Naiad."

Despite our friendship, forged by our loneliness and an innocence that did not make distinctions of rank or sex, I could not help but notice, for the first time in my short life, how much distance there was between Nebridius's life and mine. As a male child and heir to a rich father, he was taught his letters and numerals, had never known hunger or cold or uncertainty, and consequently possessed an air of confidence that derived from knowing his future place in the world. As an unlettered girl, the daughter of a craftsman, who lived hand to mouth when work was available, I was beginning to realize that I would have a very different path in life.

I sometimes overheard Nebridius's mother speaking to her maids about how, as I was poor and not a Roman citizen, I would have to rely on my looks to get a husband as I would, sadly, have no dowry. Whenever she made these comments she would be especially solicitous of me and give me sweetmeats and lengths of embroidered ribbon. When I asked Nebridius what a dowry was, he told me that it was gold or land the betrothed girl brought to her husband. How good a husband depended on how much gold and land.

"You mean he buys a wife?" I said.

Nebridius frowned. "I suppose so," he said.

"And your father will buy you a wife?"

He shrugged. We were lying side by side on the riverbank chewing on grass stalks. A breeze stirred the leaves in the trees over our heads, but it was still and hot and airless where we lay. He sat up and put his chin on his knees.

"Not for a long time yet," he said. "I'm not interested in girls. They're silly."

"I'm a girl."

"You are different."

When the days grew shorter and cold clenched tight around the campfire, my father and I turned our faces back to Carthage, I weeping to be parted from my friend.

"In the spring," I called as he stood waving at the gate. "I will come back in the spring."

But five years were to pass until I saw him again and by then we were no longer children.

CHAPTER 4

Each time we returned, my father's sister in the city, a potter's wife, bitter from the barrenness of her womb though she was a Christian, clicked her tongue with horror at my state.

"She's wild," she said and set to taming me, each winter's task, with ungentle hands that yanked the comb through the knots in my hair until I howled. My hair was washed and braided tight against my neck, my feet were shod; I learned the woman's arts and went to church although my father was a pagan and raised me to honor the gods. My father, meantime, would be gone for days, returning shuffling, heavy-limbed, my aunt's scolding the unheeded accompaniment to my joy.

"Take me where you go," I begged.

And when the air blew balmy and kind across the sea, the rains ceased falling and all the world lay greening, I forgot my coffined life and grew brown again under the sun. We did not return to the estate where I first met Nebridius despite my entreaties, for my father drank away his earnings and we had to go wherever there was work. We walked now, our mule and cart sold against my father's debts, for he would gamble when he was in his cups, trying vainly to make amends for our increasing poverty.

In the winter of my twelfth year, two years after meeting Nebridius, I began to bleed, a thing neither my father nor my aunt had told me of. In my childishness I thought that I was dying and with the wisdom of innocence I was not wrong, for my childhood died that day. Hiding the rags I stuffed between my thighs, I sensed betrayal, my nipples flowering buds, my belly curving, a changing I could not stop, the marketplace and street a strange and awful disrobing before the beast-like eyes of men. One night, my aunt confronted her brother.

"She's child no more," she said. "Come spring, she stays."

Between us lay a lamp, the flame twinned in my father's eyes. Closing them, he put out the light as if a door had closed, and surrendered me without a fight to the world of women. The next day after the evening meal when we were sitting around the kitchen table, my aunt announced to my father that if I were to become a proper lady and not a savage I would have to have my ears pierced. She took a bone needle and a piece of cork from her pocket and rose from her stool.

I scrambled to my feet, placing both hands over my ears. "Papa," I implored.

I expected him to forbid it, to tell my aunt that I was not like other girls who cared only for ornaments and finery, that I was his help and his companion and what use were earrings when we were traveling the countryside looking for work, that the ears of infant girls were pierced when they were too young to know or to remember but that I would suffer cruelly. But he remained silent, his eyes fixed on his beaker, which he turned and turned again in his hands. My aunt signaled my uncle to take hold of my head between his hands and hold it still. I screamed as the needle passed through each ear and copper wire was threaded through the holes to keep them open, but the pain of it did not burn more hotly than the silence of my father. When it was over I fled the room and flung myself on my bed. I did not weep but clenched my eyes shut to block out the sight of my father's face. Even the throbbing of my ears, the blood that ran down my neck onto the pillow, was as nothing compared to the pain in my heart. Presently, I heard my father come to the foot of my bed.

"Little Bird," he said.

I did not look at him nor give any sign I knew he was there. Instead I murmured names I had heard my aunt call him—"Drunkard," "Fool," "Unbeliever"—over and over, each word a stab more cruel than those that had punctured my flesh. After a while he went away and I gave myself up to weeping. The next day I found a pair of silver earrings lying on my pillow, each a cluster of tiny silver stars suspended from a crescent moon, and knew they were from my father.

I never wore them for him and when I did it was too late. Forgive me, oh, my father, as my son forgave me when I abandoned him in a foreign land and sailed away. Like you, I surrendered my child into another's hands and reasoned I did it only for his good.

My arms grew pale, my sandaled feet soft. Each spring I wept to see my father leave, humping his baskets down the street, a lonely shambling form swallowed up at last by a curve in the street. When he returned he looked older, more lined, his back more stooped, the blades of his cheekbones yoking his face, his soul in harness to the flesh. One day he took me with him to a house above a shop, a silversmith with wares that cast a moon-glow in the street, the same that had fashioned my earrings. The couple watched, the woman weeping, while he made a memorial for their child, tiny stones set for the smallest life, to place above her tomb.

"Say this," the husband said: "'Two years, four months, fifteen days, and nine hours she lived, Beloved One.'"

"And border it with birds," the mother said, "for we kept one in a cage and she loved to hear it sing."

He took a cough that winter and in the spring it had not abated. His eyes were sunken, fever-bright, his breathing labored as if he drew in water.

That autumn he did not return though a traveling tinker said he saw him at Hippo Regius when the pears were ripening on the trees. In the agora, the street, at the baths and temples and churches, I looked for him but no one gave me news. He was my first great disappearing and I mourned him, inconsolable, growing thin and listless until my aunt thought I would join him in the grave.

At fourteen my aunt began to talk of husbands, craftsmen's sons apprenticed to a trade, a strapping youth to give me babies, long aware of how my uncle's eyes tracked me when I moved, lingered on my breasts and thighs, a lazy, predatory look such as panthers give wild sows in the amphitheater. He had never paid me much heed before except to shove me if underfoot, shout to bring him wine, and complain I was a mouth he could ill afford to feed. I was frightened by this change.

From that time on I slept against a wall, a knife beneath my pillow; in daylight I lingered at the fountain with the women or walked the streets, a virgin seeking sanctuary in the churches of the One said to favor them. My aunt seldom complained that I was always gone. From the coldness with which she treated me, I knew she blamed me for her husband's lust. Only later when I was older and she was dead did I realize it was not I from which she recoiled but the shame of our mutual helplessness. Illiterate, unskilled, without even a child to prove her worth, my aunt must submit or else be cast off and starve. Unbeknownst to me, that very day she entered into marriage negotiations for my hand with a widower almost twice my age.

One day my aunt had gone to a birthing, leaving me alone with my uncle, and I wandered in the Christian quarter at daybreak and entered the church. Within it was cool and silent, the roof a firmament of stone. Windows high up threw spears of gold and where they touched the floor vermillion, green, and azure sprang up like flowers. At the four corners of the great floor the winged creatures of the evangelists kept watch—the angel of Matthew, Mark's lion, Luke's patient ox, the lordly eagle of John. It was these I came to see, the work of my father's hands, his astonishing, teeming imagination. More than any other place in Carthage, the church was my father's house, his monument, his memorial. It was where, once more, I was that small child who squatted at his side and marveled at his handiwork.

My only companion was an old woman standing near the altar, her veil a smoky gauze about her face, her knotted hands cupped before her breast as if to catch water from the heavens. I crouched beside a column to watch the play of light so that if I squinted just so, John's great eagle seemed to lift and hover, its wings beating dust motes in the air like chaff at threshing time. The church was quiet, the city's roar an animal kept at bay, the space around me hushed as if the place were dreaming, the muttered prayers of the old woman a kind of song. Then I heard voices. Two men talking.

"The light is pure essence," one voice said. A young man, serious.

"It's full of dust," another replied, laughing. Deep, a man's voice, but the way he spoke . . . I peered around the pillar, but they were backlit by light streaming through the doorway and I could not make out their faces.

"You're an Epicurean," the serious voice said.

"And you're a hopeless Platonist," replied the other. They scuffled briefly and then grew solemn when the old woman hissed, "Ssssh!"

I sat very still as they walked into the center of the church and faced the altar, their backs to me. Then the one whose voice I thought I knew turned slowly in a circle to look up at the roof and when he stopped and lowered his eyes he was looking straight at me.

"Nereus!" Jumping to my feet in a tangle of skirts, I ran to him and threw my arms around him, his body hard and strange, a man's body. But the scent of him, clean like pine or balsam, the scent of the woods in which we played, the scent of our childhood, was the same.

"Naiad? Is it you?" He held me at arm's length so he could see my face. "You have . . . changed." A frown appeared as he took in my woman's dress, my braided hair, and tinkling earrings. The last time he had seen me I had been wearing a short tunic with a frayed hem, my hair loose and hanging around my face, my body scrawny and flat-chested, whippy as a pealed switch.

"I have missed you," was all I could think to say. Since my father died I felt I had been in exile many years, had wandered the city streets alone in search of something precious. Now here before me stood the living bridge that joined the farther bank upon which my father stood with the nearer of my womanhood. I felt only joy at our reunion but my cheeks were wet with tears.

"I have missed you too."

He told me he was staying in his father's city house while he pursued his studies.

"More Chickpea?" I said, wiping my eyes.

And suddenly the shyness of two strangers meeting dissolved and we were laughing at the joke about Cicero, embracing, asking a thousand questions, interrupting each other as we used to do as children, finally managing to communicate in garbled form what we were both doing in Carthage.

His friend stood watching us. I think it was his silence that I noticed first, the way he held back and gave us space. I stole a glance at him: brown hair, brown eyes, light brown skin, and shadows about his chin and lip, all angles and planes like Nebridius's face, bone thickened into manhood beneath the flesh, the roundness of childhood utterly departed.

"Are you a student too?" I asked, although I knew the answer, for his hands were smooth, his fingernails trimmed, unlike my father's or my uncle's, whose hands were engrained with stone dust and clay that no amount of washing could erase.

"I am." He said it with a serious face but there was something of self-mockery in his tone as if he ridiculed himself. It was as incongruous as the expensive scroll stuck casually through his belt like a workman's tool.

"This is my friend, Augustine," Nebridius said. "We, too, have known each other since childhood."

Augustine gave a small ironic bow. "Are you here to pray?" he asked.

"No," I said. "I come to look at the mosaics."

Nebridius explained my father was a craftsman. "You remember the mosaics in our bathhouse in the country? He made them. My father says they are the best he ever saw."

I told him of my father's disappearance and how he must be dead.

"I'm sorry," Nebridius said and touched my hand.

"He used to bring me here when we were in the city and tell me that beauty is the gods' gift and without it we would die."

"Do you believe that?" Augustine asked.

"You ask a lot of questions."

He suddenly looked stricken. "Forgive me," he said. "It is a failing of mine."

But I thought of my father and how his hands created oceans and forests and all the creatures that lived therein and how living eyes still beheld his work though his were closed forever.

"Yes," I said. "I do believe it."

He looked at me a moment and then did something strange. He crouched and placed his hand palm-down on the mosaic floor. It was a kind of blessing.

"Come." Nebridius linked one arm through mine and the other through Augustine's and steered us both toward the door. We used to be the same height; now the top of my head came only to his shoulder.

As Nebridius's house lay on the hill overlooking the harbor, in the wealthy part of the city, we decided to go along the waterfront and then climb the steps up the hill.

The harbor was a huge half-circle, fronted with wharves and storehouses, storied monsters whose gaping mouths consumed the cargoes of endless ships: amphorae of Tuscan wine, Thracian silver, and pigments from the northern climes, all unloaded here, the holds regorging wine and wheat and olives bound for Rome.

Fugitive odors washed the air—spices, a hot waft of garlic and frying meat, crocus oil and animal fat, a costly unguent the highborn Roman ladies craved and paid for in gold.

"Over there is Rome," Augustine said, pointing north. He had not spoken since we left the church.

I looked where his finger pointed. The ocean stretched away into the distance, a plain of endlessness unto the farthest place I could imagine.

"I will go to Rome one day," Augustine said. "My mother prophesied I will be a famous teacher."

"An *august* teacher," Nebridius corrected.

Augustine grinned. "Her ambition for me *is* a bit obvious, I admit."

"What are you studying?" I asked.

"Nothing that interests me."

"Why do it then?"

"It's what my mother wants."

"But what do *you* want?" I asked.

"You ask a lot of questions," he said.

He had been standing in profile looking out at the ocean, now he turned to face me.

"But since you ask," he said, "I care for nothing but to love and be loved."

Then he threw back his head and laughed as if he knew he spoke the words of a cheap seducer. Nebridius joined in. But I did not laugh, for, deep down, that was what I wanted too.

CHAPTER 5

In the weeks that followed, we spent all our free time together walking in the city or sitting in the atrium of Nebridius's house under the shade of potted palms, whose wide-fingered leaves shielded us from the pitiless sun. In this green oasis at the heart of a city of stone, I listened to talk about the world, talk about books and poets and philosophers, talk about things of which I had no knowledge. For the first time, I understood that my ignorance of letters barred me from a world beautiful in a way that was different from the beauty my five senses could apprehend, that if books were word mosaics set down in sequence, I had been tasked with sorting tiles with my eyes closed.

When Nebridius had been closeted with his tutor as a boy, I had pitied him. It seemed a kind of imprisonment stuck inside while outside the sun shone bright and butterflies danced in the lilac. Now the strange words he had chanted as a boy, that he and Augustine spoke so easily as men, words like *essence, the soul's eye, light unchangeable,* were like notes of a melody half heard beneath the din of daily life, a snatch of song I first heard at my father's knee though in a different key, for my father was an artist who did not think of beauty with his mind so much as grasp it in his hands.

A kind of longing would grip me then and jumping up I would drift among the vines entwined about the pillars of the atrium, red hibiscus, orange roses, a clematis with great purple waxy flowers. There was a little yellow bird in a copper cage, and when I put my lips against the bars and made a soft clicking sound with my tongue against the roof of my mouth, it would make a sweet spider-silk of sound that floated and wavered on the air. The men's talk would cease then and when I turned I could swear the darkness in Augustine's eyes had fled and all was brilliance.

Mornings when Nebridius and Augustine were at their studies near the forum, I helped my aunt about the house. Then, snatching up a basket and a few coins, I would go to the market to buy food. As long as I returned well before sunset so she could prepare the evening meal, my aunt didn't care where I had been all afternoon. I welcomed her indifference, for, unlike other girls my age who daily carried heavy water jars on their heads or swept the steps or sat in doorways watching fractious siblings tussling in the street, I was relatively free.

One day I reached the forum at midday, a little later than usual. That morning my aunt had set me to scrubbing the kitchen floor and I had filled many buckets at the local fountain to sluice it down. By the time I was done, I was hot, dirty, and out of sorts.

The market stalls were much depleted when I arrived, the freshest produce snapped up long before, and so I was left to pick through baskets of too-soft figs, wizened grapes, stale bread, and wilting bunches of herbs. Only the fish were fresh for they were kept alive in buckets of sea water on the open bed of the fish-seller's cart and replenished by his sons whom he kept trotting up and down the hill to and from the harbor all day long. One of them, who looked about eighteen, thick in the chest and with heavily muscled arms from hauling fish all day, leered at me as I looked into each bucket vainly trying to remember what kind of fish my aunt had told me to buy. He stood too close and the smell of sweat and fish was overpowering. At last I pointed at a large silver fish with red gills.

"That one," I said.

The man scooped it up, grinning, and then suddenly swung it head first against the side of the cart with a sharp crack.

"Want me to gut it for you?" he asked, shoving the dead fish in my face.

"Want me to gut him for you?" a voice said.

I glanced round. Augustine was leaning against the cart cleaning his fingernails with the tip of his knife.

The young man stepped back, the fish still hanging from his hand, blood dripping from its mouth. "This your sister, then?" he asked, keeping his eyes on Augustine's knife as if I had suddenly become invisible.

Augustine just looked at him.

"How much?" I asked.

"It's on the house."

I held out my basket and the man laid the fish inside on a bed of herbs. I covered it with a cloth to keep off the flies.

Augustine and I left the market and wandered down the hill toward the harbor, drawn by the coolness blowing off the sea. The streets had emptied out, people gone home for the midday meal and to wait out the worst of the heat, and so it seemed the city was all our own, a kind of private kingdom and we its rulers. Augustine carried my basket and we walked side by side, close but not touching, the space between us not so much a void than a drawing in of breath before words are spoken. He told me Nebridius had been called away to deal with a land dispute on one of his family's farms a day's ride outside Carthage and would not be back until the next day. I glanced at him, surprised, for I knew Augustine had many other friends, patricians' sons like himself, who spent the afternoons drinking in the local wine bars near the forum.

"Watch your step," he said as I stumbled on an uneven paving stone, and when he put his hand out to steady me it burned.

The harbor was quiet, the sun refracting off the stone piers dazzling to the eye, blistering to the touch. The boats tied up against the jetties creaked on the slight swell, the slap of water against their hulls clearly audible, the occasional flapping of a rope a strangely peaceful percussion. In the taverns and bars that lined the quay, sailors and stevedores huddled on benches under faded awnings stretched on poles, elbows on the tables, beakers clutched in their hands, their eyes even at rest turned toward the sea.

With the coppers I saved on the fish, we bought olives and goat cheese wrapped in grape leaves and begged a clay jar from a stall owner which we filled from a fountain and swore to return. The girl smiled at Augustine and tossed her head so her earrings shimmered. She was small and pretty, her eyes outlined with charcoal like a cat's.

"Promise?" she said.

"On my honor," Augustine replied. She giggled and when we walked away I looked back over my shoulder and saw her watching us with her cat's eyes.

In search of shade we found a boat half-upturned on the beach and sat beneath it, our knees drawn up, the basket and the earthen jar between us. I took off my sandals and dabbled my toes in a tiny rock pool not yet drunk up by the thirsty sun. Lifting my face to the wind blowing off the ocean, I closed my eyes and when I opened them Augustine was looking at me.

"Here," he said, handing me the water jar.

I drank and wiped my mouth with the back of my hand.

"Now you," I said.

He drank and then placed the jar deep in the shade behind us to keep cool. We were silent looking out at the sea as we had done the first day we met. It was like being on the edge of the world.

"Tell me everything," Augustine said.

"About what?"

"About you."

And so I did, beginning with my childhood as far back as I could remember, about my father and his craft, what he taught me, how much he loved me and I him. My voice faltered then and I fell quiet.

"What are you thinking?" Augustine asked after a time.

I turned to look at him. "I chose that fish at the market because it looked like one my father once made. Each silver scale, the red line along the gills, all exactly the same. But the colors he used were not silver and red at all. He chose white and gray and yellow and black. I remember thinking: Those colors are all wrong; they will never work." I laughed. "But then it did," I said. "Work, I mean. It was completely right. When you stepped back and saw it from a distance, it was *alive*." An unexpected delight, the same as when I touched the miracle of that perfect fish with a child's finger to see if it would move, flamed up in me, and for a brief instant I saw my father walking toward me on the beach, his tablet of sketches looped through his belt bumping rhythmically against his hip.

"You are your father's daughter," Augustine said softly.

"Yes," I said. "Are you your father's son?"

He did not reply but leaning back picked up the water jar again and passed it to me, steadying its weight while I drank. I was thirsty after all that talk and drank again.

When I finished he stoppered it and set it down. "My father drinks and whores," he said. "And so, no, I sincerely hope I am not my father's son."

"I'm sorry," I said, touching his hand, which lay between us, palm up, in the sand. Briefly his fingers closed on mine and then let go.

I thought of my uncle and the misery of my aunt's life. "Your mother . . . ?" I trailed off, uncertain if this was something I had a right to ask.

"He thinks my mother doesn't know about his unfaithfulness," he said.

"Perhaps she loves him anyway?"

"Yes," he said. "Perhaps she does."

The sun had long since passed its zenith and was sinking in the west when I realized with a start that I had promised my aunt to return before sunset.

"I must go," I said, fumbling with my sandal straps.

We returned the water jar and Augustine walked me home through streets awakening to the coming evening, workmen returning to work in the last few hours of light, women throwing open shutters to catch the cooling air. At the fountain at the top of my street, I stopped. Augustine passed back the basket and I balanced it on the fountain's rim. We stood there awkwardly; all our ease together on the beach utterly fled.

"Nebridius," Augustine said. He was dabbling his fingers in the fountain and would not look at me. "I love him dearly and would not hurt him for the world."

"Me neither," I said. "I love him too."

"Yes," he said. "Of course." He gave a small bow. "Thank you for today." Suddenly I was the girl with the cat's eyes and he was the young nobleman borrowing an old jar, his faultless courtesy a gleaming armor that concealed the man beneath.

"I love him like a brother," I said.

"A brother?" Augustine repeated.

"Yes," I said and, laughing, splashed him with water from the fountain. I turned and ran up the street. At the door of my aunt's house I looked back and he was standing there in the falling dusk looking after me, water running down his face.

CHAPTER 6

"We've a guest for dinner tonight," my aunt told me one morning. "I want you home."

I was surprised for it was seldom anyone visited. My aunt had friends in the neighborhood, I knew, Christian women skilled as midwives, but they never came to the house, for fear of my uncle. In the evenings, after work, he sat at home and drank. Only when he staggered to his bed did I feel safe enough to close my eyes.

I was annoyed that my time with Augustine would be curtailed. I was already late. Every moment I did not spend in his company seemed lifeless, dull, as if all the color had leached out of the world.

By this time, Nebridius had been away a month. He had sent us word that he had been summoned by a messenger from the farm he had been visiting with news of his mother's grave illness. He had hurried to his family estate to be with her and we had not heard from him since.

Since Augustine and I first met, the upturned boat became our place of refuge, our private place. Beneath its curved and salt-scarred hull, shielded from the gaze of prying eyes, we told each other stories, laid down in words the pictures of our lives, and marveled there had ever been a time when we had not known each other, for life without the other seemed a thing impossible. The word *love* we were careful not to speak with our lips as if to do so would be to take a step irrevocable along a road but dimly figured, yet our bodies spoke it by holding hands, our eyes spoke it by seeking out the other, and when they met our joy at the miracle of the other, of that dear face, spoke it too. Sometimes we slept in each other's arms on breathless afternoons when the murmur of the sea was our distant lullaby; sometimes we wandered along the beach, hand in hand, the water at first so cold it made us cry out; sometimes I lay with my head resting in his lap while he read me poetry, the tragic love of Dido, Queen of Carthage, and her consort, Aeneas. And when he came to the part when Aeneas abandoned her and sailed across the African ocean to the farther shore of Italy, Augustine would touch my face and say: "I would never leave you."

When I entered the house that evening, I expected to hear my uncle's angry shouts, my aunt's shrill scolding at the lateness of the hour. Augustine and I had lost track of the hour and we had had to run all the way home. I was hot and tired and longed only for bed. Instead, all was quiet except for the low murmur of voices coming from the kitchen. Unwinding my head scarf and trailing it behind me along the floor, I carried the basket into the kitchen. My aunt and uncle were sitting at the table and with them a man I didn't recognize.

"This is my niece," my aunt said, getting up. The man also rose although my uncle stayed seated. "My dear brother's girl."

My father had never been dear to my aunt that I could tell and she had never called him anything but lazy and good-for-nothing and worse. I shot her a look and saw that she was smiling at me, a kind of stretching of the lips for appearance's sake but her eyes were black with fury at the way I looked—hair escaping from its coil, my clothes in disarray, my hands and feet grubby, my lips when I licked them tangy with salt.

"Excuse me," I said. "I'm very tired." I longed to lie on my bed and think about the day, the waves crashing on the shore, the quality of Augustine's silence when he listened to me talk, the sound of his voice when he replied. I was already turning to go but my aunt had crossed the room and half led, half dragged me to the table, her fingers digging into my arm.

"Have some wine," she said, pouring me a beaker. "There's someone I want you to meet."

I glanced at the man. He was wiry and slightly stooped in the shoulders with thinning brown hair combed forward over his brow. His eyes were heavily wrinkled at the corners as if he was always squinting in the sun although his skin was pale. He smiled at me tentatively. He looked very old to me, perhaps thirty or so, but seemed harmless enough. I drained my wine, nodded to him, and started to get up. I had eaten very little that day and the wine made me dizzy.

"Sit," my uncle said.

"If I may?" the man said, darting a look at my aunt.

She nodded.

"My name is Paulinus," he said, addressing me. "I am scribe to the bishop."

Now I realized why the skin around his eyes was so worn. He took dictation all day. That also accounted for the pallor of his skin, for it seldom saw the sun. When he picked up his beaker I saw the fingertips of his right hand were stained with ink. The rounding of his shoulders was from perching on a stool and bending over parchment like the scribes of the Roman tax collectors who sat in the forum recording the coins people dropped reluctantly into the iron-banded money boxes guarded by soldiers.

"Paulinus is a Christian," my aunt said.

I looked at her and back at him. For a moment, I thought my aunt had hired him to tutor me in letters, and then all at once I understood. This man was to be my husband. This night was to have been our betrothal dinner.

I pushed myself up from the table so that my stool scraped the floor.

"If you will excuse me," I said.

Paulinus looked down, his face so dejected I almost felt sorry for him.

"You will stay," my uncle said in a voice I had learned to heed. I sat.

"I understand," Paulinus said. "It is too sudden." He looked at my aunt accusingly, and, briefly, I disliked him a little less. He was not a bully.

"She'll do as she's told," my uncle said. "It's settled."

From within the folds of his tunic, Paulinus withdrew a small package, placed it shyly on the table, and pushed it toward me. "For you," he said.

I glanced at it but did not touch it for fear it would be taken as a sign of my consent. It was a tiny alabaster box tied with a red ribbon. I pictured his ink-stained fingers fumbling with the bow, his brave little token of hope. It made me pity him.

"Thank you for your kindness," I replied.

Paulinus was leaving, my aunt escorting him to the front door. I heard her speaking to him in soothing tones and could imagine what she said: She doesn't know her mind; she's young yet; she will obey.

Left alone with my uncle, I could feel myself shaking but it was not from fear. Was I now to be bartered to a stranger and sold off like a bucket or a cooking pot?

I thought of Nebridius and Augustine, who walked the city at will and never incurred disapproving or lascivious looks, of the way they talked of their future as if they had only to reach out and take it. Whereas I was handed mine full-formed, an entire map of my life stretching into old age—wife, mother, drudge.

My aunt returned and I saw her jerk her head at my uncle indicating he should leave. I tensed, expecting him to refuse, but he got up. He stood for a moment looking down at me. I stared back, my chin raised.

"You will marry him," he said, "or I will throw you into the street."

When he had gone, my aunt and I sat in silence. I expected her to berate me for coming home so late, for spoiling the dinner, for refusing Paulinus so rudely; instead, she seemed lost in thought. The oil lamp guttered, throwing wavering shadows on the table, on the little box with the red ribbon. My aunt took it up and, untying the bow, took off the lid. She withdrew a slender gold chain and held it up on the end of her finger where it dangled there, a shining filament.

"A generous gift," she said.

I said nothing. I was thinking of the feel of the water jar as Augustine lifted it to my lips, the coolness of the water in my throat, the hot nearness of him.

My aunt sighed and dropped the necklace back into the box, replaced the lid, and set it aside. Without the ribbon the box looked like a sarcophagus, a design of vine leaves etched faintly around its sides, a tiny coffin for one girl's life.

"He is a good man," she said, quietly. "A *good* man."

I knew she was comparing him to her husband. For the first time in my life I wondered how old my aunt was, how long she had been married, and if it had been a love-match or arranged. I could not imagine her young, could not imagine a time when her hands were not red and ugly, her face not scored with lines, her hair not lusterless and brittle.

Instead I said: "My father would not have done this."

She gave a humorless laugh. "Your father was a dreamer," she said, "with no more idea about the world, about a woman's life, than a child. No," she said, her eyes glittering but whether from anger or sorrow I could not tell. "Your upbringing was left to me to sort out."

She struck the table with the flat of her hand so that the box jumped and the lid fell with a tiny clatter.

"When your father brought you home that first summer, you were a sight, I can tell you. Hair so tangled it took weeks to comb out the knots and crawling with lice." She shuddered. "You were like a mangy dog and with manners to match. You ate your food like a wild beast and flung yourself about when I tried to dress you, scratching and biting, refusing to wear shoes."

I remembered only snatches of what she described, the way the walls of the house pressed out all the air, the painful clang of copper pans instead of the delicate tic-tic of the chisel on terra-cotta or the trill of birdsong in the trees, the suffocating constriction of the shoes and dresses I was forced to wear. Yes, I thought. Sunlight in a box.

"You are a young woman now," my aunt said. "It is time to think of your future." She dipped the edge of her stole, the one she only wore to church, the one she had put on in honor of Paulinus, in a cup of water and before I could draw back, rubbed at my face. "See," she said, showing me the smudge of dirt and sand on the cloth. "You act like a child."

When I did not reply, she got up stiffly, as if all her bones ached. "The wedding will be in a month," she said and left the room.

Early the next morning I waited until I heard my uncle leave for the potting factory in the western district of the city hard by the clay pits, a long, low building filled with the hum of potters' wheels endlessly turning, and rack upon rack of drying vessels. My father had taken me once when I was small.

I heard my aunt moving about. Once she tapped on the door and softly called my name, but I pretended I was sleeping. Then I heard her leave and remembered it was the day she went to the women's baths. She would be gone most of the day.

I had lain awake all night turning over and over in my mind all that had happened the evening before. I wondered when Paulinus would come again and what I would do if he did. I knew I could not be here but had nowhere else to go. I heard a knock on the front door.

Thinking it a neighbor wanting to borrow oil for frying or a broom, I opened the door. Augustine stood there as if conjured from my mind. It was the first time he had come to the house.

"You cannot be here," I said to him, though my heart pounded in my chest. "I am alone, and my aunt and uncle would not stand for it."

"I came here only to give you this," he said, putting something in my hand.

I looked down and saw a shell the size of a robin's egg, a creamy helix lined inside with mother-of-pearl as delicate and pink as a child's ear. I lifted it to my lips and it tasted salty, put it to my ear and heard the memory of the sea trapped within.

"It's beautiful," I said. "Thank you."

Behind his shoulder, a woman banging at a rug with a stick was frowning at us. By tonight my aunt would have been informed of this strange young man who visited her niece when she was alone with her hair loose about her shoulders like a slut, her head shamelessly uncovered. By tomorrow, the whole street would know.

"Will you meet me at the church at noon?" he asked. "There is something I would ask you."

Just before midday, I slipped quietly from my aunt's house. Inside the church was deserted. A few leaves had blown into the open doors and made a scratchy sound under my sandals. Augustine was waiting for me at the door and led me toward the altar in the middle of the nave.

Then, still holding my hand, he turned to me. "Before we take this path, you must decide if this is a journey you want to make with me."

I began to speak but he placed a finger on my lips.

"Hear me out. You know I come from a family of landowners, that my father is a Roman citizen, that I am the youngest son."

I nodded.

"Then know this: I will inherit nothing. I must make my fortune by my wits."

"I understand," I said. "My father had to make his way in the world with only his skill to keep body and soul alive."

"No," Augustine said, sorrowfully, "you don't understand. If only it were so simple. I have certain . . ." He stepped back, frowning. "*Obligations.* I am expected to succeed in my chosen profession, but to do so I shall have to marry." He raised his arms and then let them drop heavily to his side. To marry *well,*" he said.

I thought of Paulinus and the way he had presented himself in the best possible light—a steady job, a rich gift to show he had the means to support a wife. By contrast, Augustine was pointing out all the obstacles that lay in our way. If what he was saying was not so serious, his misery so acute, I would have smiled at the irony. And smiled, too, because he had given me yet another thing to love. His honesty.

Interpreting my silence for dismay, he went on in a low voice: "Believe me when I say, I would marry you if I could, but I am not free to do so; my family would never permit it, not even if we had a child. Do you understand? I can offer nothing but myself. I offer you my love and my fidelity, but, under the law, you can only ever be my concubine."

Concubine. Common-law wife. In the eyes of the law the terms were much the same. The emperor Vespasian had had such a concubine—a freedwoman named Caelis—whom he had loved many years but only lived with after his wife died. A former secretary in the Imperial Palace, she had been much respected for her wisdom and integrity. To be a mistress of a married man was a shameful thing, censured by Roman law and the Church alike; to be the concubine of a man who was faithful was another thing entirely.

I thought of the alabaster box sitting on the table in my aunt's kitchen and then of the shell Augustine had given me. One gift was man-made, one was of nature. It seemed to me that I would rather follow my heart and make my own destiny than have it given to me whole.

"I would rather be your concubine than another's wife," I said.

"You are sure?" he asked.

"I am sure," I replied.

Augustine looked at me for what seemed a long time, then took my hand in both his own.

"Do you take this man to be your wedded husband?" he said softly.

"I do."

Taking off his iron citizen's ring, he slid it on my finger. It was so big I had to make a fist to keep it from slipping off. Then we kissed as we had seen married couples do in church, our only witnesses the eagle, the angel, the ox, and the lion my father had made. I did not realize until many years later that Augustine had not spoken a vow to me but only I to him. This was the bitter part of the honesty I loved, not the sweet.

He accompanied me to my aunt's house, where I gathered up what few possessions I owned and left for good. I could not write a note but I left a copper bracelet threaded on a ribbon I had worn as a child. It was a gift, but more than that it was my way of asking for forgiveness, for although I did not regret the decision I had made, I knew it would break my aunt's heart.

We left the house and ran hand in hand through the streets, so eager to be in each other's arms we did not heed the people in our path but barged right through a group of slaves in the market buying food, a huddle of important-looking men on the steps of the law courts, a gang of urchins tormenting a dog, heedless of the slaves' indifference, the men's angry shouts, the boys' lewd jeers. At the *insula* where Augustine lived he led me up a flight of stairs to the second floor. Outside the door, he paused. I looked at him questioningly. With a solemn look and with such care he might have been lifting glass, he picked me up in his arms, kicked open the door, and carried me across the threshold.

He put me down in the middle of the floor and closed the door. Finding ourselves alone at last we looked at one another shyly, almost anxiously, as if only now we realized the momentousness of what we had done, what we were about to do. Even now his eyes pleaded with me to be quite sure of what I did, for society decrees that once a woman gives herself to a man, forsaking all others, if she does not remain true, she is forever marked a whore.

I looked about me and saw a room small and cramped, a narrow bed pushed against one wall, a table and bench below the open window, scrolls heaped untidily in a basket, a tunic hanging on a hook. A cracked cup and half-eaten roll lay on an upturned bucket beside the bed.

"It's not much," Augustine said ruefully, following my gaze. "In fact, it's pitiful."

I removed my veil and stood there holding it. He took it from me awkwardly and hung it on the hook. Perhaps it was this simple act of courtesy such as a husband might make for his wife when they returned home from market, perhaps the sight of our two garments hanging there, the darker cloth of the tunic now overlaid by the veil's gauzy weave, but in that moment all my shyness fled. Of doubt, I had none; nor later did I have regret. The ancient playwrights tell us that life is fated and all we do predestined; the Christians say we have a choice which path we take, the right-hand turning or the left, and whether we end up in paradise or hell is of our own devising. I do not know who is right and who is wrong, not then, nor now. I only know that I could not do other than to love him. And so I chose the way ordained for me and spoke the words he said to me that first day:

"I want to love and be loved." And when he came to me I trembled not from fear but from desire.

CHAPTER 7

When she heard of what I had done, my aunt found out where we were living, and one morning when Augustine was at his studies, she showed up at our door. Thinking Augustine had returned early and forgotten his latchkey, I jumped up and opened it eagerly, ready to fling myself into his arms, for even an hour apart was too long. She pushed past me into the room.

Her eyes took in the way I had pinned up my hair as a married woman, the rumpled bed and sweat-soaked sheets, that I was still in my shift though the sun was high, the day well begun.

"He loves me," I blurted out before she could throw her accusations in my face.

"So he says now," she said. "Just wait. Once you become fat or sick with the bearing of his brats, he will cast you aside. Such is the fate of whores."

She did not sit but walked restlessly about the room so I was forced to press myself against the wall so small was the space. She said I would have nothing, not even my good name, and any children I bore him would belong to him to do with as he wished.

"We are married," I told her, showing her the citizen's ring on a ribbon around my neck. "This is his pledge."

"You think that ring will protect you when he casts you off? You think it will save you from poverty and shame?"

Before I could slip the ring back under my shift, she caught at it and pulled. The ribbon broke and the ring fell to the floor, spun, and rolled into a corner. I scrabbled for it and snatched it up, holding it in my fist as I had done when first Augustine gave it to me.

"Why do you hate me?" I said. "Why have you always hated me?"

Like metal foil crumpled by a fist, her face caved in upon itself. Before my eyes she turned into a crone.

Sorrowfully, she looked at me and then slowly turned away.

I leaned out of the window and saw her emerge from the staircase into the courtyard. Although I saw her one more time before her death, this is the image that has remained with me all my life. A woman bereft, arms wrapped about her body as if to hold herself inside, the death-throes of her heart a thing too terrible to behold.

My earliest memory is of a woman singing, a gentle, happy sound that filled me with contentment. When I was four and my father took me with him, I dimly remember being frightened by shouting, tears. After that a distance grew between my aunt and me, the woman who had sung the lullaby vanished and left behind a hard and bitter woman, someone I could not love. May the gods forgive me but I hated her for her unhappiness.

And so I pulled back from the window and closed the shutters. When I looked again, she was gone.

Never have I known such happiness, such joy, as those months of our first love in Carthage, my orphaned heart unfurling like a flower beneath the sun of his loving gaze. The world, it seemed, had poured its riches on us, a cornucopia of youth and love and pleasure, the only shadow Augustine's fear of what his mother would say once she knew of our joining, a melancholy coming over him as we lay in each other's arms at night, the time when fears arise and grow to monsters in our minds.

During the days while Augustine studied, I often took myself to the baths, mornings being the time when women were allowed to bathe, and amidst the squeals of children, the gossiping of matrons, the quiet patter of slaves' rope sandals on tile, I sat solitary in the steam room and hugged my happiness close.

Used as I was to seeing the nakedness of women in the public baths, I now looked upon their bodies with a different eye, one made knowledgeable by the loss of my girlish innocence, a change I did not mourn but gloried in. It was as if I was now part of the continuum of female flesh from youth to old age, the slender bodies of the daughters with their pointed breasts and slim thighs glistening with oil beside their mothers' ruined bodies slack with childbearing, legs marbled with broken veins. The ancient crones seemed nothing more to me than tents of sticks and leather and were so fantastical they did not seem human.

I smile now to remember this. Yet the ruin of women over time did not frighten me for I thought my love exempted me from the drudgery and disease that caused such decay as surely as if I had been blessed with immortality. I was Venus come to earth, the huntress Diana, and looked on mortal flesh with pity and contempt. At sixteen I could not see the future even as it was figured there before my very eyes. Of the decay of men's bodies I knew nothing. The only man I saw naked was Augustine and when we parted he was in the prime of manhood, his body sleek and muscled, his belly flat, his hair without a trace of silver.

Thus he remains in my mind's eye though I know that soon I will look upon his body's ruin, the end of all our mortal journey if we live so long. As I sit in this courtyard waiting for night to fall, I fear the change that time has wrought in him, that if he has become a stranger it will be like arriving at a place I thought was home to find nothing but an empty building, windows eyeless, walls collapsed, no trace of those who lived there long ago except perhaps a broken cup where once lips, warm and pliant, were laid against the rim.

One night during our early months together, Augustine told me of something he did a year before in Thagaste before he came to Carthage. He said that he and some friends stole into a farmer's orchard and plundered his pear trees.

"We did not do it for hunger," he said, "but to despoil his trees."

The farmer, he told me, had a name for pride in the town and often boasted that his fruit was the best in the neighborhood, indeed in all the region thereabouts. He was often seen walking in his orchards handling the fruit that grew upon his trees as if, Augustine said, he were Midas and they were made of gold. That night he and his friends crept over his fence and climbed the trees. They ate a few pears and deemed they were as ordinary as others they had eaten, and then, laughing, they plucked all they could and threw them down on the ground to carry away for the pigs.

"But something came over me," he said. "Even as I was laughing with my friends I felt as if I stood apart from myself and saw what I was doing, that I loved not so much the fruit of our theft but the act of destruction itself. Each pear I threw down was like a part of my soul that I despoiled."

He turned to me, his face troubled. "The worst of it," he said, "is that the knowledge of this gave me a kind of joy."

"You were but a boy," I said. "Now you are a man."

"I was *myself*," he said. "And what I did that night, the sheer delight in doing wrong, haunts me." He clasped me tightly in his arms. "Oh, my love," he said. "How will I keep you safe?"

"From whom?"

"From me."

"Do not be foolish," I said, taking his face between my hands and kissing his brow, the corners of his mouth, his lips. "You will never harm me."

With daybreak, Augustine's fears of his own nature dispersed. All except one and it was not so much fear as the sliver of a shadow that fell between us, the first one we had known.

During our talks on the beach, Augustine had confessed to me he was a Manichee, a secret follower of Mani who taught the world was divided into good and evil, light and dark, and that these opposing forces were always at war, each striving for ascendency over the other. All humans, Augustine explained, were little worlds and joined in this great battle, our flesh forever at enmity with our spirit. At first I laughed at this for when he told me we were lying in each other's arms, his hand stroking my hair which he always loosened when we were alone together for he loved it so. And later, when we lay together, his unerring instinct of how and where to touch me and for how long, his delight in my body and the pleasure he could give me, made his notions about the world appear incongruous and absurd. Yet he said that when our bodies convulsed in ecstasy it was because our souls had found release like birds who fly their cages.

One night, as we lay side by side, our bodies not touching for we were sheathed in sweat and the air was too hot, he asked me what I thought of having a child.

"To tell you the truth," he said, and from the way he said it I could hear that he was smiling, "I do not think I could share you with another. Babies are greedy little things, you know, jealous of anyone else coming near their mothers."

"I didn't know you were an expert on babies," I laughed. But then I fell quiet for I realized suddenly that I knew nothing of babies, had never even held one in my arms.

"You forget my brother and his wife have children," he said. "I would have you know that I have held and walked and jiggled infants plenty in my time. But," he went on, his voice growing serious, his hand reaching for mine, "it is for you to say, for you only to decide. None other has the right."

I remember turning my head on the pillow to look at him, his face a dark shadow against the lighter shadows of the room.

"A child," I murmured. Our child. All at once my heart quickened and turned over. Placing my hand on my belly, I pressed down. I felt the concavity of my womb like an empty bowl waiting to be filled. Augustine placed his hand over mine.

"Yes," I said, rolling toward him. "I want your child."

CHAPTER 8

We had not been able to afford to send a messenger to Nebridius to inform him of our union and so we waited with some trepidation for his return to Carthage. Not knowing whether he would be happy or sad for us was the one shadow in those sun-filled days of our first love. Except when he was at his studies, Augustine and I were now inseparable and we feared Nebridius would feel excluded as if we had gone into a house together and locked the door against him.

He returned late on an early autumn day just as the light was fading.

I did not know that he had returned until I met Augustine in the forum and there he was beside him.

"Nereus," I cried and flung myself upon him. Then I held his body away from me as he had done to me when we met again in the church months before and looked into his face. It was more gaunt, his body leaner, more angular and there were shadows behind his eyes as if in the weeks we had been apart our happiness had battened on his, diminishing him as we thrived. His mother, I knew, had died.

"Naiad," he said, kissing me on top of my head. "I am happy for you both."

When I would have embraced him again, so overjoyed was I to see him, he gently held me away. This new constraint between us at first confused and then grieved me for I remembered how, in childhood, we had swum in the river or sprawled on the bank to dry, wholly unconcerned about our nakedness. But in the time it took for Nebridius's mother to take sick and die and be put in the earth, the girl he once knew had forever vanished, replaced by a woman marked by the intimate touch of his best friend, forever untouchable and set apart to all other men.

As for Augustine, never did he show jealousy of the love between Nebridius and me but accepted that, like twins, we were two trees grown so close their branches appear as one. Nebridius was the link between the time before and the time after, between my childhood and adulthood, and so he became the guardian of my past, the only one who had known my father and his craft and the savior of a future I did not yet know.

As we strolled with linked arms through the streets, I in the middle, Augustine on one side, Nebridius on the other, it came to me that all my aimless wandering about this city, my restless searching for something I could not name, had led me here, precisely to this moment. I knew then that forever I would be held in balance between these two men, that somehow all my happiness and well-being would depend on them, one my dearest love, one my dearest friend. Later, there would be another—my son, Adeodatus. To this beloved trinity, I gave myself body, heart, and soul.

Augustine and Nebridius had another friend called Alypius, who loved the games beyond all measure and often begged us to go with him to watch men die for sport in the arena. My own age and from a wealthy family in Thagaste, Augustine's place of birth, he loved to wager on the gladiators, who would win and who would die. Later, when I witnessed it for myself, I could not understand his love for carnage nor his delight when the man he had bet against lay defeated in the dirt, the crowd booing and jeering, his life hanging on their whim, the roar of "*Mitte!*" "Let him go!" or "*Iugula!*" "Kill him!" his own man strutting round the ring in triumph, sword held high.

Augustine, too, had no love of the games and I often heard him remonstrate with Alypius, trying to get him to see that to profit off the blood of a man was unclean, sinful even. But Alypius would not heed him. By temperament he was quiet, his manner toward me reserved, and apart from gambling, his interests seemed wholly intellectual. At Nebridius's house—we never invited anyone to our room now—Alypius would talk for hours in the evenings about his compulsion. I would become sleepy and long for Alypius to leave, but he talked on and on until Augustine told him flatly he had to go.

"You should see Alypius when he's at the games," Augustine told me when I was complaining that Alypius was so withdrawn that it cast a damper on the time we spent with Nebridius when he was present. "He's a completely different person, laughing when his horse or gladiator wins and then sunk in deepest gloom when they lose. It's bizarre. He is like a man possessed."

Later, thinking over what he had said about his friend, I concluded he was right. I had never seen Alypius in the grip of this strange obsession but I knew how much my uncle had frightened me when he was drinking, the sudden rages, the way he clenched and unclenched his fists.

"Let's call him Janus," I said.

"Mmm?" Augustine was almost asleep.

"Janus," I replied. "Because he has two faces."

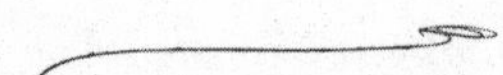

The next day Alypius turned up at our door at daybreak. We had forgotten that Augustine and Nebridius had arranged to go to the games with him, but Alypius had vowed that if his friends accompanied him this one time he would quit his compulsion forever.

"One last time," he pleaded.

My father had never taken me to the games. He believed that the arena was an accursed place of death. He could not understand the willful destruction of anything that was beautiful—man, beast, or artifact.

"Your father was a wise man," Augustine often said.

But I was curious to see what my ears had often heard—the roar of animals rising from the amphitheater—and I confess that I wanted to see the other face of Janus. So I persuaded Augustine to let me accompany them.

In my heart I was afraid to witness the suffering of others but most of all I was afraid I might discover that I enjoyed it. My aunt and her Christian friends condemned the spilling of blood for sport, said it was barbaric, unnatural, that human life was sacred. I knew that in the time of the Emperor Diocletian, thousands of Christians had been executed in the arena, some whole families burned to death or torn to pieces by wild animals, babes in arms and little children clinging to their mother's skirts in terror. I have heard that, in Rome, so great was the slaughter, so unending, that the crowds began to riot, and the emperor, fearing for his life, made a proclamation that the purge be ended, that Christians waiting in cages underneath the arena be given amnesty. People in Carthage still talked of the black pall of greasy smoke that hung over Rome for weeks, the stench of burnt flesh that clung to clothing and permeated the taste of their food. Even though we had a Christian emperor now, the horror of that time was remembered, and the power of the emperor's edict feared.

When we descended to the street from our apartment, we joined others who were already walking toward the amphitheater. The trickle soon to become a torrent as the morning wore on. On game days, the city was like a giant lake slowly draining down roads and alleys, flowing to the stadium. The shops were shuttered, the usual commerce of the day suspended, the city as silent as at a time of plague. On the air the roar of the gathering crowd came to us distantly, the sound as familiar to citizens of Carthage as the booming of the sea against the cliffs of our coastal city.

Alypius strolled beside us blithely talking of his future winnings, how he would pay his landlord and pay Augustine back for the money he often lent him, in spite of the fact that we were poor and barely scraped by on the meager stipend his father could afford his younger son. I glanced at Augustine, eyebrows raised, but he shook his head to warn me to remain silent.

I stole a glance at Alypius as he walked beside me. He was indeed a different person, putting a hand on my arm while we walked. Augustine noticed I was uneasy and, with a graceful movement of his arm, swept me across to his other side so I now walked between him and Nebridius. I gave him a grateful smile. Nebridius took my other arm and we continued.

Alypius led us to a private box. His family was rich, his father influential on the city council and I, a woman, was allowed to sit in it because of this. Otherwise, I would have been forced by custom to stand with slaves and poor male citizens on the very top tier of the stadium. I was glad of this. It allowed me to hold tightly to Augustine's hand, but it also meant that I was much closer to the arena and could make out the faces of those doomed to die. I determined that I would keep my eyes shut, although I could not block out the sounds even with my stole drawn close about my head. But when I heard the roaring of a lion and the rasp of metal as it was released from its cage, my eyes flew open.

An enormous yellow lion emerged, its mane tattered, its side scarred from previous battles. Its flanks were sunken with hunger, one of its ears torn like a battle standard after the fight.

The crowd began to chant, "One Ear, One Ear," and I saw it run at a barrier between the crowd and the arena, causing the people sitting there to scramble back. Then the beast lay down in the sand, motionless except for the tip of its tail, which twitched lazily from side to side, yellow eyes surveying the stands with a kind of indolent contempt. The lion instantly sharpened to alertness when a gate creaked open and a rhinoceros trotted out, its gray hide plated like armor, its nostrils blowing as it picked up the scent, a cruel tusk set between tiny black eyes.

I glanced at Alypius, who was sitting forward in his seat shaking the bone betting tokens in his hand, his body taut, his eyes feverish as if another inhabited the house of his body. Even Augustine's eyes were fixed on the arena and his hand had tightened around mine.

The lion was stalking the rhinoceros now, moving slowly, shoulders hunched, belly close to the ground, its huge paws taking almost delicate steps. Its prey snorted uneasily and lowered its head. Then the lion sprang, clawing at its prey's soft underbelly, a great gash opening in its flanks. The crowd roared. Giving a great bellow, the rhinoceros lashed its head from side to side, its horn scything wickedly through the air. But the lion leapt easily out of its reach and continued to circle the rhinoceros, waiting patiently for a chance to inflict another terrible wound.

I could watch no more and buried my face in Augustine's shoulder while the sounds of the death-struggle below beat at my ears and the copper smell of blood grew stronger. At last it was over, and when I looked again, the rhinoceros was a gray hump in a welter of gore, the lion tearing great gobbets of flesh from the carcass. At last its handlers appeared and, prodding it with long spears, forced it away and into its cage. Attaching hooks to the corpse, they harnessed it to mules, rearing as they caught the scent of the blood, and dragged it away, a great smear of red trailing behind.

I glanced at Alypius, who had the look of a man sated by sex, eyes now dulling, forehead beaded with sweat, mouth slackening. I looked away, sickened.

The trumpets sounded and the gladiators strutted into the arena. Every man, woman, and child in the Roman world knows what they look like even if they have never seen them fight: the *retiarius,* armed with trident and net, his left shoulder covered with armor; the *murmillo,* a fish-like crest upon his helmet; the *thraex,* carrying a scimitar and small square shield. Small boys squat in the street and, within a circle drawn in the dirt, enact fights with figures made of sticks, the net a scrap of muslin. Alypius stirred from his torpor and leapt to his feet, and when the clank of weapons echoed around the stadium he screamed out encouragement to the fighter he had put gold on that day.

I rose and pushed along the seats, out of the box and up the steps to the back of the stadium, the highest tier, fighting my way through, pushing at the crush of bodies, deafened by the screams. Behind me I heard Augustine call my name, but his next words were drowned out by the roar of the crowd.

The fight to the death horrified me, but the bloodlust of the crowd who moments before had been ordinary citizens horrified me even more. I saw the girl with the cat's eyes from the stall at the harbor, the one who had lent us the water jar. Leaning out across the barrier she was screaming, "*Iugula! Iugula!* Kill him! Kill him!" lips peeled back, teeth glistening, her painted eyes crazed with a kind of murderous joy. I bumped into her as I tried to force my way past, and she greeted me gaily although she did not recognize me, all trace of her monstrous passion slunk back below the depths. I shuddered to think of what hidden horror crouched in other people's breasts waiting to be let out, like the trapdoors in the arena of the Colosseum in Rome where lions, crocodiles, hyenas, and all manner of fearsome beasts would suddenly appear at the feet of those destined to die. It frightened me to think that beneath the surface of ordinary life nightmares lurked. I wondered what evil lay coiled within my own breast.

Augustine was right: the world was a place of evil. Only love could transform it and make it beautiful and good.

Appearing beside me, Augustine took me in his arms and held me to him, holding my head tight against his chest as I have seen mothers of newborns do.

"Forgive me," he whispered. "This is a terrible place. I should never have let you come. Nebridius says he will stay with Alypius while I take you home."

As we left the amphitheater, I looked down into the arena despite myself. A slave in the guise of the god Mercury was touching one of the gladiators, now crumpled in the sand, with a red-hot cauterizing iron to see if he was dead. He did not move. Slaves dressed as Pluto, god of the underworld, dragged the corpse away by the heels. The sweepers began to rake the sand level like a scribe scraping his wax tablet clean so he can mark it again, like Alypius erasing all memory of his losses and placing another bet, like my father sickened with drink only to raise the wineskin to his lips yet again.

I wondered then at the compulsions men lay upon themselves—violence and the lust for power—while women bore the burden. My life, I vowed, would be different.

CHAPTER 9

There was no more shadow cast on our happiness that autumn except for Augustine's increasing frustration at what he regarded as the pointlessness of his studies. He railed against the method of learning passages from rhetoric and literature by rote and the lack of critical discussion about content in the classroom. Nebridius's city house increasingly became a meeting place for the more serious students, an ad hoc university, where discussions of literature, philosophy, and theology raged long into the night. The brotherly affection with which Nebridius treated me rubbed off on the others and I became a kind of sister to the group: Nebridius first and last amongst our friends; Possidius, at fourteen the youngest of the group; gentle Antonius, who every time I looked at him blushed to the roots of his hair; stubborn Marcellus, who would not be budged from his argument by reason yet would suddenly abandon it on a whim and laugh uproariously about it after; Zosimus, who was to become a serious and revered bishop though I knew him as a great teller of jokes. All those future lives held in that courtyard long ago and at the center, Augustine. He was the sun around which we lesser planets danced, the great light of his intelligence, his wit, his humor, and his unfailing generosity, the radiance he shed effortlessly.

In this way I was thrown more into male company than female, a rarity for our time when men and women spent much of their lives separate converging only at table or in bed. The talk about philosophy and literature, astronomy and religion was intoxicating although my untrained mind was frequently bewildered.

During this time I mastered letters and began to read and write Latin and Punic with fluency. All those soft late summer and fall evenings we spent seated at his desk forming words or I reading them aloud, hesitantly at first and with many errors, my finger moving slowly along the page and then faster with more confidence. I would be perched at the foot of the bed, Augustine stretched out on his belly, his chin propped on his arms, murmuring a correction here and there but mostly quiet, listening. And when I looked up his eyes were fixed on me and filled with light, the same look he gave me before I knew he loved me.

"Don't stop," he would say. "Don't stop."

My father had talked of beauty in a way that was not abstract but made incarnate by his art. He spoke of colors and lines and how shapes should complement one another, how proportion was all important, and as he spoke his fingers showed me what he meant, sketching figures in the dirt beside the campfire or arranging bits of tile.

When I first met Augustine, he spoke of beauty as if it had no material form but was something invisible but necessary, like air. But his actions told a different tale. I remembered the way he had stooped and touched my father's mosaic in the church as if by touch he could feel the beauty of what was made and so come to know my father's spirit. He loved to take down my hair and run his hands through it, and holding its weight back from my face he would kiss my forehead, my nose, my neck and throat, and then slowly undress me, planting kisses on each part he uncovered, my falling hair a cover for us both as he knelt before me, a veiled place, a tabernacle in which we found each other. He worshipped the beauty of my body with his body but talked about it with his mind. And he was never so lost in speculation that his eyes did not seek me out, his look saying: "I am a fool to talk thus. I know it." And he would give that ironic quirk of the mouth I loved so much, a look so boyish, so self-mocking, that it was all I could do not to throw my arms around him.

One morning we left the city and, passing though the western gate, walked out into the countryside beyond the walls. It was late autumn now and the evenings were often chilly so I took along the cloak Augustine had given me on my birthday two weeks before. It was of emerald wool—to go with my eyes, he said—and lined with fur. He also gave me a silver ring to wear upon the fourth finger of my left hand and on the inside it was inscribed: "My heart rests in thee." I learned later he had paid for the cloak and ring by selling some rare scrolls he possessed to a dealer in the forum. When I found out I wept for I knew how much he loved them.

His own birthday was approaching—November 13—and I already had a special gift to give him.

It had cost me nothing; it was to cost me all.

A road ran from the gate straight as an arrow toward the west where first the Phoenicians, those seafaring ancestors of my mother's Punic race, landed. Wide enough to let two carts pass side by side, the road was busy with vehicles of all sorts: lumbering carts piled high with stacked amphorae of olive oil from olive groves that grooved the lowlands and lower slopes for miles; other carts laden with bushel upon bushel of apples, plums, pears, and grapes, the mountains to the south and the sea to the north kind to crops and fruits of every kind. Once we were passed by a messenger on a galloping horse, its hooves sending up a roiling dust storm that made us cough and covered us with grit; a person of wealth was carried by in a litter but whether man or woman we could not tell, for the curtains at the windows were drawn shut.

We walked hand in hand, my cloak over my arm, a basket of food over Augustine's, but soon I tired and we left the road just as it descended into a shallow valley no more than two miles from the city where a tiny stream meandered busily to and fro like a little dog nosing for a scent.

I spread my cloak beneath an apple tree near the stream and we lay down on our backs and, shielding our eyes, looked up at the sky.

"An elephant," I said, "about to raise its trunk."

"Where?"

"There," I said, pointing to the north where serried banks of clouds were rolling in from the sea.

It was a game we sometimes played leaning on our window in

our room, a game my father and I had played to pass the time when we walked from site to site. He called it making "cloud mosaics."

"That's a rhinoceros," Augustine said, squinting. "See. It has a horn not a trunk."

"You took so long to find it, the cloud changed shape," I protested.

He laughed. "An elephant, then, who got his trunk caught in a door."

I thumped him on the shoulder and he laughed again.

Perhaps it was the sound of his laugh that made me ask what I had puzzled over for months. Shifting closer to him, I laid my head in the crook of his arm. Immediately he pulled me closer and taking up the edges of the cloak covered me for he had felt me shiver. We lay there for a while, cocooned together, the only sound the trilling of the stream, the distant cry of a hawk.

"Augustine?"

"Mmm?"

"Why are you a Manichee? Mani teaches that this world is evil, yet you love it so."

During our walk I had watched how his eyes took in the late flowers growing in the ditch, the bare branches of the trees swaying in the wind, their shadows checkering the stones beneath our feet. I recalled how he had watched the furling of the ocean on the shore, rubbed silk between his fingers in the market, held lemons to his nose to smell their scent. Never have I known a man so attentive to beauty nor so tender to all living things. Once when I was looking out the window into the courtyard watching for his return, I saw him pick up a baby bird where it had fallen to the ground and, climbing the wall that ringed the courtyard, place it gently in its nest.

He was silent for a while and I knew he was thinking. Never did he dismiss the questions I asked as stupid or banal as I had heard some men do to their wives but always considered them with utmost seriousness. So much so that I sometimes smiled to myself when I saw two little frown lines appear between his brows, his eyes taking on an inward gaze as if he looked at pictures in his mind.

"I look at the world and as well as beauty, I see sadness and evil. My mother's God is supposed to be all knowing, all loving, but how could such a God allow us to suffer? It seems to me that only an evil God could delight in our pain. Ergo: To posit one good and one bad deity perpetually at war is the only rational explanation.

"My mother says that we have free will and that God allows us to do evil but then brings good out of that evil. I cannot understand how that can be so. Good and evil are opposites and one cannot lead to the other. They can only coexist separately."

"What about the Christian God, who is said to be all good, all knowing?" I asked. "My aunt says it is we who have transgressed, bringing evil into the world. There's a story the Christians tell about it in the book the Jews have."

"Adam and Eve?" He laughed derisively. "That's just a folktale dreamed up by an illiterate tribe.

"Plato is interesting," Augustine went on. "He tells a story, too, but it is much more sophisticated and free of contradictions. He said the world is like a cave and outside the cave is a great fire. The gods—not people, you understand, but great ideals like Truth and Justice and Goodness—pass back and forth across the fire, and within the cave we only see the shadows on the walls and that is how we know that they exist. This metaphor makes much sense to me as well."

I thought about this a while. "It seems to me the world is like a giant mosaic formed from my father's art—his masterpiece. But from the moment the plaster dries and we walk upon it, it begins to turn to dust. It is the ruin of the world and all its beauty that you hate, not the world itself."

In one swift motion, Augustine rolled over so he was looking down into my face, my head still pillowed in the crook of his arm. "You are a marvel," he said.

He saw I thought he teased me. "No," he said. "I am quite serious. Not all the students I have ever known or am likely to know could have understood my philosophy so well. Before you put it into words I didn't know myself."

"It is because I love you that I see you truly," I said. "My love is a kind of knowing."

He stared at me.

"What is it?" I asked.

"Remember that bird in a cage at Nebridius's?"

"It is a sun lark."

"The first time you made it sing I thought: This beautiful girl is that little bird whose song escapes the bars of its cage. I have never in my life heard music clearer, more melodious, than your song."

"My father called me Little Bird," I told him, "in the Punic tongue." Never had I told a living soul of this before.

After that day, he sometimes called me Little Bird when we were alone, and I could swear I heard the cadence of my father's voice beneath his own as once I had seen his tunic showing through my veil.

On the morning of November 13, Augustine's birthday, I woke when it was still dark and lay listening to his breathing. The day before I had gone to the baths and washed myself with care, oiling my body, brushing my hair until it shone. After that I went to the market and bought a tiny cake of almond paste and honey and a bunch of dried lavender tied with a bow of grasses. I also bought a little flask of wine. When I got home Augustine had not yet returned from his lessons so I hid them underneath the upturned bucket by our bed. He thought the scent of lavender was in my hair, the almonds from the oil on my body.

I knew at once when he awakened. I always did. There was a difference in the air, a tremor, as if the world had shifted minutely on its axis when his soul grew conscious. Later I would feel the same vibration when his soul was ready to leave this world. But on that day, when he turned eighteen, he and I were as gods immortal.

"Happy birthday," I said.

"Thank you."

A dim gray light was creeping through the shutters. I could just make out his face.

"I have a gift to give you."

"You are my gift," he said.

"I have another." And taking his hand, I placed it on my belly. "Here it is."

For a moment he was still and then comprehension flooded him. "Is it true?" Swiftly, he sat up and took my face between his hands.

I nodded.

"You are with child?"

"I am." I had known now for a month, waiting to be certain, waiting for this day to tell him. But like the man he was, Augustine had had no clue not even when I tired more quickly, had bouts of sickness in the morning and could not look at food, or burst into tears when the strap of my sandal broke. I smiled at his stunned expression.

Reaching down, I drew out the cake and lavender and wine. I gave him the cake and flowers, poured the wine into the single cup we shared, and, handing it to him, said: "To our son."

He drank and passed the cup back to me.

"To our daughter," he said.

I drank.

Augustine took a sprig of lavender and threaded it in my hair and then broke the cake in two and passed me half. We ate cross-legged on the bed, our simple meal a solemn, holy Eucharist.

CHAPTER 10

In the spring a letter came from Monica that Augustine's father, Patricius, lay dying and he must come at once to Thagaste. He gave excuses and delayed for he hated his father, a drinker and a bed-swerver, an insult to his mother Augustine considered mortal and would not pardon, hoping meantime he would die. Then came a letter from his older brother, Navigius, sending money for the journey and beseeching him, in Christ's name, to come at once. So at sunrise one morning in a mule-drawn gig he hired, for I was seven months gone with child and wearied easily, we set out along the coastal road southwest into Numidia and then turned inland due south toward the mountain range and forests, a place I had never gone before.

We spoke little on that journey, hearts stunned by the breaching of our secret love as if we stood together on a deck and watched our ship drive toward the rocks. We knew a reckoning was near and dreaded it, the mountains close-threatening, each peak distinct as if papyrus-cut, a portent and a sign.

And yet the beauty of our first journey is with me still like ephemera of dreams that come unbidden to the mind long after sleep is past, clear as if I looked on them again and know them real: the seabirds shouldering the following air, cutting and dipping like Icarus gone beneath the cliffs, their cries a paean to their daring; the salt on his lips as we kissed; the dust so thick and choking in the first spring heat, we resembled those sad shades who wander on the nearer shore, no coin to pay the ferryman. We bathed in rivers that ran like molten silver through plotted fields, our teeth aching from the cold, my belly buoyant on the swell, toes sifting velvet mud. I washed my hair and combed it on the riverbank, my fingers carding it like skeins of wool as he watched me.

"My mother's hair," I told him. "Or so my father told me."

"My mother also," he said and then grew silent, the dread we felt returning as if the sun had dimmed and all the birds gone silent.

We reached the outskirts of Thagaste a week later. Augustine pulled up beside a wayside shrine where oaten cakes lay moldering on moss–grown stones beside a spring, encircling them a frailty of wild flowers woven in a wreath and long since dried, the god, it seemed, indifferent to decay. I climbed down and sat beside it.

"Are you well?" He knelt beside me and, smoothing back my hair, peered up into my face.

"She will hate me and the child," I said, tears trickling down my face. I cried so easily now it sometimes made Augustine smile but not today. He took me by the shoulders and gave me a little shake. "Don't be silly," he said. "My mother will love you and the babe. It's me she will be angry with and not for long. My mother is too good to stay angry. There is nothing to fear from her."

I looked at him doubtfully.

He took my hand and, lifting me, helped me brush down my

dress. We washed our faces in the spring beneath the shrine and then went on through country lanes, around the town until we came to a road where stones were piled on either side like ruined pillars. He turned in there and set the mules to walking.

On either side were vineyards with orchards and olive groves planted on the slopes where the ground began to rise toward the mountains.

"Siesta," he said as if to explain the emptiness of the fields. "My mother insists the servants rest until it's cool."

Our African spring came early and already in April the sun was high and warm, coaxing out all manner of field flowers and a froth of apple and pear blossoms whose heady scent made me dizzy.

Ahead, saffron-colored tiles of a villa's roof showed through dark-green cypress trees planted all around to give it shade. As we rounded a bend someone came running, a middle-aged man, sun-lined and thick in the shoulders where his tunic stretched taut. He took the bridle of the leading mule and walked beside us, face upturned and joyous.

"Cyrus," Augustine said, clapping a hand on his shoulder. "How are you?"

"Well, young master," he said and then nodded to me. "Mistress."

I looked down, shy at such a formal greeting from a servant as if I were far above him and not a mosaic-layer's child who had slept outdoors and often went hungry.

"Does my father live?"

"He does," Cyrus said, "but sinking fast. Thank God you came in time. Your mother has been praying for your swift return."

The path opened onto a round courtyard fronting the house. Terra-cotta urns with ancient rosemary bushes, cut in spiral form, stood on either side of the doorway, and a woman, small and fine-boned as a bird, her dress the color of cream and of such simplicity that, at first, I took her for a servant, was shadowed there. Her ice-brown hair was parted in the middle and drawn in graying wings over her ears then gathered at her nape. She wore no jewelry except a plain gold band on her left hand, which burned in the sunlight as she held it out.

"My dear," she said, taking my hand to help me down. "Come in and welcome." I knew her now; she was the domina of the household, Augustine's mother, Monica, come out into the sun like a peasant's wife to welcome me to her home.

Without another word she led me in, still holding my hand, Augustine following. No word he spoke to her, yet I could feel a silent conversation going back and forth as if they signed by thought. She led me through an atrium, where a fountain fell in sparkling shards, and then on into a room shuttered to the heat, cool and whitewashed as an anchorite's cell with the sound of wood doves purling in the eves and the soft plash of the fountain outside the door. A large bed was pushed against a wall, on a ledge above it a cross fashioned out of sticks joined with a leather thong; an oil lamp on a chest, beside it bread and cheese and apples, a pitcher of water and a cup, a bowl for washing, an ivory comb and pins, a small stone jar before a bronze mirror; a single chair and a footstool in the corner by the bed, a carven cradle, black with age and lined with a coverlet of blue-dyed wool. When I saw the careful preparation, how every object in the room bespoke one woman's thoughtfulness for another, I began to weep, tears of gratitude and exhaustion streaming down my face unbidden and unstoppable as rain.

"Hush, child. Hush," said Monica, embracing me and rocking back and forth the way mothers comfort children when they are hurt in soul or body or imagine themselves so. Short as I was, I had to bend to lay my head against her shoulder. Her hair smelled of sandalwood, and faintly in her clothes was an acrid tang of wood-smoke as if she herself stirred the pot before the fire, which, I later learned, she did. Then stepping back, she pushed me gently down on the bed and, lifting my legs along its length, began to untie my sandals.

"You must rest," she said, placing the shoes on the floor. "You have had a wearying journey." Bending down she kissed me on the forehead and, motioning Augustine out, softly shut the door. In that moment, before I slept, I loved her. And yet a tiny corner of my soul, one deep in shadow and almost unregarded, felt suborned, as if her kindness was a trap and I must be on my guard.

When I awoke the shadows were long in the room and for a moment I did not know where I was. Then I heard the sound of voices in the corridor near my door and backless sandals slip-slopping on stone, pottery clinking, the smell of cooking meat, which made my stomach twist with hunger. I arose and put on my sandals, dashed water on my face, and twisted up my hair. Then I opened the door and looked out. A woman carrying a jar was passing in the atrium. She smiled and beckoned.

"The mistress said to take you to her when you awoke."

I followed lagging, my eyes seeking out the home of him I loved as if to catch his imprint there and so, in holding it, possess the years that I had missed. Here he was born, wrinkled and mewling, sleeping with his fists bunched up beneath his chin, his mother's foot gently pressing that ancient cradle, perhaps singing a Berber song from her ancestral tribe to lull him into dreams. There he walked his first steps pulling a toy horse on a string, tottering and unsure. There crouched beside the fountain he lined up stones for soldiers, miniature battles for which he wove a grass crown for his head, acclaiming himself *imperator* on the field. Such I have seen young boys do in the forum, their older sisters a row of mocking monkeys squatting on temple steps, scornful of the bellicose strutting of little men.

The servant was standing at a door with her arm held wide to indicate I should enter. Voices murmured, and then sudden silence. I was certain they had been talking about me. Feeling as if I were intruding, I hesitated. Augustine rose at once and came toward me, taking me by the hand and drawing me farther in as if he thought I would run away.

"Here," said Monica, patting the couch on which she sat.

Unsure, I glanced at Augustine. I wanted to be near him, and the distance across the room from where he stood and where his mother sat seemed so great. He smiled and nodded slightly as if to say: I am here, my love.

"And place a footstool by her, Augustine." Then she gestured across the room. "This is Cybele."

From a corner a shape resolved itself amongst the shadows, an ancient crone bent double so her head craned up to see. Her head was almost hairless, her mouth a stitched and crumpled gash, which champed toothlessly at nothing.

"Cybele was my nurse," Augustine said, "the tyrant of the nursery."

"And mine," laughed Monica. "She is the true domina of this house." Cybele's clawlike hand plucked at her dress as if she was cold, and when she spoke it was in a Punic dialect of the tribe of the Garamantes that my father taught me when I was a girl.

"Seven moons," I answered in that same language.

Again the nod, a kind of grimace for a smile, which I returned.

"Excuse me, mistress," a male servant said, coming into the room, his tunic's crimson braid at neck and hem proclaiming him steward. "Cook asks if you want to check the roast. He says it's done."

Monica stood up. "Thank you, Marcus. I quite forgot." Then to me, "Forgive me, my dear."

She moved like a girl though I knew her to be almost forty. Beside her, with my growing belly, I felt stupefied and gross, a placid heifer gazing blankly over the paddock fence.

Cybele seemed to have fallen asleep, a pile of clothes heaped on a chair, her breathing almost nothing in the stillness of the room, a mouse's breath, no more.

Augustine tucked a rug around her legs and then whispered: "Come." He took my hand and helped me rise for I found it hard to get up from a sitting position now that I was so weighted down by the baby. "Father asked to see us when you awoke."

And so he led me, still clasping my hand as if to keep me near in this strange place where he was at home and I was not. We crossed the atrium at the center of the house, an old-fashioned design the way the Romans used to build their villas when first they came to Africa, to another room, spacious and airy, lamps burning around a bed, a burnished nimbus as if a mist of gold had settled there. A shape lay there so still it seemed an effigy, covers drawn tight across the chest, hands clutching the sheets as if to delay the body's passing. The face I saw seemed molded out of beeswax, an *imago* of the living. I saw the covers rise and fall minutely and the orbs beneath the blue-veined lids move side to side as if he watched a phantom game of catch.

Beside the bed a young man sat, some years older than Augustine but clearly of his blood. He had the same dark hair, the same brown eyes, although a fraction taller and heavier of build. He rose when we entered, embraced Augustine, and bowed to me.

"I am Navigius," he whispered. Then to his brother: "He fell asleep just now but if you wait awhile he might awaken." He put a hand briefly on Augustine's shoulder, bowed once more to me, and left the room.

There was an odor in the room of putrefaction as if the body had already begun its slow descent into the earth, a viscous slide of parts unjointing, and I recoiled, my hand going to my belly as if to ward off that thing called Death from him whose life had barely begun. I have heard it said that pregnant women must not go near a death chamber for fear the child will catch the taint and I believed such notions until I learned what all must learn if they live as long as I: that life is a kind of dying, there is no border over which we cross from one to another but dwell always in its precincts.

Augustine's face was stone, as if his father, Medusa-like, had reached out and touched his heart. I looked to see if I might glimpse anything of the son in the father, but the figure before me seemed hardly human, so still he lay, so absolute his last composure. His hair was white and sparse, his nose jutted blade-like from his face, on his neck and arms brown blotches showed, the dying body's harbinger. Then, horribly, like a half-crushed spider, a hand unfurled and crawled toward me.

"Come closer," the effigy said.

"It's me, Father."

"Not you. The girl."

His filmy eyes flared briefly as he looked on me. I recalled Augustine saying he always had an eye for a comely girl, that he would put his hands on the servant girls.

"Pretty," he said. It seemed a kind of horror that despite the dissolution of his body, it still retained the urges it was powerless to satisfy. His hand gripped mine.

"Remember this," he said to me, glancing at Augustine. "God's hook is in his heart."

CHAPTER 11

Patricius lived another day and then died, his going hard and pitiless. During his illness, he had consented to be baptized and a priest had come and chanted words, a censer swinging smoky arcs that made Patricius choke, baptized him, then anointed him with olive oil smudged on forehead, eyes, mouth, ears, feet, and hands, a greasy cross that glistened in the lamplight. Then he took a piece of bread, made signs over it, and fed it between Patricius' blue-tinged lips. I was ashamed for his helplessness, his heaving breaths, while the living stood around his bed like Olympian gods as if impervious to the rigors of their mortal flesh. Used as I was to pagan corteges in the streets of Carthage where keening women tore their hair and painted mummers mocked the foibles of the corpse, this tearless Christian gravity seemed an insult to the dying, as if the living grieved not at all, and I could not imagine Christ's mother would not have beat her breast beneath the cross and called down curses on her son's murderers.

After the burial the tranquil waters of the household closed soft and seamless over the dead man's memory, its surface placid and untrammeled. Augustine's married sister and her husband returned to their nearby farm, and Navigius became paterfamilias in his father's stead, his wife the domina, though she ceded authority to Monica in all things.

One evening Navigius's wife, Perpetua, knocked on the door and came in before I could ask who it was. She stood by the door watching as I arranged my hair in preparation for dinner.

"It is shameful to wear it thus," she said. "You should wear it loose like an unmarried woman, for you are no true wife to Augustine." Then she was gone.

My eyes filled with angry tears. Since coming here I had known only kindness from Monica, Navigius, Cybele, and the servants but I had noticed that Perpetua often looked at me coldly. She was older than I by five or six years and already the mother of a four-year-old son and eighteen-month-old daughter. Brown of hair and skin like a nut, she was as tall as her husband and strong and shapely of limb although her waist had thickened with childbearing and there were dark shadows under her eyes. The daughter of the landowner who farmed the property adjacent to Navigius's land—for with the death of his father ownership had passed to him—Perpetua was my social superior, as was Monica, but I had never been made to feel it until now.

My fingers fumbled and my hair unraveled and fell down.

"Hades!" I exclaimed and threw the brush across the room just as Augustine came in. Then I was angry at myself because I couldn't bend to pick it up so big my belly had grown. Defeated and a little ashamed at being so childish, I flopped down on the bed. Never had I felt so ugly and useless as at that moment.

"What troubles you, Little Bird?" Augustine asked, stooping to pick up the brush. He came and sat beside me and took my hand.

I told him what Perpetua had said.

"Come," he said, kissing my fingers one by one. "Let's pin it up magnificently and we will watch her turn puce when she sees you at dinner."

I smiled a little at that.

"For that is what it is, you know. Envy. And she is frightened of the responsibility of being the mistress of this farm. You must not mind her unkind words."

Later, after dinner when I was getting ready for bed, there was a knock on the door.

"Enter."

It was Perpetua, her face blotched as if she had been crying and I wondered if Augustine or Monica had spoken to her.

"I'm sorry for my words," she said. "They were unforgivable and rude. Here." Clumsily she pressed an ebony comb and several silver-headed ivory pins into my hands. "To put up your hair."

"Thank you," I said, taken aback and touched, more by her courage than by the value of the gift. "They are exquisite."

At that she blushed with pleasure. "You forgive me?" she asked, and the way her voice rose uncertainly at the end made my heart twist. "Truly?"

I smiled at her. "Of course I do."

"Oh, I'm so glad." Impulsively she put her arms around me and kissed me on each cheek. "Sisters ought not to quarrel."

"Would you like to stay?" I asked as she turned to go.

She looked at me surprised—I was surprised myself—then smiled, the first I had seen and it lit up her face. In that moment she looked very young and very pretty. "But you must sit in the chair and put your feet up," she said, pushing me down and stuffing a cushion behind my back. She lifted my feet onto the footstool.

I groaned at the relief. My back was a misery to me whenever I was on my feet and even when I lay flat on my bed. I was also very tired for the baby chose the nighttime hours to move about and it was difficult to sleep and I tossed and turned all night. To give me room, Augustine had insisted from the first on sleeping on a pallet on the floor. Monica had not approved of us sharing a room under her roof but relented when Augustine told her flatly we would move into an inn in Thagaste if she insisted we keep separate rooms. I could have wept with relief. We had hardly been apart and being now so advanced with child I felt vulnerable and fearful in a strange house.

"As you wish," Monica said to her son, patting my cheek. "It is just as well for the baby most likely will choose to come in the night."

As I came to know her, I realized this was ever Monica's way, to make her charity appear a thing of necessity or merely common sense so the gift of it could be accepted more easily.

"Better?" Perpetua asked.

I realized my mind had wandered, something it was prone to do now I was pregnant.

"Very much," I said. "Thank you."

"My back felt like it was breaking when I was carrying Cecilia." She poured some water into a cup and passed it to me. "Here, drink this. You must let me know if there is anything you crave and I will try and get it for you. I wanted calf's liver. Couldn't get enough of it. Can you imagine?" She wrinkled her nose. "Can't stand the sight of it now."

I told her I longed for pomegranate juice and she said she would see what she could do, that she knew a neighbor who grew them and would walk over the next day and beg some fruit.

And so we sat on for an hour or more and talked of pregnancy, its joys and ailments, childbirth and how the first labor could take hours, of how to breastfeed infants and care for them. She was astonished at my ignorance until I told her I was motherless.

"Sisters?"

I shook my head.

"Ask me whatever you want to know," she said.

And so I did and as I saw her devotion to Navigius and her children, her love and respect for Monica and Augustine, how kind she was, how eager to be helpful, I came to love her. She was the first friend I ever had who was a woman; more than that, she was a sister to me.

The next day, good as her word, Perpetua brought me a cup of pomegranate juice she had squeezed herself. She watched, smiling, as I drank it down greedily, declaring it the most delicious thing I ever tasted. Perpetua told me the neighbor, an old man named Silvanus, said I could have as many as I wanted and he sent a blessing on myself and the child.

Except for that one instance with Perpetua, no cruel words were ever spoken in that house about my status or my swelling womb, though as I lay awake at night sleepless with the movements of the child, I heard Augustine's voice across the house vehement, intent, the way he spoke when he was laying out his reasoning to a skeptic and in response the low murmur of a woman's voice. When he came to bed later, moving quietly so as not to disturb me although I was awake, I felt his sadness, a burden heavier and more bulky than the one I carried in my womb.

As my belly grew and the days got hotter, my ankles swelled and my breath seemed harder to get so I was forced to sit long hours in a wicker chair with my feet up. As I watched the daily business of the house go on around me—servants crossing the courtyard on errands, the sound of shutters opening, water sluicing the tiles, the flap of a cloth out of a window, voices calling, the sound of little Cecilia crying or Julius playing—I felt heavy as a boulder in the middle of a chattering stream. At first it irked me to be so useless, but as the days and weeks passed I found a kind of quiet contentment gradually descend on me.

Cybele often sat with me during the mornings when Augustine was out on the property with Navigius and Cyrus, the foreman, discussing the farm and ways in which the land could be made to yield more, for Patricius had let it go badly in recent years. Perpetua and Monica were busy running the household, a thing they did together in remarkable harmony considering it was Perpetua, not Monica, who was now the domina of the estate. Even so, Perpetua would come out to visit with me from time to time and ask me if I needed anything. I see her still, perched on my footstool in the shade, leaning forward, gesticulating with her hands, her eyes gleaming with fun, or seated with her little daughter on her lap, who stared at me solemnly, thumb in mouth, a little slick of drool glistening on her chin. In those talks, Perpetua confided to me how much she loved her mother-in-law yet felt overawed by her, too, how she despaired of ever measuring up.

Monica had instructed the serving girls—Livia and Marta—to make sure I received everything I needed, but, typical of her, she often came to check on me herself. I learned from Monica how a domina should care for her household. She was a far different mistress from Nebridius's mother, who had lain all day on an opulent divan attended by her maids, her only exertion to give orders to the steward and the cook. By contrast Monica worked side by side with her servants in the kitchen, the distillery, the spinning room, and storeroom. I never knew a more diligent or more competent housewife; I never knew a more harmonious household despite Monica's unhappiness with Augustine for his Manichaean beliefs, which, as a devout Christian, she regarded as heretical.

The company of women was, for me, a revelation, my childhood having been spent largely in the company of men. Shyly, I had kept to myself at the women's baths in Carthage, content to watch and listen silently as I bathed myself or rubbed oil onto my skin. Compared to the talk of men in Nebridius's house in Carthage, I found women's talk mysterious, largely taken up with childcare and how to treat sickness. In my foolishness and pride, I thought that only talk about intellectual things like the soul and mind and ideals was interesting or of value. It was like admiring an apple tree for its lovely blossoms and never guessing one could also eat its fruit. Cybele sat spinning wool, the spindle madly twirling in her expert claws, plucking at the lyre of her web like Arachne, a marvel to see so straight and fine a thread emerge from such crookedness. For household tasks I was useless except to wind the thread she spun and place it, rolled in balls, in a basket at my feet, a heaping mound of goose-eggs to be kept for dyeing in the winter when their drabness would be changed to robin's egg, leaf, and crocus as if spring came premature but welcome. Or birthing peas from pods to rattle in a bowl set in my lap, a bowl I couldn't see except through touch so great had I become, while within the baby danced and nudged my belly's shiny dome like kittens wriggling in a sack, my outer self inert and supine, gasping in the heat of summer as I awaited my baby's birth.

At noon, after the midday meal, the house and fields fell silent, stupefied by the heat. That was the time Augustine would return from working on the estate and we could be alone. He would come and sit with me in the courtyard where sometimes there was a breeze. Sometimes we lay together on the bed in our room his body against my back, his arms around me, for my belly was too big for us to lie face to face. Smoothing the damp tendrils from my forehead, he would blow gently on my neck or waft a fan to cool me. The tiny life inside me was like a winter-lit brazier and I suffered cruelly from the heat. He loved to rest his hand on my belly and feel our child moving within.

"Augustine?" I said one afternoon when we were lying thus on our bed.

"What, my love?"

"I have heard you arguing with your mother late at night."

He sighed. "It is not you we talk about," he said. "It is me. My mother is worried about my soul. She says the Manichees have no true understanding of God and the world. It is nothing to be worried about."

"It's because she loves you."

"Yes," he said. "She does."

We lay there quietly for a time but I could feel Augustine was not at peace from the feel of his body against mine though he kept quite still and I knew what troubled him.

"Augustine?"

"Mmm?"

"You mustn't worry. I am not going to die in childbirth."

"Hush," he said, his arms tightening around me so strongly it hurt. "Do not speak of dying. I could not bear to lose you."

"You will never lose me," I said.

"Nor you, me."

In the evenings, the whole family gathered in the courtyard where it was coolest and after dinner, Augustine and I read stories aloud, my tongue halting over words still new to me. Monica would listen, her fingers busy with sewing or sorting herbs for drying. Like most women of our time she could not read or write but made her accounting of the household goods by cutting notches on a stick, which the steward transcribed into the estate records. At first I was proud of my ability to read while she could not—without patrician birth or Roman citizenship, it seemed the only mark of distinction I possessed—but she listened so intently, with such humble attention, sometimes asking me to repeat a sentence or two so beautiful it was, she said, that my pride was overborne by her pleasure.

Then one morning in mid-July as I was bending awkwardly to

wash my face, a filament of pain glowed briefly in my belly, then went out, then came again.

"Augustine," I called. "Augustine." But I knew he could not hear me for he had risen early to ride with Navigius to a neighboring vineyard three miles distant to buy an oil press.

The servant girl, Livia, passing by my door heard me and ran to tell Monica and Perpetua and soon all the household knew my time was come upon me. Cyrus was dispatched on a fast horse to fetch Augustine. I was frantic to have him by me despite Monica's saying that birthing and death were mysteries only women had the strength to bear.

At last he came and found me sitting on the bed, my knees drawn up against the pain that came with regularity now though still quite spaced apart. Perpetua was braiding my hair into two long plaits, which she put forward over my shoulders so they lay on my breast.

"It is more comfortable thus," she said. "When the time comes to push, your hair will not irk you when you lay your head against the pillow."

Augustine sat down beside me and I laid my forehead against his breast relieved beyond measure that he was there.

"Tell me what to do," he said.

"Don't leave me," I implored.

All day I labored, the pain a cresting, roaring thing that bore me up and up until it peaked, then down I rushed panting in its wake to flounder for a while in temporary calms. And as the day progressed the swells increased and I a straw doll on its surface whelmed over, battered down but still afloat, no will at all but to survive this endless pounding. The others there became another species entire as if I gazed through liquid crystal at a dry terrestrial world in which, once beached, I knew I could not live.

As lamps were lit, I felt a gushing drench my legs. I looked up appalled but Monica smiled.

"Your waters break," she said. "It is a sign the babe is near." Then to Augustine, "Help me lift her. We must change the sheets." And to a servant woman standing by, "Fetch hot water, Marta. Towels. A sharp knife and put it in a flame to cleanse it."

She then instructed Augustine to sit behind me and lift me so I was half sitting, supported with his hands under my arms.

Sometime during the night, I know not when, my strength gave out and sinking ever deeper down a darkening well, the filmy light receding far above, I would not rise up toward it even for the sound of Augustine's voice saying my name or for my baby's struggling life but let myself be swallowed by the darkness and the peace it brought. I felt my mother near me then and like a moth-wing brushing my ear, someone whispered: "Live."

"The babe is stuck," I heard Monica say as if a long way off. "We must turn it."

From worlds away I felt her reach between my legs and enter there, while with the heel of her other hand she pressed on my belly with unbearable force.

"Now push," she commanded. "Push hard."

Like plants whose roots finger rocky desert places yet somehow drink water from the air and live, her words called forth some power within me and I bore down with all my strength, my body splitting, heaving like the earth that throws up mountains and so redraws the geometry of what we see. And blindly groping down, I felt him slide eellike from my living core, a molten rush, delivery of twins, he and I, our new life in this new world announced by wailing and blood and with the afterbirth, dawn breaking.

CHAPTER 12

Packed with cloths to stanch the bleeding, I held my son in my arms and looked and looked and looked on him, was drunk on looking, as if to stamp each nail, each eyelash, each perfect part so miniature, so complete, this masterpiece of flesh and bone and sinew, blood and pumping valve into my heart's soft wax forever. With misty eyes that peered up at me and frowned in puzzlement to see such radiance there, my little flower upturned to this first sun, his mother's joyful face.

Adeodatus, we named him. Given by God. And leaning forward Augustine put a timid finger in our son's crumpled fist, which curled around it like a morning glory at dusk and made him laugh out loud so tight the grip.

Cybele sat with me and brewed up potions for me to drink to stop the bleeding and ward off infection, bitter cups of bark and leaves and nameless somethings taken from a calfskin pouch around her neck and powdered in a pestle, her lips moving spell-like all the while. My young flesh grew stronger hour by hour and the next day I was taking steps across the room, Augustine's arm about my waist to support me, Cybele nodding in approval from her chair. My breasts swelled up like gourds as my milk came in and it was such exquisite agony to feel my baby's tender mouth draw off that throbbing fullness, his tiny throat pulsing like a sparrow's heart, eyes closed as if in disbelief of such abundance.

I was nursing Adeodatus when Monica came and asked if she could sit with me.

"I love to watch you," she confided. "It reminds me of when I was a young mother like you." She smiled at me and smoothed down the covers on my bed. "I shocked Patricius by insisting on nursing my own babies, did you know?"

I shook my head.

"Oh, yes. He told me I had to hire a wet nurse."

Looking down at my son, the warmth of his swaddled body like a tiny package in the crook of my arm, I could not imagine giving up this moment even if Augustine asked me to, nay commanded as Patricius had done.

"What answer did you give him?" I asked.

Monica laughed. "I said that if he wanted to give birth to the next child then he was welcome to do so. Until then, he should keep his mouth shut."

I could not imagine Monica saying such words to her husband and told her so. She laughed.

"Neither could he. You should have seen his face." She watched as I put Adeodatus on my shoulder and patted his back.

"Here," she said, slipping a cloth between his cheek and my shoulder. "You'll need this."

As if on cue, Adeodatus gave a tiny hiccup and a thin trail of milk ran out of the corner of his mouth.

"But you know," said Monica, "a woman becomes a tigress when she becomes a mother. There is nothing she will not do to protect her cub."

She took him from me then and laid him in the cradle, which had been pushed next to the bed.

"Now," she said. "Try and get some rest. It is wise to sleep when he sleeps as he is likely to be awake all night." She kissed me on the forehead as if I, too, were a child. "He has spent so long in the dark warmth of your body, he thinks night is day and day is night."

One day, when I was drowsing in the sun, Adeodatus sleeping in a basket at my feet, the lavender I had been tying in bunches so they could be hung on a beam in the kitchen to dry spilling off my lap forgotten, Monica sat down in a chair beside me. Picking a stem off my lap she rubbed the blossom between her fingers then brought it to her nose, inhaling its fragrance. Leaning her head against the chair, she closed her eyes against the sun.

"When I was carrying Augustine, I had a dream," she said quietly. "I was walking in the lane behind the farm and I came across a youth, a beautiful boy on the cusp of manhood with dark hair and quick, sad eyes. He was very thin but his clothes were not ragged and his sandals were tooled leather, expensive. Reclining on the grass beneath a pear tree heavy with fruit, he seemed to be waiting for someone. I greeted him but he did not reply. I asked him whom did he seek?"

I glanced at her at the mention of the pear tree. I was certain Augustine had never told her about his adolescent crime. Monica's eyes were still closed and she did not notice my disquiet.

She went on: "'I am hungry,' the youth said. I gestured at the pears. 'Eat,' I told him. 'I cannot pluck them,' he replied. 'I must wait for them to fall.' As I was considering these words, strange even for a dream, he changed before my eyes and grew older and more wasted and I knew that time had passed though I was the same. I knew that he would die if he did not eat so I reached up and plucked a pear to give to him but the young man had vanished and when I looked in my hand so had the pear."

Monica opened her eyes and looked at me. "I was much troubled by this dream so I went to a priest and asked him what it could mean. He told me the young man was the child in my belly, a boy, who would not receive true nourishment until he was a man and that I would offer him what he craved. 'But he disappeared,' I told the priest. 'It was not he who went away but you,' the priest replied.

"I thought the priest was speaking nonsense," Monica said, a tiny smile on her lips. "'How can a child starve and live until he is a man?' I asked. The priest said that there were many things that kept us alive and that food was only one of them. After that he would say no more and I feared it meant my son would not live to manhood and he could not bring himself to tell me outright."

She reached for another stem of lavender and twirled it in her fingers. "I remember when I birthed Augustine. The labor was long and hard like yours. Everyone thought I would die, for he was large and I was small and I had lost much blood. There was much wailing and carrying on, the midwives wringing their hands, Patricius burning incense to the household gods he honored."

She laughed. "The smoke almost choked me," she said, "but he thought he was helping so I said nothing.

"I was not afraid," she said, "for I knew I would not die. I knew this child, of all my children, would be great although he is the most difficult."

I was about to protest when she leaned forward and touched my arm. "Forgive me, my dear. 'Difficult' is a harried mother's word." Leaning back again in her chair, she continued. "I knew not how but that he would come to rule over others with his words and that his name, *Augustus*, Great, would live on down the ages."

She laughed. "And so while the others were rending their clothes and planning our funerals, I delivered this great child and lay back exhausted. It was his cries that roused the others and they rushed to tend him, quite forgetting me.

"Men need women to push them out into the world. But the labor does not end when they are delivered from our bodies. Indeed, it has only just begun. It continues throughout their childhood and adolescence, even into their manhood. As our children increase, so we decrease. When they are ready to be born into the world, into the life that God ordained for them, that is when our task is done."

Monica settled back in her chair, fingering the cross at her throat. "Augustine is the second son, as you know. It is Navigius who has inherited all this." She waved her hand taking in the courtyard, the house, and the fields beyond. "Augustine must carve a way for himself in the world. Even his father understood this and was willing to pay dearly for his education."

Monica turned to face me. "You are wondering why I am telling you this?"

I nodded.

"I tell you," she said, "so you will understand that Augustine has a destiny." She ran her hands over her skirts as if by smoothing out the creases she could erase the hitch and snag of her thoughts. "I do not know what that destiny is but I know that he is, even now, starving for something he has not yet found."

I picked Adeodatus up and as my milk let down, the exquisite relief of it made me dizzy as if pressure were being drawn from around my heart.

Monica knelt and began to gather up the spilled lavender, laying each stalk carefully in a basket so as not to shake the flowers loose.

"You must forgive me for speaking," Monica said. "But I am a mother and I must. Augustine is my child as Adeodatus is yours."

I looked down at my son's face and thought there was nothing I would not do for him. Nothing at all.

"You remind me of when I was young, of a time when my life was before me and I could have chosen to be better, to have *loved* better."

She put the last of the stems in the basket and stood. Suddenly she stopped and leaning down she touched my cheek lightly with her knuckles as a mother will do to a sleeping child to see if the fever has abated, fearful lest she wake him.

"When the day comes when you perceive the hunger in him, I hope you will forgive us." She made as if to go back inside the house and then stopped again. "I am sorry for the death of your father," she said. "It is hard to be a woman without protection."

When she had gone, I sat rubbing stray lavender blossoms between my fingers much as Monica had done but not to release their scent, more to feel something in this world alive the way my father was not, for even his memory was less tangible than this single stem and the seeds falling onto the stones. I knew what she was telling me, that without a father I was alone. Her son could be no true husband to me under the law and that his destiny—his hunger as she had called it—would take him from me. Not now, not tomorrow perhaps, but one day.

The shadow of the roof had moved across the courtyard and the sun now fell directly on my son's face. Screwing up his eyes, he began to wail so I stood and, shushing him, paced to and fro, where Monica herself must have paced with her children in her arms. The image of her young motherhood, here in this very place, my feet treading the very tiles upon which she walked, transposed itself as if I were she and this, my son, Augustine. And all at once I felt unmoored, drifting, without home or husband or standing in this world, with only the warm weight of my child in my arms and my absolute necessity to his life to anchor me. I wondered at Monica's talk of what was needed to stay alive, for when I looked at the face of our son, I knew that therein lay all my heart's nourishment and I had no more need to search for it than I did for the sun above my head. Like my newborn son now gazing on my face with blind necessity, I had fixed all my happiness on him whom I loved and the fruit of that love. Of the riddles Monica spoke, I knew only the faintest shadow. What I did know was that I was on one side and Monica's God was on the other. And Augustine was in between.

CHAPTER 13

I never saw Monica angry but once in late summer when the wheat stood high in the fields, rippling in waves when the wind blew, and the grapes began to plump and darken on the vine. Adeodatus was now two months old.

A childhood friend of Augustine's from Thagaste, I forget his name, fell sick with a fever and looked to die, so his parents brought the priest to him, though he was a Manichee. I was not there myself but heard that at his bedside Augustine argued with the priest, denouncing the sacraments of the Church as so much hocus pocus and the priest left in a rage, the friend unshriven. Word soon got back to Monica.

A few days later I was walking at the back of the house near the paddock under a giant oak. It was shady there and quiet and Adeodatus had been colicky and restless all that day. As I turned the corner of the barn, I heard voices.

"A pagan I could understand." It was Monica and her voice was raised more with fear than with anger, it seemed to me, "for the worship of false gods is naught but ignorance. Your father was such. But you of all people should know better, you with all your learning, your philosophers, your great intellectuals."

This last said with utmost scorn.

"But to deny Christ and all the goodness of this world, that beautiful girl and your little son included, when you know better is not mere foolishness but willful heresy."

"Mother," Augustine said, and I could picture him writhing under the lash of her words, trying in vain to make her stop.

"Do not 'mother' me," she retorted sharply. "Since when have you minded anything I tell you? No, for once listen to me, Augustine, and listen well. I was willing to overlook your heresy for the sake of that sweet girl and her baby, my grandson. Yes," she said. "Do not look at me that way. For *them.* No matter you have made promises to her that you cannot keep. No matter you brought a child into this world with no means to support them."

"I have been offered a teaching post in Carthage," Augustine said stiffly. "The messenger came this morning."

I knew of this. He had told me that very morning. A part of me was overjoyed to be returning to Carthage for I missed Nebridius and the city, but, most of all, I missed being alone with Augustine as we had been before. A part of me was also sad to leave this peaceful place and the company of Monica and, most especially, Perpetua.

But Monica continued as if she had not heard him. "No, that is nothing compared to the happiness of these two souls you have so carelessly taken into your hands because you must have what you must have."

"I love her," Augustine replied. "She is the only woman I will ever love."

My heart leapt at that. He had often told me so but to hear it spoken to another was an exquisite joy.

"I know," Monica said. "But can't you see that makes it so much worse? For if you loved her you would never have entangled her in your life. You would never have given her a promise you could not keep."

Monica's voice came to me clearly. She spoke the words with great clarity as if she knew it was her only chance to say them.

"And so I sought to repair the damage you had done her. With love. And care. And, God be praised, those two beautiful children survived the ordeal of birth when they so easily could have died."

"I thank you for that, Mother," Augustine said.

Monica continued, "She is a child. But you, my son, are not."

"Enough, Mother!" Augustine shouted. "She came to me freely. You make it sound as if I tricked her. I did not. I told her of my situation and she came to me of her own accord. Truly, you know nothing of her or me or of our love for one another."

Never had I heard him speak so to his mother. Nor had he ever raised his voice to me in anger.

He said more quietly and I could hear him striving for control: "I will not listen to you speak of her that way, Mother. She is no child. She and our son are my life."

"By child I do not mean simple in her mind or heart, Augustine." Monica's voice was patient though infinitely weary. "I meant she is *innocent* as a child. And you have put both her and your son's happiness and their immortal souls in danger through your selfishness."

"I will not listen to this," Augustine said.

I thought then he would walk away but he did not. Instead

there was a silence that stretched on and on so I could hear cattle lowing in the fields and far off the tock-tock of goat bells on the mountain slopes. Somewhere in the distance a dog barked. It seemed strange to me the world was so indifferent to the human drama in its very midst, so lovely and serene it was on this late summer's day. If overhead black thunderclouds had suddenly appeared and hurled down lightning bolts it would have been more fitting.

"Think my son, I beseech you. *Think.*" I could imagine her grasping the front of his tunic and shaking him.

"Your father, God rest his soul, was a man who gave himself up to the world and all its delights. He drank. He whored. Do not look so shocked; of course I knew. No, my son, do not look away in shame. I was a wife before I ever was a mother. Children, especially sons, forget this. It is the truth and I am not afraid of it."

"I hated him for what he did to you," Augustine said in a low voice. "For what he was."

"I know you did, my son. And perhaps I am to blame for many a time I played the wronged wife, the martyr. I only know I forgave him in the end."

I caught a glimpse of her dress as she showed briefly at the corner of the barn then turned and disappeared. She was pacing up and down, her hands clasped before her.

"That was your father," she said. "And then there is me. I am a Christian, commonly thought throughout the neighborhood to be a saint. Hah!" Her laugh was bitter, filled with desolation. Suddenly I glimpsed Monica's dreadful loneliness and, commensurate with it, her courage.

"I raised you in the Church and thought I taught you well.

What pride! What I really taught you was to see your father's face imprinted on the world and make you fear it. Fear you would become like him. And so you follow the teaching of Mani, for it gives you a perfect mirror in which to see the division in your nature your father and I created."

Monica continued: "I was willing to bear all this because it is, in part, my own doing. I hoped that with the death of your father you would learn to forgive him and forgive that which is like him in your own nature. But you have not forgiven. Augustine, my dear, clever son, you are no longer a child. Only a child makes a mirror of the world and thinks his own image is the only truth. You are a man, Augustine. You are now a father. You must look through a window and see the world as it really is, not split like two halves of a broken cup but whole and undivided. How else can it hold wine?

"But even if you persisted in your childish beliefs, I could bear it and simply pray harder for your soul. What I cannot bear, my son, is when you put another's soul in mortal danger. You had no right to send the priest away from the bedside of your friend. He is dying and will not recover. Even if you do not believe in the Church's sacraments, a true friend would give a dying man whatever he desired to bring him comfort. His soul stands on the edge of this world and the next. Are you so arrogant you place your own intellectual purity against the happiness and salvation of another? That is wrong and I will not stand for it. It is good that you have won this post for you cannot remain under my roof."

Her voice was so low I could barely make out the words.

"I do not do this on account of that lovely girl and my grandson.

I will always and forever love you and love them, my son, but for now you must go. It is best."

I did not hear or see her leave. She must have gone a different way back to the house along the path behind the henhouse, which stood next to the barn. At last I heard Augustine's footsteps approaching and stepped out from my hiding place.

"You heard?" he said.

I nodded. I did not know what to say. His face was pale but whether from anger or sorrow I could not tell.

Augustine put his arm around me and we walked slowly back to the house. "Are you and the baby strong enough to travel?" he asked.

"Even if I were not I would go with you," I said. "But, yes, we are both well."

He kissed me. "If we pack tonight," he said, "we can leave for Carthage in the morning." He stopped and turned to me. "I'm sorry, my love. I know you have been happy here." He stroked his son's cheek with a finger.

"Yes," I said. "But I am happiest with you."

We did not end up leaving in the morning after all for a messenger arrived late that night saying Augustine's friend was on the point of death and was asking for him. Augustine left in haste and by midmorning had not yet returned. The cart with our few belongings, provisions for the journey, and many gifts from Monica and Perpetua was standing by the front door, the mules harnessed, their tails flicking irritably at the flies that swarmed about them. Still Augustine did not come.

When I had told Perpetua we were leaving the following dawn, she burst into tears. Cecilia, toddling at her feet, began bawling too.

"I will miss you so much," she sobbed, scooping up Cecilia and hugging me so the child was squashed between us and wailed even louder.

"You must come and visit us," I said. "In Carthage. We will take the children to the beach and to the children's puppet shows in the forum. You will meet Nebridius." I had told her of my childhood friendship with him.

She cheered up a little at that.

"Here," I said. "Help me pack. I don't know if I have enough clean breechcloths for Adeodatus."

And so I distracted Perpetua from her sorrow and she grew a little happier though not consoled. We plumped Cecilia down in the middle of my bed with some walnut shells to play with and she soon forgot her tears. Adeodatus slept peacefully in the cradle.

Augustine rode up at midday, his face closed to me. All he told me was his friend had died an hour ago. I put my hand on his arm but did not speak. I had no words for his grief but my heart grieved with him. It was too hot to set out then so Augustine ordered the mules to be unharnessed and we went into the house out of the sun.

"We will leave tomorrow before dawn," he said.

The day passed strangely, a kind of non-day, a marking of time until our departure. The servants went quietly about their tasks and even Perpetua's children played quietly as if they sensed the heavy mood of the household. Augustine spent a little time in conversation with Navigius in the atrium while I sat with Perpetua, Monica, and Cybele in a sitting room and passed around Adeodatus so they could take their farewells and kiss his little oblivious face as he lay dreaming in their arms.

After dinner, Monica took me aside.

"This is for you," she said. "It was my father's."

It was a wax tablet bound in silver with a silver stylus attached to it on a silver chain. As I turned it over in my hands it grew indistinct for my eyes had filled with tears.

"Thank you," I said. "Thank you." Suddenly I was sobbing, a mirror image of the day I arrived, me crying, Monica comforting me. Yet this time I wept out of a kind of sorrowful joy. Sorrow to be leaving, joy to have found someone such as she. It was a far different leave-taking from the one I gave my aunt.

"If you rub the silver with chalk from time to time," Monica said. "It will keep bright."

I smiled then through my tears. This piece of practical advice was so like Monica.

"Good," she said, wiping my cheeks with her thumb. "That is better. Now get some rest, my dear. You have an early start in the morning."

We left when it was still dark, the birds still silent, the stars still not faded from the sky. Marcus, the steward, and Cyrus held torches. Monica and Perpetua with their hair still in sleeping braids stood with Navigius in the doorway. I hugged Perpetua one last time and Navigius gave me a chaste peck on each cheek.

"Be well, sister," he said.

Then I turned to Monica. We embraced in silence and then she drew me a little apart from the others.

"Remember this," she said softly. "Men think themselves strong, though they are weak; women are strong, though we are thought weak. It falls on us to bear the sorrows of this world." Then she made a tiny sign of the cross with her thumb on her grandson's forehead and kissed him. "Take good care of them both."

"I will," I said.

Augustine kissed his mother's hand and bowed to her. I saw the pain at his formality flit across her face though she smiled at him. Then she reached up and cupping her palms on either side of his face she looked deep into his eyes.

"A wise man once told me," she said, "the son of so many tears will not be lost." And pulling down his head she kissed him on the forehead. "Go with God."

Augustine embraced his sister-in-law and brother, shook Cyrus's hand, and helped me up into the cart.

As we pulled away, I looked back. Monica and Perpetua stood there waving; then we turned a bend in the road and they vanished from sight.

CHAPTER 14

Thus we returned to Carthage, retracing the road we had traveled five months before, I holding our child upon my knee or suckling him in my arms, Augustine driving the mules that pulled our cart, the darkness that had settled on him since the death of his friend lifting fraction by fraction as the miles flowed beneath our wheels. In a wicker basket on the seat between us I could hear the jostle and knock of the wooden bosses of Augustine's scrolls, those most precious instruments of his livelihood containing tales of others' lives like Dido and Aeneas, Orpheus and Eurydice. With the securing of a position as a teacher of rhetoric in Carthage, Augustine was full of hope that at last all his desires would come to pass. And because he wished it, so did I.

Monica had pressed amphorae of wine, food, and cooking utensils on us as well as a gift of fine linen baby clothes woven by her own hand. I held them to my cheek, their scent and softness, the tiny regularity of the stitches, a remembrance of all that I loved about this woman. She had given us the names of Christian landholders who would be glad to shelter us on our journey, but we seldom stopped there, preferring to sleep out in the soft African night with an ocean of stars above our heads like myriad eyes, bright and watchful.

We were young and hopeful as only the young can be. Augustine's bruised soul soon mended, and after its ordeal in childbirth, my body soon healed and one soft night, the air fragrant with the smell of apples and cut wheat, I took him once again to my bed.

There were many travelers on the road: farmers on their way to market driving patient oxen pulling loaded wagons. Field slaves bending in the vineyards straightened up, fists knuckling their backs in brief respite from their labor, and stared at us as we passed. We pulled aside when the rich passed by, their body-slaves roiling up the dust as they tramped by shouldering their mistress's litter, and sometimes a curtain would twitch aside and a lady's face would look out and smile to see my son so round-eyed at the spectacle. The land lay rich and replete as far as the eye could see, the wheat stirring and riffling in the wind, the vines marching in serried ranks to the furthermost distance where terra-cotta tiles glowed among the deepest green of ancient pines like molten honey in the sun.

The heat of our African summer had faded the land to yellow, but all about us, in hedgerow and ditch, field and orchard, flowers grew rampant. As my father and I had walked together on our journeys, we would play a game, matching colors we saw with stones he used to make his pictures: jasper for poppies, lapis for streams, ivory for jasmine, amethyst for violets. Seldom was I at a loss and my father laughed with pride at my knowledge of his craft. Now I pointed to flowers and cattle and sheep and birds and named them for my son in Punic, my mother's tongue. Augustine laughed and told me he was too young to understand, and, besides, Latin would be his language, but I replied that words were music and when he was older he would recognize their melody like a lullaby sung to him while he slept and, in so remembering, give honor to the grandmother he never knew.

One afternoon near the end of our journey, after a trying day with Adeodatus who had cried and cried, his face flushed, his body hot and squirming in my lap so I could hardly hold him, we turned into a gate that led to a large estate. As we passed the regular plantings of poplars on either side of the road, I remembered a summer long ago when my father and I had trudged wearily up this same road at dawn.

When the house came into view I knew it. It was Nebridius's.

"We must rest here," Augustine said. "The babe is unwell. Perhaps there is someone here who can physic him."

The same steward who had approached my father to consult with him on the work he was to do came out to greet us. He did not recognize me so changed was I from the scabby-kneed urchin who had once run riot with the master's son seven years before. The dominus had received a letter from his son saying that we might visit, the steward said, and bowing led us indoors.

This was the first time I had entered through the front entrance but inside it was as familiar to me as my own home. The polished marble floors where Nebridius and I had run and slid, whooping with merriment until shooed away by cross servant-girls who said we tracked in dirt from outside and the floors only just swept. The rooms where we played hide-and-seek behind the stiff, gilt-legged couches, their plump and tasseled cushions handy missiles for us to throw. The fountain in the central atrium where we had sat on blistering noontimes when the rest of the household lay flattened by the heat, idly flicking water at each other before drifting to the kitchens to see what we could filch, for in those days we were perpetually hungry and the cook was kind and winked at our thefts. Our preferred playground, however, was the gardens, woods, and fields that surrounded the property and I determined to explore all our secret places on the following day, the landscape of a time before Augustine and I met yet linked to the future by our love for Nebridius.

The steward informed us that the family was away, staying at a hunting lodge in the mountains to escape the heat of the plains surrounding Carthage. He showed us to a guest room. As I laid Adeodatus on the bed to change him I wondered if it was fate or chance that had returned me to this place.

Augustine had never been to Nebridius's family estate before so it was I who led him to the bathhouse behind the main building.

Strange it was to return to this place with my own child, my father's grandson. As I stepped from the dazzling light of outside into the half gloom of the bathhouse, I half expected to hear the sound of my father's voice calling to me to hurry, Little Bird, bring water, the plaster sets; I expected to hear the chink of tiles being sorted, the slosh of water in a bucket just put down.

It was here my father had labored so long and painstakingly that summer, and I entered with a prickling of my scalp as if I would see him crouching there still fixing the tesserae into the mortar before it dried, quickly yet precisely, the motion of his fingers never faltering. It was a wonder to me that however small the area he worked, he could always keep the greater design in his head even without the underdrawing he had sketched in charcoal before the plaster was spread. He told me the lines he made with charcoal were drawn onto the tablet of his mind and so he could remember them even when obscured. I thought then that all his love and patient teaching were the shadowy lines that lay beneath the design of my life, hidden yet immutable, never to be erased, dictating who I was and would always be.

Adeodatus fussed and moved restlessly in my arms. Kneeling, I placed him gently on the floor and took off his clothes, and then I undressed myself until I was only wearing my shift.

"I must cool him," I told Augustine.

"Be careful," Augustine replied. "The steps are slippery."

Augustine steadied me as I carefully descended the steps into the pool, Adeodatus naked in my arms. Sitting on the middle step, the water lapping around my waist, I held Adeodatus in the crook of my arm and scooped water over his limbs with my hand, stroking his hot little body to gentle him. At first he flinched to feel this strange sensation on his skin and then he began to move his arms and legs as if he were trying to swim.

Augustine laughed. "My son the water beetle." Stripping off his clothes, he slipped into the pool beside me. Taking our child from me, he stepped down until his feet rested on the bottom and waded out to the center of the pool where he stood, chest-deep, holding his son in his two hands on the surface of the water.

Adeodatus was quiet now and blinked up at Augustine astonished that his world should suddenly turn to liquid as if he had been changed into a fish. I laughed out loud at his look of surprise, so comical and innocent it was, the sound echoing in the vaulted chamber. A shaft of sunlight slanting through an upper window drew Adeodatus's eye from his father's face down to where the sun shone full on me.

"Look," Augustine said softly.

My infant son was smiling at me, the first smile he ever made, as if astounded to discover his mother's face. Laughing with delight at this miracle of his first knowing, I waded out toward him.

"Your grandfather made this place," I told him, tickling his tummy. "Isn't it beautiful?" Then I put my arms around Augustine's bare back so I could hold them both and laid my cheek against it.

In the center of the ceiling was Neptune, god of the deep, part man, part fish, trident raised aloft, sea monsters curled around his torso, giant sinuous bodies, webbed, scaled, and finned, monstrous mouths agape, the design seeming to churn yet ever still, the bright reflection of the pool rippling continuously over its surface so that the ocean seemed alive.

Not for my father a mere catalogue of creatures raised in nets and brought dripping to the marketplace, a sight unremarkable to any householder or market slave. He had reached inside his mind and made a drama of his own devising, a thing of power and mystery, a language for the awe that mariners felt, the tales they told in taverns of monsters glimpsed through waves as tall as mountains as if they swam behind a wall of glass.

Although the bathhouse was roofed and had windows set in each wall to aid in heating, my father had ordered extra windows cut high up near the roof so sunlight fell upon the floor. As the sun altered its position in the sky, a shaft of light lit up the precious stones he used as accents and flung back brilliants of amethyst, carnelian, and lapis lazuli.

"This is his greatest work," I said. "He never made a better."

"No, you are mistaken," Augustine replied. "*You* are his greatest work."

CHAPTER 15

We stayed four days at the home of Nebridius, until whatever childhood ailment that had afflicted Adeodatus passed, and then continued on our way toward Carthage, such a familiar route the shade of my father seemed to walk beside me as if I were a girl again and we were going home, the job done.

We reached Carthage as the west flamed crimson like a praetorian's cloak flung carelessly across the sky, the last in a long line of weary travelers eager to pass through the city gates before curfew, the soldiers stationed there shouting at us to get along, impatient for the taverns. Behind us the northern gates groaned shut, the crossbar clanged on iron brackets then the creak of leather greaves, the tramp of hobnailed boots as the soldiers marched away.

We made our way to the apartment Nebridius had rented for us. It was on the ground floor of a six-story insula near the street of the silversmiths where in daytime the air was filled with the sound of the workmen's tiny hammers, the soft clash of wares hanging from their stalls, and the bitter odor of molten metal. It was not far from the shop where my father had made the memorial for the little girl not many years before.

Our door opened directly onto a small courtyard with an enormous fig tree planted in the center, which made the courtyard dark but blessedly cool on hot days; near it was a well that gave sweet water and a communal oven for baking. By day the women of the insula would congregate in the courtyard washing clothes and hanging them to dry on the low-hanging branches of the tree or slapping flatbread between their palms, gossiping as their children played in the dirt or tottered at their skirts; by night the courtyard became the gathering place of men, their drunken shouts and braying laughter making sleep uneasy. My son had never known the clamor of a city and in those first weeks was fretful, but he soon adjusted and after a time was able to sleep through even the loudest din, an unlooked-for boon for his tired parents.

For my part I sometimes missed the peace and privacy of our first apartment but with Augustine teaching now and gone for much of the day, I was grateful for the company of women. On becoming a mother, I had forever left that solitary state of girlhood behind, and if I sometimes pined to be alone with Augustine as we used to be in our first love, a quick glance at my sleeping son's face soon banished such foolish thoughts. It was as if Augustine and I had been in a beautiful bubble but when my body spilt open in childbirth, the shimmering membrane broke and we were delivered to the world.

At night our music was shouts and too-loud laughter in the courtyard outside our door, cries of tired children refusing to go to bed, and when the men had emptied their wine skins and gone in to their wives, the rhythmic pounding and groans of sex through the parchment thinness of the walls.

Augustine would put down the scroll he was reading and we would exchange a glance. Then he would grin at me, saunter over to where I sat curled in a wicker chair pretending to ignore him and nuzzle my neck, nibbling my ear until in mock exasperation I put down the book I was reading.

"Let's join in," he would whisper. "Feel free to make all the noise you want."

To my surprise I did not fall with child again as if the trauma of Adeodatus's birth had dealt me a secret wound. I think Augustine was relieved. He had been in terror for my life. Except for the crones, the women in the insula were all in a perpetual state of breeding and when I saw their hollowed eyes and the lines etched cruelly on their faces, grown swiftly old with all their cares of motherhood, I was glad to keep my youth for yet a little while. They pitied me in a kindly way and one girl no older than myself, already swelling with her third babe, offered me temple remedies made of disgusting things that I thanked her for and secretly poured away. I won their trust by minding their young ones so they could rest in the searing heat of our summer noontime and in this way gave playfellows to my son and earned friendship for myself.

My closest friend in the insula was Neith, older than myself by a decade and married to a leather-worker. A large-boned woman and rather plain of face, she had such grace of body she drew the eyes of men. She had four children living but had miscarried two while another had died of fever while yet an infant. When I placed my hand upon her own in sorrow, she shrugged and said her mother had birthed nine sons and herself, a daughter, the only one to live.

"It is our destiny," she told me.

We were in the courtyard. It was now December, cold at night and in the early morning but warm enough at midday to sit outdoors. I was seated on my doorstep where a shaft of sunlight warmed the stone; Adeodatus was sleeping in a basket by my feet, lulled by the sound of Neith grinding almonds with a mortar in a stone pestle.

"It's for a cake," she explained. "Mena's birthday is today."

Her three-year-old daughter, Mena, was squatting in a corner of the courtyard digging up dirt between the tiles with a stick and humming tunelessly to herself. At the mention of her name she did not look up as any ordinary child would. Mena was deaf. She had been born with hearing and was just beginning to babble when she caught a fever. When she recovered, Neith noticed that she no longer turned her head when she called her daughter's name.

"It nearly broke our hearts," she told me. "It was like she fell into a dark well." Her eyes had filled with tears but she shook the memory off and picking up her daughter, cuddled her. "But it could have been worse," she said. "At least she lives."

That was typical of Neith and one of the reasons I loved her. Beneath her no-nonsense ways, she had great courage. I suppose she reminded me of Monica.

Though Neith loved all her children dearly, Mena was the one she cherished most and would fly into a fury if she caught the others teasing her. Their favorite game was to shout into her ear and when she didn't jump, they whooped with glee and pulled mocking faces behind her back. Neith would come storming outside, her youngest on her hip, and deal out slaps all round even to children not her own, the courtyard that had echoed with the sound of childish laughter a moment before now loud with lamentation.

It was Neith who taught me how to fold a cloth and sling it round my front to hold Adeodatus.

"Now you have both hands free," she said, knotting it behind my back and tugging on it to make sure it was secure. "And when he gets bigger and can hold on, you can swing him round the side onto your hip or on your back."

I looked down at Adeodatus's face peeking up at me out of the cocoon against my heart and smiled. Now I could read a book and hold him at the same time, a problem I had tried to solve in vain.

Neith studied me with hands on hips, head cocked to one side. "You don't know much about mothering," she said.

I confessed that I did not. And when I told her I had no mother she clicked her tongue as if I were one of her children who had carelessly dropped something in the street and lost it.

"I'll have to take you in hand then," she said. "As if I don't have enough to do."

Despite her gruff words I knew she was quite pleased to have an apprentice.

My barrenness set me apart from the women of the courtyard, who spoke of men as if they were a different species, strange in all their habits, prone to snap and snarl, creatures whom they must humor and feed and clean up after if they would keep them tame. It was not so between myself and Augustine and I often saw a wistfulness come into the other women's eyes when they saw us together, how we laughed and joked, how we touched each other in passing as if we always had to bridge the gap that separated us, no matter it was only air. Especially they noticed how Augustine treated me as an equal and when he was at home performed tasks they deemed women's work like cleaning leeks or changing and bathing the baby. One girl, Lena, even asked me if I had given Augustine a charm to make him so compliant. I laughed out loud but then saw that she was serious, for her husband was a man most simple—sex and food, she told me sadly—and when he was sated did not seem to notice her at all.

Neith's husband, Tazin, was a decent man, hard-working and much in love with his wife, following her every movement with a dog-like gaze, adoring and devoted. Augustine would sometimes sit out in the courtyard with him, a cup of wine at his elbow, and watch admiringly as Tazin worked a piece of leather he brought home in scraps to make his children's shoes.

"Tell me more of this man you follow," Tazin said, matching upper and lower strips of leather and grunting in approval. "He sounds a bit of an oddball to me." He began piercing the edges of the leather sole with an awl.

Augustine took a sip of wine. "You're right," he said. "I don't know why I bother. To tell the truth, I'm becoming impatient with how tidy he makes everything appear, split neatly down the middle—good and bad, flesh and spirit, what have you."

Tazin grunted again. He was not a learned man but not stupid by any means and asked deeply intelligent questions, ones that sometimes left Augustine at a loss at how to answer them.

"I can't see it myself," Tazin said, biting off the waxed thread he was using to sew the leather and threading another length through the bone needle. "Seems to me the world is too much of a jumble, too messy, to be put in boxes like different colored buttons. Take our daughter Mena for example." He held up the little pair of turquoise slippers he was making. "These are for her, by the way. It's her favorite color." He smiled briefly to himself as if he were picturing her face when he gave them to her and resumed stitching. "Anyway, where was I? Oh, yes, Mena. According to the world, Mena's nothing—not only a girl-child but deaf as well. One person actually asked us why we hadn't exposed her outside the walls when we learned she'd lost her hearing." He said this last with the barely controlled rage I had seen in his eyes when people pitied his daughter and treated her as if she were an imbecile.

"I'm sorry," Augustine said.

"What seemed to Neith and me a curse turned out to be a blessing. Her ears may be deaf but her heart hears everything. Mena is special. She is a gift from the gods." He put down the shoe and leaning forward looked directly at Augustine as if to challenge him. "Tell me how something so good can come out of something so bad?"

When Augustine made no answer, Tazin sat back. "It seems to me," he said, "that although the roots may be in darkness the flower grows toward the light. Root and flower are one, not separate. Mena is our flower."

Neith was a devotee of Astarte, the Punic goddess of fertility and war, and one day in early spring she took me to her temple to give an offering of honey for my failure to quicken. I did not tell her I was relieved I was not pregnant, for it was an honor to be invited to her worship.

"You must not tell your man," Neith said, as we hurried through the streets. She did not know Augustine was a Manichee but she knew he was different from the other men and held his learning in great esteem. My own love of reading she thought odd, a strange aberration brought on by my failure to get with child.

"You'll soon be cured," she said.

I was carrying Adeodatus in the sling swiveled round on my hip for he was ten months old now and heavy. With one chubby hand clutching tightly to my dress, he pointed with the other at all he saw, his little imperious finger a demand to name the strange new world to which he had awakened from his dream of infanthood. Recently, he had learned to pull himself up on furniture and, holding on, had begun to take little steps, grinning madly as if he were the first person on earth to discover he had legs. In the evenings when Augustine was home, Adeodatus had made up a game where he would totter stiffly from my chair to Augustine where he sat at the desk reading essays his pupils had written. At the touch of his little hand, Augustine would lay down his pen and grab him up. Then, with a whoop, he would lift him high above his head.

"He flies!" he would say, zooming the little body to and fro. "He's turned into a bird!"

I would look up then from my book and watch them and my heart would beat with violent love, my son's joyous shrieks, his father's teasing, the sweetest music I ever heard except for Augustine's soft "I love you" when he and I lay holding one another after lovemaking or if I should happen to glance up and find his eyes upon me.

"He'll be walking soon," Neith told me one day after she had seen Adeodatus pull himself up and take two steps. "Then watch out."

Aside from frequent trips to the market to buy food and twice weekly visits to the women's baths, once when Neith and I went alone, once when we took all the children to bathe them in the children's pool, it was almost the first time I had left the insula all winter and the spring sun felt heavenly on my face and shoulders, the colors of the street so bright they almost hurt.

"The goddess does not look kindly on the ways of men," Neith said as we were walking, "for they swim on the surface and know nothing of the deeps."

I thought of Augustine and all his ardent talk of things far above the life we women live and knew that Neith spoke true, that somehow the wisdom of which he so often spoke lay not above in realms of light but in the deepest things of blood and flesh and bone.

And in that instant and for the first time since I loved him, he appeared to me lost or, rather, seeking something he could not find. I thought of the quarrel I had overheard between him and Monica when they spoke of his father, Patricius, that man of appetite, and the contempt for him I heard in Augustine's voice. It came to me then as I walked with Neith that Augustine was searching for a father he could respect and love. I wondered if perhaps that had been one of the things that had drawn him to me—except that I had known a father's love before I lost it whereas Augustine had never known it. I wondered if one could lose something one never had or perhaps find something one didn't know was lost.

The temple of Astarte stood in an area of the city unknown to me. Not built in the Roman style with portico and columns, all hard lines and masculine symmetry, it seemed to emerge out of the very earth itself, an ancient rounded cairn with a dark opening in the center through which we passed by bending low. The air smelled sulfurous, decaying, and I could hear the faraway sound of water as if a river gushed beneath our feet. Hosts of black flies circled in the noisome air, crawling horribly on Adeodatus's face until I covered his head with my veil to keep him from breathing them in.

Neith bowed low with palms pressed together and, edging forward in the gloom, placed a tiny clay pot of honey upon the rough stone altar and then backed away, chanting in a low and guttural tongue, one I did not recognize. The statue on the altar was of a woman in a pleated dress with the crescent moon upturned upon her head like the horns of a great bull. Her lips were smiling but her eyes, wolflike, regarded us with feral and pitiless intent. Eggs lay broken on the altar, some fresh, some rotting, and heaped upon the floor a coil of glistening offal, a woman's afterbirth. More dreadful still the tiny corpses of stillborn children like dolls discarded carelessly after play, their blackened faces cauled as if they peered through membranous windows to another world.

I watched as Neith touched her forehead to the altar then backed away. Outside in the blinding sunlight, she put a hand on my shoulder. "Now you will quicken with child again," she said.

I thanked her but found that despite the warmth of the sun

I could not suppress a shudder. The temple seemed more to me a place of death than of life—of flesh but not of soul. Breathing in the clean air again, I understood why Augustine preferred the airy realms of spirit.

CHAPTER 16

Those years we lived at the insula were some of the happiest of my life, marred only by one incident that broke my heart.

It was in September almost two years to the day since we had moved in. It had been a hot day and I had been looking after Neith's children for she was in her ninth month of pregnancy, big as a whale, hugely swollen about the legs and ankles, and finding it hard to catch her breath. I had moved my wicker chair outside for her and she was sitting in the shade of the fig tree in the courtyard fanning herself with a palm leaf, her feet up on a footstool. She reminded me of myself that summer so long ago now it seemed. Adeodatus was just over two and had changed from a sweet little baby into a rampaging toddler. I had a task just keeping him under my eye, let alone Neith and Tazin's little tribe.

Five-year-old Mena was sitting at her mother's feet, tickling them with a chicken feather she had found and laughing when Neith wiggled her toes, an odd sound like the creaking of a gate.

"You look like the Queen of Sheba sitting there," I said, handing Neith a cup of water I had just drawn from the well so it was icy cold. I dipped a cloth in the bucket and laid it on her breast to cool her.

"A fat sow is more like," she said with a tired smile.

I stroked her sweat-soaked hair back from her face. "It won't be long now," I said. "You'll soon be sylphlike again."

"Hah!" she snorted. "I was never sylphlike to begin with, as well you know. But," she added, touching my hand, "it's nice of you to lie. I don't know what I'd have done without you."

"Coped," I replied, squeezing out the cloth and dabbing her forehead. "As you always have. As we women always do."

"Isn't that the truth."

At that moment a crash came from my apartment followed by a howl and running in I found Adeodatus lying on the floor, a stool upturned beside him, his father's oak gall inkpot overturned and a black lake already spreading over his papers and the desk.

"Oh, Hades!" Picking up my son, I checked for damage but he wasn't so much hurt as shocked by his tumble and his wails were those of fear of being punished.

I stuck my head through the door of our sleeping chamber. Neith's youngest children were sitting on my bed playing with the clay animal figures I had given them earlier. Sitting cross-legged on the floor beside the bed was Gil, their nine-year-old brother, a reluctant watchdog.

I smiled at him guiltily. So concerned was I for their mother, I had quite forgotten them. "I know you're bored, Gil," I said, "but watch them just a little while longer. I promise you can go out to play soon."

He folded his arms and stared stonily at me but did not move from his spot. Despite his surly expression he was a good boy who would grow up to be a good man just like his father, Tazin.

"Thank you," I said. "I will buy you something nice tomorrow."

Holding Adeodatus on my hip so he wouldn't paddle his fingers in the ink, I was mopping up Augustine's desk when I heard another crash followed by a piercing scream. This time it came from outside.

Running out I saw that Neith had tried to stand and crumpled forward, tipping over a little table with her cup on it. Mena, who had her back to her mother, played on regardless. This picture of Neith in agony and Mena innocently unaware has stayed with me all my life. I see it as a frozen tableau, perhaps entitled: "The Mother."

At the scream, the other women of the insula had appeared in the courtyard. They clustered there in a group, looking at Neith, none of them seeming to know what to do. I handed the still wailing Adeodatus to Lena and went to Neith.

"What is it?" I said, taking her by the shoulders and supporting her.

"It is time," Neith said, then doubled over again, gasping. "Ye gods!"

It was then I saw the water at her feet and mixed with it, blood.

"Take the children away," I told Lena, "and send someone to fetch the *medica*." To Maris I said: "Send Gil to fetch Tazin."

Both Lena and Maris were staring at Neith, their faces fearful and bewildered.

"Go!" I said and they ran to do as I had bid.

Mena played on.

When Augustine returned at sunset he found our apartment a different place. Many lamps from the neighboring apartments had been brought in and all were lit—the inside of the bedchamber was bright as day and stifling. There had been no question of getting Neith up all those stairs to the fourth floor to her own apartment, so I had helped her into mine and laid her on our bed.

I was seated on the edge of the bed holding Neith's arm; Tazin was seated on the opposite side, holding the other. When she reared forward in agony, we braced her and held her up. She had been laboring like this for hours. And for hours, her blood had flowed from her body, a deadly little stream, the merest trickle but dark as heart-blood, dark as artery blood is dark.

Her face was waxen and bloated, unrecognizable, her eyes rolling back, her mouth set in a rictus of torment. I do not think she knew who we were nor what was happening to her. I pray that she did not. We had sent Mena away, but later I spied her crouching in the corner, eyes fixed on her mother's face, a high-pitched keening issuing from her throat such I have heard a leveret make when it is taken by a fox.

Tazin's face across the bed was as expressionless as a carven idol in a temple; from between lips that never seemed to move he chanted invocations to the ancient Punic gods in a guttural dialect I did not recognize, a deeper counterpart to his daughter's lament as if they prayed in tandem, a sound that stood the hair up on the back of my neck. Sometimes he spoke his wife's name. That, too, was an invocation.

Augustine came to me and touched my shoulder. Then he

moved me gently away and took my place for he could see I was exhausted.

I moved to the foot of the bed where the midwife, sleeves rolled up and bloody to the elbows, was wiping her hands. She had just examined Neith, feeling for the child inside her. She looked at me and with a tiny gesture shook her head then she drew me to the door.

"The baby is dead," she whispered. "I must cut it out."

I shuddered when she explained what she must do but I nodded and straightway began to gather what she required—hot water, clean cloths, a needle, and sheep gut for thread. From her basket she withdrew a linen cloth, which she laid on the foot of the bed; on it she placed the dreadful instruments of her art—a long bronze needle with a blunted end, a length of garroting wire attached to the eye, one end running down the needle's shaft and wound around a wooden toggle; a long-handled bronze spoon and knife, its blade serrated and razor sharp. She was as calm, as practiced, as if she laid a table for a meal.

When all was ready, I lifted Mena in my arms. "Come, little one," I said though I knew she did not hear me. "This is something you should not see." I carried her, unresisting, to Lena's apartment three floors up. Entering, I passed her to Lena then checked on Adeodatus; mercifully, he was sleeping. I stood a moment looking down at him, then briefly touched his head. He shifted and put two fingers in his mouth but did not wake.

"Will my mother die?" a voice asked from the darkness.

In the light from a single oil lamp I saw Gil. He was hunched on the floor by the side of the bed, his back against the wall, his knees drawn up against his chest, minding his siblings still as if

I had forgotten my promise earlier to let him go out and play. I went to him and, kneeling, touched his shoulder. I do not know why I did not gather him in my arms and crush him to my breast as any mother would who seeks to comfort a child who is frightened, lonely, and bereft. Perhaps it was his faithfulness, the dogged patience of his vigil, the way he spoke so calmly, but it conferred on him a kind of dignity. In that moment, he seemed to me full-grown and not a child at all. And so I told him the truth.

"The baby is dead," I said. "We are trying to save your mother now."

He nodded once then turned away, dismissing me.

The sight of him, alone and watchful, came near to breaking me.

When I returned to the bedchamber, the midwife had already begun.

"You must help me," she said. She handed me a cloth and pointed to a bowl of water. "You must wipe away the blood so I can see."

And so I did, closing my mind to what she withdrew piece by piece from Neith's body though my eyes remained wide open.

Neith was quiet now, sunk almost in a coma, her breathing shallow, her eyes flickering behind swollen lids, her only movement now the pull and tug inside her belly as the midwife went about her bloody business.

No longer needed to hold her up, Augustine had moved to stand behind Tazin who sat on as before, his hand on Neith's arm, as if he had not noticed his wife no longer needed his support.

At last the midwife stood back and, with the edge of her sleeve, wiped her forehead. "It is done. I can do no more."

Like a butcher in the market who hands a housewife the calf's liver she has just purchased for her family's dinner, she folded the corners of the waxed cloth around Neith's desecrated child—it was a daughter—and gave it to me. "Take this and burn it," she instructed.

"I will do it," Augustine replied. He took the bundle and left the room.

For three days we sat, Tazin, Mena, and I, by Neith's bedside. Augustine left in the morning and returned at dusk to silently hold my hand or briefly rest his hand on Tazin's shoulder. Every day when he returned, he went upstairs to spend time with Adeodatus who was missing us; at night he slept holding him in his arms.

As for myself, my own child I barely saw except when Augustine brought him to me to nurse from time to time and hold tight, too tightly, for he fussed and squirmed upon my lap until his father took him away.

Tazin did not move nor speak nor would he eat the food I brought him. I sometimes dozed in my chair but when I opened my eyes, I saw Tazin's face, withdrawn into itself, blank as before, and knew there was no change. Neith slept on, neither moving nor even seeming to draw breath so I had to lay my ear close to her lips to hear if she still lived. The bleeding between her legs had stopped the second day and spots of color showed now in her cheeks; the swelling, too, had vanished. We hoped then she would recover. But despite the herbs I mixed in water and trickled between her bloodless lips, on the second night she took a fever and soon was burning up, her head moving fretfully from side to side on the pillow, mumbling words we could not understand as if she were an actor in a dream.

Then on the third day, a little after sunset, she opened her eyes and they were lucid.

"Bring my children to me," she commanded.

I left to fetch them and then gathered them around her bedside, watching from the shadows as Neith bid her children farewell one by one, laying hands on each and kissing them. Then she reached for her husband's hand and Tazin bent over her. When he raised his head again, Neith was gone.

CHAPTER 17

Dry-eyed I washed Neith's body and wove flowers in her hair; dry-eyed I stood beside the funeral pyre outside the city walls and watched her burn, her ashes sealed into an urn; dry-eyed I welcomed mourners to my home and served them wine and funeral meats.

Augustine and I took away the bed in which she died and bought another. I scrubbed the floor where she had bled and the courtyard tiles but no matter how hard I rubbed there still remained a stain.

"Do you want to move?" Augustine asked one evening. It was a month after Neith's death.

I was sitting in my chair, the same chair I had carried outside for Neith so she could rest in the shade of the fig tree. I remember how hot she had been, how she had wiggled her toes to make Mena laugh.

Mena. She could not hear and so had never learned to speak. Now she no longer smiled or laughed but watched the dumb show of the world with too serious eyes and made her silent judgment upon it.

"No," I told Augustine. "Neith's children need me."

Since their mother's death, I had become a sort of stepmother to Neith's children, nursemaid rather, for they did not treat me as a mother, their little bodies stiff in my arms when I embraced them, eyes that followed me without interest. All the fun, all the noise and naughtiness of normal children had died with Neith and in its place a perfect and most unnatural acquiescence.

"Eat this, little one," I would say. Or: "Wash your hands." "Time for bed." In each and every thing required of them they were compliant to a fault. Like wild animals kept too long in captivity, their spirits dwindled with each passing day, their movements became more sluggish, their eyes more dull. I watched them turn to shades before my very eyes and could do nothing.

I had tried to speak to Tazin about my fears but he just stared at me as if, like Mena, he saw my mouth moving but heard no words.

After the funeral, he shut himself away in their apartment with the children. No sound emerged, not even the sound of weeping. After three days, I knocked and entered.

Tazin was sitting in a chair with Mena on his lap, the other children huddled at his feet. The room stank of unwashed clothes and bodies, a slop bucket in the corner was filled to the brim with human waste, rotting food lay uneaten on the table, all the meals I had prepared. The only sound, the buzzing of a thousand flies. But the most disturbing thing of all was not the filth but the stillness: Tazin was a man whose hands were seldom idle, always he was working on something or other whether it was shoes for the children, a leading harness for the latest baby newly walking so, looped over her arm, Neith could keep the child from stumbling, a leather jerkin for Gil, the boy's pride and joy because it was a miniature of the one his father wore. Now Tazin's hands lay empty, lifeless, not even lifted to caress Mena's curls as he had been fond of doing so that in her silent world she could feel the touch of her father's love.

Turning on my heel I went straightway to fetch Augustine. Tazin did not resist when Augustine pulled him to his feet and sleepwalked him down the stairs to the courtyard. I followed with Siri, the three-year-old, in my arms, leading Mena by the hand. The others came after, Gil bringing up the rear. While Augustine fed them, I knocked on Lena's and Maris's doors and told them what I'd found. Their husbands fetched us bucket upon bucket of water from the well and we scoured Tazin's apartment—I did not think of it as Neith's—from top to bottom.

After that, despite the lateness of the hour, we women bathed the children in the courtyard, washed and combed their matted hair, and dressed them in clean clothes we borrowed from those neighbors who had children the same or approximate age. By this time the other women of the insula had joined us, even old Sylvia who seldom emerged from her top-floor apartment for her joints pained her and she found the stairs difficult. For the first time since Neith's death the courtyard echoed with the sound if not of happiness, then a kind of contented hum we women make when we go about some common task.

"Do you have any scissors, Maris? These knots are impossible to comb out."

"Has anyone seen the oil flask? I swear I put it down a moment ago."

"Stand still, honey, while I dry you. Sylvia, pray pass me that dry towel."

Tazin watched dull-eyed, nine-year-old Gil standing beside

him. The boy's childlike body proclaimed him subject still to women's rule yet since his mother's death his soul had passed beyond our hands. By some collective mother's instinct we knew this and left him in peace.

The water from the well was cold and could not be heated; the children squealed and did a little dance of protest, making us women smile. Perhaps it was this childish sound that roused Tazin; perhaps he heard Neith's voice, her brisk, no-nonsense way of speaking, echoed in our own; perhaps her shade compelled him. I only know that all at once he stirred and taking a bucket and sponge from Lena, silently began to wash his children's bodies. Gil watched him for a moment then began to do the same.

After the little ones were bathed, Augustine and I carried them indoors and sat them round our table. I closed the door so Tazin and Gil could strip and wash unmolested by women's eyes. Then I heated wine, sweetened it with honey, and gave it to the children to warm them and make them sleepy.

"You are worn out," Augustine said, putting his arms around me.

"The children need me," I repeated.

I had the words but I could not find the strength to tell him why I had not yet wept for my friend.

If I could, I would have told him the torch the priest thrust deep into the oil-soaked wood of Neith's funeral pyre, he thrust deep into the center of my soul. Neith's body burned and turned to ash; my soul burned still.

Two days before the Roman festival of Saturnalia, when master and slave exchange roles and the world is topsy-turvy for one brief night of the year, Tazin knocked on our door.

"Come in, my friend," Augustine said.

It was four months since we had lost Neith and Tazin was much changed, thinner in the face, his beard going to gray, the skin around his eyes perpetually creased with tiredness and whereas once he had been a straight-backed vigorous man, he now walked with a somewhat shambling gait as if he were twenty years older. He had not done what many widowers with young children do—marry again. Indeed, he had confided to Augustine when they had sat out in the cold under the stars one night that he would never wed again.

I had just put Adeodatus to bed and was folding laundry at the kitchen table. I paused to listen.

"For Neith was all the mother they ever knew or wanted and all the wife," Tazin said. "She can never be replaced. Not to them, not to me."

A long silence followed, then Augustine's voice, so low I strained to hear: "The measure of love is to love without measure."

I heard the soft chink of cups as if they saluted one another.

This time Tazin refused the drink Augustine offered him. Declining a chair, he stood somewhat awkwardly in the middle of the room as if he were about to make a speech.

"I have come to bid you good-bye," he said. "And to thank you for all you have done for us. We are moving to Hippo Regius. I have a cousin there." He took my hand shyly. "A better friend Neith never had," he said, his voice becoming hoarse. "She told me once, soon after you moved in, that you were a woman made of iron."

I smiled at that for Neith had said the same to me one day when she came upon me on my knees in the courtyard rinsing out Adeodatus's breechcloths in a bucket. I had been irritable, exhausted from nursing an infant all night, and liberally splashed with dirty water. When I would have politely thanked her for the compliment—for although a familiar face in the insula, she was still a stranger to me—she spoilt it by adding: "Prone to rust when wet."

We howled with laughter, holding onto one another and upsetting the bucket. That seemed even more hilarious and set us off again. We only stopped when six-month-old Adeodatus cried with fear at seeing his mother act so strangely. I think that was the first time we knew we would be friends.

"I made your son these," Tazin said. He handed me a pair of child's boots made of soft kid, dyed leaf-green and tooled with gold arabesques and stars; the tassels on the ends of the laces had silver bells. Truly the shoes were a work of art and much too beautiful to wear.

"Thank you, Tazin." I kissed his cheek.

He ducked his head in embarrassment, then pressed a tiny object into my hand. "This is Neith's. I found it when I was packing. I know she wants you to have it."

I looked down and saw a tiny bronze figurine of a Punic goddess. It was not Astarte, for it did not have a crescent moon, but another goddess.

"She is the consort of Anzar, the god of rain," Tazin explained. "Neith had a special devotion to her."

I kissed it, then closed my fingers around it. It fit perfectly in my palm, entirely hidden in my flesh. Bereft of words, I nodded. For the first time since Neith's death I felt tears cloud my eyes. Perhaps it was the rain god who blessed me, perhaps Neith herself, but suddenly I was weeping, a flood I could not stop, a tempest so violent it made me shudder. I held onto myself and collapsed forward. Like my aunt. Like Neith when her pains had come upon her. Then Augustine's arms were about me, holding me.

Neith, I wept. *Friend. Woman of Iron.*

And then all at once I was laughing, tears raining down my face. *Prone to rust when wet.*

The next day I bid Tazin and the children good-bye, holding the little ones tightly one by one. I stroked Mena's head and put a honey cake in her hand. She looked at me as her father lifted her into the cart and fluttered sticky fingers at me, a tiny gesture of farewell. Gil I did not shame by hugging but shook him solemnly by the hand.

"Take care of your brothers and sisters," I told him.

He nodded, hitched his belt the way his father did, then swarmed onto the bench beside Tazin all arms and legs and scabby knees. I hid a smile. Augustine, Adeodatus, and I, Lena and Maris and their families, and even ancient Sylvia leaning on her stick waved until they turned a corner.

CHAPTER 18

"It is good to see you smile again," Augustine said, stroking my cheek. We were lying in each other's arms worn out, close to sleep. I had come to him parched, starved for his touch, a wanderer in a desert who, half-crazed, glimpses city walls in the distance but fears it is a mirage. The frenzy of our joining, the sweet long drawn-out violence of it told me it was no illusion but fact. And from the ardor of his caresses, I knew that Augustine, too, had been in exile though I did not know then how far he had roamed within the desert of his mind.

It was the night of Saturnalia and the streets rang with drunken laughter and shouts. We did not celebrate Saturnalia with pagan customs but by going to the theater, something we had done often before our son was born but seldom since we returned to Carthage.

One evening we got dressed up—I in a new dress Nebridius had given me for my eighteenth birthday in the autumn, Augustine in a tunic I had embroidered at the neck and hem—and strolled through the darkening streets to the theater. The night was cold and I walked with my green cloak wrapped around me. Adeodatus was riding on his father's shoulders, his splendid green boots drumming on his father's chest, eyes fever-bright in the moving torchlight, a chubby finger pointing out things for naming—"What that?" forever on his lips—the whole world a puzzle and delight until we took our seats. The cadence of the poetry soon lulled him into drowsiness, his chin sinking, then jerking upright, then sinking again, two fingers slipping slickly from his mouth as he sank deeper into slumber from which nothing, not even the audience's thunderous applause, could disturb. I drew my cloak around him and the warm hump of his body curled against mine made me long to be with child again.

I sat with my son in my lap, Augustine's arm around me, and listened to Virgil, that greatest of all the Roman poets, tell of the tragic love between Dido, Queen of Carthage, and Aeneas, who forsook her for a kingdom, a story engraved on every Punic heart down to the last syllable and trope, be it the most scabrous beggar on the temple steps or the wealthiest citizen in Africa Province, a story that bespoke a Roman's callous disregard for our native soil, that most lush of all soils, a land despoiled and then abandoned. This, for me, was heaven.

I close my eyes and Dido is in her tower, the ships of Ilium unfurling in the offing, the air so bright, so glassy, she sees her lover, Aeneas, standing at the prow, so clear she can almost touch him though his back is turned. He gazes toward Italy, the Rome that is yet to be.

And behind the Queen, in her chamber, the bed where once he

lay still holds his shape, the pillow the hollow of his head though the sheets are cold. No child of his to hold.

The audience groans, a woman sobs aloud, and no one silences her. Our hearts are Dido's, her anguish our own. She our queen and we her people, who know what the Romans will never know—that love is more than duty. That love is all there is.

Augustine's arm tightens about me and I lean against him.

"I love you," Augustine whispers in my ear.

"As I do you."

After the performance we stood on the terrace overlooking the ocean, as the theater was set on the clifftop east of the city. A vast blackness stretched before us, behind us the still-illuminated theater and the lights of the city. Augustine was holding Adeodatus, for he had grown too heavy for me to carry when he was sleeping.

"Remember I said that one day I would leave Carthage and cross the ocean to Italy?" Augustine said.

The gale blowing off the sea was bitter but I did not move closer to him, instead I shifted a little farther away, only a step, but it seemed a great distance. I nodded but I did not know if he could see me in the dark.

"I have decided to apply for a position in Rome," he said. "Carthage is too far from the center of things. There is no future for me here."

The wind buffeted me and I braced myself against it, my veil snapping out behind me like a banner. But it was not the wind that chilled me as I waited for him to continue but a terrible fear. The nothingness that stretched endlessly away would be my life if he should go away. I gripped tightly to the balustrade.

I will not stand in his way, I thought. If I have to I will let him go.

When I still did not look at him, Augustine put himself between the parapet and me. The wind instantly stilled.

"You are thinking," he said, "that I would leave you here."

When I did not reply, he encircled me with one arm and drew me to him while with the other he still cradled our child. He laughed softly. "Do you think I would go without you? Do you think me Aeneas, my love? And you Dido, Queen of Carthage?"

I shook my head, ashamed for doubting him, but that vision of the blackness that lay beyond remained with me.

"Come," he said. "It is cold. We should go home."

Side by side we walked back through the night-lit city, so familiar I did not need to think which turn to take, which street, for I had lived within its walls all my life. Never had I considered leaving Africa, the land of my heritage, the land that was as known to me as my own body, as my lover's, my child's. As we walked my fears receded and were replaced by an eagerness so intense I had to stop and catch my breath although the hill we climbed was not so steep. Not to tread on different soil, hear different tongues, taste different foods, see different customs, suddenly was a thing unthinkable though I had not been discontented before. I took Augustine's hand.

For you, I vowed, *I will go to the farthest reaches of the empire. Say but the word and I will gladly make the wilderness my home.*

In my simplicity and ignorance of how the world works, I thought that when Augustine spoke of Rome it was a fact accomplished, for

I could not imagine him wanting something and it not straightway being given him. But after he began applying for teaching posts in Italy and wrote endless letters to would-be patrons who might sponsor his career, stand friend to him at the imperial court in Milan, months dragged by and soon it was more than a year since we had stood that night on the terrace.

Augustine was increasingly discontented with his position as rhetor in Carthage. He often told me hair-raising tales of what his students got up to in the classroom, their rudeness, their drunken pranks—once they put a dead puppy in his scroll case—their cruel bullying of the younger students, fourteen-year-old boys away from home for the first time and easy prey.

"The jokes I can put up with," he told me one night as we were having dinner. "Even their immense ignorance. But the worst is they change tutors behind my back to avoid paying my fees, these so-called sons of noblemen who have no respect for anything except their own pleasures."

He looked at me despairingly across the table, and for the first time I noticed dark circles under his eyes put there by the burdens he carried, how to clothe and feed us, his guilt over the poorness of our lodgings but most of all, his monumental boredom in his job, a torture for one so intelligent, so quick to apprehend the world. And deeper than mere boredom, a restlessness of spirit that drove him ever to seek that which was just beyond reach and, when he grasped it at last, to discover that it was not what he wanted after all. Sometimes, in the darkest part of the night when I could not sleep, a voice whispered that one day he would find that I was not what he had wanted after all and he would seek another.

"Unless he is rich and can do as he likes," he said, "a man is like a mule harnessed to a heavy load and beaten up the road. He longs for freedom, to be forever free of the whip that drives him, the taste of the iron bit in his mouth, the blinders over his eyes so he can only see the path laid out before him." He gave a small smile. "Forgive me," he said. "I am more than usually self-pitying tonight."

I touched his hand. "Mule is right," I said. "But that is a good thing: you are more than stubborn enough to find a way."

He laughed as I had intended he should and we spoke of other things. But I did not forget his restlessness and prayed that he would find what he was searching for and soon.

At this time, he was engaged in writing a treatise on aesthetics entitled *De Pulchro et Apto—On the Beautiful and the Fitting*—dedicated to Hierius, a man he had never met but who was famed in Rome for his oratory.

"I must flatter him before he will assist me to a post." He pulled a face. "I think academics are the vainest creatures alive. They long to be admired."

"I thought women were supposed to be the vainest?" I teased, sitting down beside him and scooting along the bench so I could read what he had been writing.

"That's a myth invented by . . ."

"*Academics*," we both said in unison and burst out laughing.

He flung down his pen, pulled me to him, and buried his face in my hair, his favorite position when we were alone and sitting side by side. I could feel his weariness in the tension of his body.

I read aloud a few sentences of what he had written.

"'What then is beauty and in what does it consist? What is it that attracts us and makes us love it? Unless there be beauty and grace in those things, they would be powerless to win our hearts.'

"The yeast in the bread," I murmured, almost to myself.

Augustine raised his head from my neck. "What did you just say?"

I repeated it.

He frowned. "Explain."

I smiled inwardly, for I had heard him use the same tone when Nebridius said something that puzzled him but piqued his interest. I could imagine him commanding his students in the same voice, intense, almost stern, his eyes fixed on them like an arrow, like a hawk ready to drop down on a hapless rabbit. No wonder they played tricks on him. He must terrify them.

"I mean," I said, "that the Manichees are wrong when they say the material form is a cage in which the soul is trapped like a bird beating its wings against the bars. Beauty or soul, it seems to me, is more like yeast in bread. When I bake bread I mix it into the flour and the dough rises, but if I cut the bread I can't find the yeast like some lump in the middle. It's mixed right through because it *is* the bread. *Ergo* . . ."

Augustine had taught me this term and I was quite proud of using it, especially when I saw him blink.

"Beauty and form," I went on, "soul and flesh cannot be divided except perhaps by death. As you say, it is the *form* that draws our love but that form is indistinguishable from the beauty. Or rather, it *is* the beauty."

I felt a little breathless after this speech and a little ridiculous. He was the teacher, after all. Touching his face, I felt the roughness of his unshaven jaw, smoothed my thumb over the dark circles under his eyes. "I do not love merely your body nor do I love merely your soul. I love them both but not as halves of one whole, but one whole itself, as yeast and bread are one loaf. *Both* are you. Both are Augustine."

He was looking at me in a way I could not interpret and then he threw back his head and laughed, so long and so loudly I feared Adeodatus would waken in the next room.

"I don't believe it," he said at last, wiping tears from his eyes.

"It makes no sense?" I asked.

"On the contrary," he said. "It makes perfect sense. Your analogies have taught me more than all the philosophers put together, including Cicero."

"I think best in pictures," I said.

CHAPTER 19

Some days later, an old friend of my aunt's came to me and told me my aunt was dying and asked to see me. While my conscience had told me I should make my peace with her, I had not had the courage to visit her since returning to Carthage.

It was strange to walk the streets alone in the district where my uncle's house lay, for I had not returned to the neighborhood since the day I left with Augustine almost seven years before. No one spoke to me or raised a hand in greeting, so changed was I from that wild girl who roamed the city years before. Even the fountain looked the same, the chips on the rim that I used to run my fingers over so familiar I could find them with my eyes shut. I marveled that so much could remain the same when I was so changed.

With each step I had taken across the city, I was retracing my past, returning to the place where, for good or ill, I had begun my life. Now I must return and somehow set things right. The image of my aunt in the courtyard, my last sight of her, haunted me. My own motherhood, the bright flame that burned within me for my child, a flame devouring all other loves except two, my love for my child's father and my own, had also burned in my aunt. This

I now knew beyond all certainty. For what else could cause such agony, such sorrow in a woman unless she be parted forever from her child?

A lump rose in my throat when I remembered the hardness of my heart when I left her house. That I had done so partly out of fear, to proclaim that her sad woman's life had no correspondence with my own, did not absolve me.

When I arrived at that familiar door, I hesitated. I think if I had heard my uncle's voice from within I would have turned and walked away, but I could hear no sound of voices except the noises from the street.

The door was unlatched, so I entered. No lamps were lit, and dirt gritted the floor beneath my sandals, a sad decline as my aunt could never abide disorder and filth in her home. The kitchen, usually so immaculate, was in disarray with dirty pots and knives piled on the table, a platter of stale bread and olives, a wedge of moldy cheese, and the appalling smell of rancid fish heads in a cauldron on the hearth as if my aunt had been making soup when she suddenly took ill.

I pulled aside the curtain to the bedchamber at the back of the house. In the half-light I could make out my aunt lying on the bed, a tiny shrunken figure like a doll, a soiled coverlet molding her stick-like body like a shroud that scarcely rose and fell so light her breath.

"It is I," I said, crossing to the bed.

Her eyes opened and fixed on me.

As when a breath of wind shivers the surface of a pool, so her eyes seemed to flicker, change, become at last quiescent as she recognized me, and her sparrow-bone hand rose up from beneath the coverlet and grasped my gown with surprising strength. I bent low and put my ear against her working mouth.

"You," she said and closed her eyes.

I thought at first she had gone but then her eyes opened again.

"When my brother brought you to me, a motherless scrap, filthy and neglected, I thought that God had answered my prayers." She spoke in a harsh whisper so I had to strain to hear.

Panting as if she had run a long race, she gestured at a clay cup that stood on the floor beside the bed. I filled it with water from a jar in the kitchen and held it to her lips. She followed me with her eyes as if she feared I would abandon her in that wretched room with the sounds of the living heard but distantly, the sun falling on neighbors, friends, strangers, even the very stones in the street outside her door, never again to warm her skin, the hearth in her kitchen cold and unswept.

I did not know where my uncle was but I wondered that two lives, albeit lived in enmity all those years, could have become so separate, so estranged, that one would let the other cross beneath that dread portal, death, alone and quite friendless.

I sat down beside the bed and took her hand in both my own.

"Hush," I said. "I am here."

"When your father brought you to us, you were so beautiful," she said as if she hadn't heard, as if she had a speech by heart and must get it out before memory failed. "I sat by you while you slept and could not believe how perfect you were, the creases in your wrists, your ankles, your hair mussed and rubbed away from sleeping on your back, your tiny hands, your sweet, milky breath on my neck. You were the answer to my prayers. I loved you. And I longed for you to love me as well." Exhausted, she fell back on the pillow gasping. I helped her to another sip of water and dabbed her mouth with the corner of my veil, she who had prided herself on the cleanliness of her home now lying in a nest of squalid rags.

"When your father returned from his travels," she went on when she had recovered, "you forgot me. He who had not bathed you or sat in the doorway with you on his lap so you could see the sights or sung to you to make you sleepy, now he was the one you turned to as a sunflower lifts its face to the sun. And when you were four he took you away." Her voice sunk to a whisper as if the words bruised and must be handled gently. "Ever after, this home became a prison to you, I your jailor. I wanted only to protect you, to save you from the life of disappointment and grief that has been my own lot." I knew what I must say but I could not. My pity and remorse were sharp flints in my mouth.

"Lift me up," she commanded. "There is something under my pillow."

I put my arms about her shoulders and lifted her, the weight of her body no more than my six-year-old child's, and felt beneath her pillow. I withdrew a small box and put it in her hands.

She lay awhile holding it. "Take it," she said at last.

Inside was an iron key, the key to her bank box, her savings, the money she had received at all the births she had attended over the years, she said, hidden from a husband who would drink it up as he had drunk up her heart's blood and all her hopes. Lying at the bottom of the box beneath the key was the copper bracelet and the length of ribbon threaded through it, the same as I had left the day I quit her house forever.

"Only give me a Christian burial," she said. "The rest is yours."

She closed her eyes. I stayed with her as evening fell and lit a lamp so she would see me keeping vigil. I held her hand and whispered to her though I do not think she heard.

Sometime in the night a tremor shook her and her eyes flew open. When she saw me she smiled, a look of great beauty and tenderness. "My daughter," she said. Then: "I would have loved to see your child."

"Mater," I replied, stroking her face. "Forgive me for not loving you as I should have."

But her eyes fixed like agates in a frieze and looked on me no longer, neither did she hear my too-late confession.

Kissing her on the forehead, I crossed her hands on her breast. Then I took the wooden cross she had nailed to the wall above the bed and, placing it on her chest, tenderly drew the coverlet over her face. The rest of the night I spent sweeping and cleaning her home so she would not be shamed. At dawn I went to fetch the priest.

I spent most of the money my aunt had left me on a lavish funeral. Her bier was placed before the altar in the church in the center of her brother's—my father's—glorious mosaic; the lion, the angel, the eagle, and the ox a fitting escort from this world to the next. With a priest leading the way, choir boys singing so sweetly, the bell-like purity of their voices so ravishing passersby stopped in the street to listen, some crossing themselves, some weeping openly, we processed to the church of St. Flavius by the southern gate beneath which lay the catacombs of Christians. Here my aunt was interred in a stone sarcophagus I had had carved, instructing the stonemasons to adorn it with *putti*, chubby infants with creased wrists and ankles, dimpled knees and elbows, romping in a field of flowers. Denied babies in life, denied the sight of Adeodatus, in death I gave her children of stone. It was both a tribute and a penance, for I had given her a heart of stone when I should have given her one of living flesh.

CHAPTER 20

Another year passed, one in which we heard Augustine's treatise on beauty had been received with admiration and acclaim in Rome and in Milan, but still he received no word of a teaching position.

Then one morning in spring, a messenger arrived at the house with the offer of an academic post in Rome.

Suddenly, after all this waiting, we were leaving. This longed-for event brought a kind of sweet melancholy. It made me look on Carthage, the city of my birth and all my life, with different eyes. Perched above the ocean and open to the cooling winds and scorching Numidian heat as if it hung suspended in the heavens, it came to seem a place of light and grace. The opulence of its colors enraptured me as when Augustine and I were first in love and saw with the self-same eyes oranges piled in the market place, blood-red pomegranates in their woven baskets, their seeds Persephone's brief parole, blue linen curtains snapping in the breeze, in the forum brocaded cloaks of every hue clasped with jeweled brooches about the throat, everywhere a richness as if the city said: "Remember me."

The prospect of leaving Carthage acted like a tonic on

Augustine and he grew cheerful again. I heard him humming to himself sometimes when he was grading student papers in his study, a thing he had never done before.

Each night when we lay in each other's arms we talked of Rome, what it was like, its ancient history, the sights that we would see there.

"It is not the seat of government any longer. The court is in Milan," Augustine said. "But the Curia where the senators voted is still there. The rostra outside the Curia is still there, the very place where Cicero stood and gave his speeches to the mob, where Caesar and Mark Antony stood. And Sulla surrounded by the heads of his enemies taken in the proscriptions. All this remains."

"I would visit the Temple of the Vestals," I said. "But not the Colosseum." I shuddered remembering the killing I had seen in the amphitheater in Carthage.

"We will visit all but that," Augustine replied. "Oh, my love, this is a new life for us."

I kissed him. "Yes," I said. "But it will break your mother's heart. And Nebridius will be sad too."

"Nebridius says he will come and visit," Augustine said. "He is as eager as we are to see Italy. So have no fear for him, my love." Augustine knew how much I would miss my friend. I would miss Monica, too, for I had come to look on her as a mother.

We had sent a message to Monica letting her know of our plans, and she came to us at once. Except for that one time in Thagaste when I overheard the argument between Monica and Augustine, I have always known her serene like a still pool on a summer's day, its surface only riffled by the wind but not disturbed. But when we told her of our move, it was as if we had heaved a stone into the middle of that calm. Monica was proud of Augustine for being offered such a post, but she was also troubled. For Christians, Rome was an evil place, the site of great suffering and persecution. And for the Punic people, Rome was the ancient enemy of Carthage, conquered by Scipio Africanus five hundred years before.

"But also a holy site, Mother," Augustine reminded her. "For Peter and Paul were martyred there."

I was sitting beside her on a couch and had taken her hand when Augustine had begun to speak. Adeodatus was at school. He had been excited as only eight-year-old boys can be, seeing adventures around every corner. When we told him we would have to take a ship and sail across the ocean his joy knew no bounds, and that night we heard him moving about in his room and talking to himself when he should have been asleep.

"I am happy for you, of course," she said, "I shall miss you but that is nothing. The only thing that troubles me is that I feel your destiny lies here, my son. In Africa."

"Mother," Augustine said, coming to sit the other side of her on the couch and taking her hand. "Why else did you and father pay so much for my education if not for advancement? Carthage is well enough but it is still so far from the center of things."

Then she sat up straighter, the stiffening of her spine a kind of spiritual resolve. "Of course you must go," she said. She laughed, a little shakily. "*Of course* you must. Forgive me. I am a selfish old woman."

She kissed Augustine then turned to me and did the same. "I will miss you both."

In this way, she gave us her blessing. She never seemed braver to me than at that moment. Later, I would remember her courage and seek to emulate it.

On the day we were to sail we left in the late afternoon—for high tide was at dusk—and descended to the outer harbor where a merchant ship lay, which would carry us to Rome. Monica and Nebridius accompanied us. I held Adeodatus by the hand, Monica held his other, Nebridius was on my other side. Servants followed behind, pulling a cart carrying our few belongings, mostly clothes and scrolls.

When we arrived at the harbor we walked out along the long stone jetty to the very end where the ship was moored. Up close it seemed enormous to me, the portals along the hull above the water line where the oars would emerge, dark empty holes. Within were benches where slaves were chained, their strength the power that would speed us through the water if the wind failed.

Now that the moment to depart had come, I felt a lifting of the heart as if the wind filled it and strained it at its mooring, eager to be gone. But I dreaded saying good-bye.

I hugged Monica tightly and when I would not let go she gently disentangled my arms. "God be with you, dear daughter," she said and briefly rested her hand on the top of my head as if in blessing.

Then Monica turned to her grandson and kneeling put her arms about him and pressed his head tight against her breast. Adeodatus was freely crying now but I saw Monica whisper something in his ear that made him smile. Releasing him she put her hand briefly upon his head and then drawing out a little wooden ship from the folds of her skirts she gave it to him. "Here," she said. "Now you are Captain Adeodatus."

I embraced Nebridius.

"Do not weep, Naiad," he said. "I will come and visit soon."

Then turning to Augustine. "My friend," he said. "Make sure you live up to your name."

Next he picked up Adeodatus. "So, Captain," he said. "Remember to steer by the stars and make sure you keep these landlubbers, your parents, in check."

Augustine went to speak to the captain and when he returned told us the sailing was delayed because a shipment of wine had not arrived from the vineyards north of the city and the captain had to wait for it before casting off.

"He says we can stow our belongings now," Augustine said. "But if the shipment doesn't arrive in the next hour, he says, we will miss the tide and have to wait until the next high tide tomorrow."

Monica looked into Augustine's eyes for what seemed a long time. Then she embraced him. She looked so small in his arms as if she were the child and he the parent. I looked at Adeodatus's curly head at my elbow and knew that one day it would be the same for me—he a full-grown man, me an old woman stooped with age, although Monica was not bent but ever straight like a centurion's spear.

"You get your things on board," Monica said. "I will visit the shrine of St. Cyprian to pray for a safe voyage. I have never been and have always wanted to go." She turned to Nebridius. "Would you mind accompanying an old woman?" she asked.

Nebridius took her hand and put it through his arm.

"We will return in time to see you sail," Monica said.

Augustine put his arm around my waist, his hand resting on our son's shoulder as we watched Nebridius and Monica walk away. Once Monica stumbled but Nebridius steadied her and, looking back over his shoulder, nodded at us. She will be all right, his gesture said.

We boarded the ship and the captain showed us to a small cabin in the stern, hardly more than a kind of cowhide tent stretched on a frame. Inside were sleeping pallets and two buckets. Immediately on stepping from the gangway onto the deck I knew I was in another world. And in my breast I felt a kind of strange unraveling, which terrified and exulted me all at once. When I pictured that upturned fishing boat on the shore under which Augustine and I had sat in the weeks before our union, I saw it as a sign, a portent of the future. We had so often talked of what lay beyond the sea's gray line, the coast of Italy, Ostia, Rome's great port, that now it seemed as if the strength of our imaginings, of Augustine's longings, had conjured up the fact.

While I stowed our things inside the tent, Augustine followed Adeodatus around the deck to make sure he did not get in the sailors' way as they continued their loading.

The loading had been completed and the sun was saffron in the west when the captain raised his voice.

"Cast off," he shouted. "Ready to weigh anchor."

I turned to Augustine in surprise. "I thought we were waiting for a shipment of wine? Monica and Nebridius will return and find us gone."

He looked away and said in low voice, "I could not face seeing my mother weep as we sailed away."

I stared at him and imagined Monica arriving and finding the ship sailed, her son gone. I thought of how I would feel if my son deceived me and stole away.

Standing at the rail we looked back toward the shore and watched as the lights of the harbor receded then winked out, drowned in darkness so inky vast it seemed we floated in a void.

CHAPTER 21

That first night on board Augustine was quiet, and I knew he hated himself for the way he had deceived his mother. I was silent, too, still angry at him for causing Monica such sorrow.

"I can't help seeing my mother's face when she found the ship gone," he said to me when we were lying side by side on our pallets, our son snuggled in between us, the curtain drawn across the opening.

I did not reply.

"You are right to be angry," he said after a moment. "I should not have done it."

The misery in his voice made me relent a little. As with the theft of the pears in his youth, he was brooding on what he had done and felt a terrible remorse, a punishment far greater than my censure. When I told him this he replied: "My relief that we could slip away without my mother knowing convicts me in my heart."

"Write her a letter begging her forgiveness and give it to the captain," I said. "I heard him say his ship returns to Carthage as soon as they unload and take on more cargo at Ostia. She will receive it in a month."

This comforted him a little and soon he slept.

Augustine, Adeodatus, and I spent many hours standing at the bow watching as, bladelike, the ship cleaved the waves, shouldering up great gouts of spray that sometimes drenched us, making us laugh out loud. We saw schools of sleek gray fish racing alongside the hull as if to outstrip us to our destination, leaping gleaming and supple from the waves as if they sought to fly. I knew them to be dolphins for I had seen them figured in my father's mosaics in the bathhouses of the rich, but to my son all he saw was a miracle and a delight, and I thrilled with him as he drank this new world in with shining eyes, the sorrow of his parting from his grandmother all forgotten as is the way with children. One moment they are inconsolable, the next, lit up with joy.

I had often taken Adeodatus to the harbor to watch the boats, and now his joy knew no bounds that he was sailing in one. He spent hours squatting beside the sailors watching what they did, cording and coiling rope, turning great capstans, fishing off the side. I would hear his voice high and continuous, questioning them in all they did, and their replies, gruff but kind and astonishingly patient. When I rebuked him once for pestering the sailors, a seaman, whose face was so seamed by the sun he looked ancient though his movements were supple like a much younger man, said: "He don't bother me, mistress. I have one just like him on shore."

At night, the sailors would sit on the deck and tell stories of their seafaring, some so fantastical that I smiled to myself although Adeodatus's face was solemn and rapt. Tales of enormous fish that could swallow ships whole, of fish that flew, and others with swords for snouts, and of great storms when Poseidon heaved up the waves like mountains so high the sailors called on their mothers and the gods.

"You'll give him nightmares," I said.

"He's a little man is what he is," one sailor said and ruffled my son's hair.

One morning Adeodatus shouted, pointing over the side and there before us swam a swordfish just as the sailors had told him. He looked with triumph at me and the sailor who had told him grinned.

I learned then that stories that seem improbable can oftentimes be true and that what we think we know about the world is just a tiny portion of what lies therein, and I wondered if in other lands there lived beasts that could live in water and in air, could cross that frontier of elements that keep us back from so many of our desires, and if the boundary between them was so frail, perhaps so too is the one that separates the living from the dead, from myself and all those I love whom I have lost.

A dreamlike state enveloped us, days filled with sunlight, the creamy churn of waves as the ship plunged and reared like a mettlesome horse, the flash of silver spray against our faces and, at night, a canopy of white-hot stars in a blackness so deep it seemed as if I could stretch out my hand and plunge it wrist-deep into the velvet of it.

Only one thing marred our crossing and this was the misery of the galley slaves. Becalmed for a time after leaving port, I found myself staring trancelike at the oarsmen as they strained continually at their task, their muscles bunching, their sweat blackening the benches on which they were shackled, a brutal yet even motion that moved us swiftly through the water despite there being no breath of wind. Men chained to their relentless work, an overseer prowling constantly among them on a gangway set between the benches, his whip flicking over their heads, drawing beads of blood on their arms and shoulders, the monotonous boom of the drum like a monstrous heartbeat as much a tyranny as their chains. Their ceaseless labor reminded me of Sisyphus in hell.

When Adeodatus would come and stand beside me to watch, I put my arm around him and moved him away, pointing out something else.

"Let him be," Augustine said. "It is good for him to know there are poor unfortunates in this world. Otherwise, he will have no gratitude for his own happiness."

Despite this shadow, the crossing was to remain in my memory a brief, idyllic interlude when we had laid down one burden and not yet taken up another, when all seemed possible and the gods seemed to smile on us, when our ship pointed north toward a coast as yet invisible but waiting.

On the fourth day the wind picked up and the sails were unfurled. The next morning we came in sight of land, a thin wavering strip like a line of charcoal drawn hesitantly on the sky where it meets the sea. Fishing boats clustered about us as we drew nearer the shore, and a huge flat-bottomed barge approached that was to tow us into the inner harbor, its many oars lifting and falling in tandem like the legs of a giant water beetle scudding on the water. As we drew closer

I saw a sprawling metropolis spread out along the shore and thought I looked on Rome. I had heard it had seven hills and was puzzled by its flatness. When I asked a sailor who was coiling rope nearby, he grinned, revealing a mouth filled with rotten stumps.

"Ostia," he said, spitting over the side, "the port of Rome."

It began to rain, the first we had felt since our African spring, and as we tied up to the jetty low gray clouds rolled in from the sea concealing the wharves as we made our way to the pier, arms clutched around our belongings, uncertain of our balance on the slippery gangplank. The entire voyage had only taken five days, yet I felt as if a hundred years had passed since I had left Africa.

My first step on Italian soil was unremarkable, earth like any other. It was the smell that was different, an overpowering stench of rotting things, a choking miasma that seemed to settle on that low-lying place like a suffocating blanket.

"It's built on a salt marsh," Augustine said when he saw me wrinkle my nose. "It's always silting up. The Emperor Claudius had it dredged, but that was a long time ago and the sea is reclaiming it again."

By comparison, the port of Carthage smelled sweet, scoured clean by wind and salt, the city on the cliffs above airy and untainted. I had imagined Italy to be a place of marble and gold-leaf and endless tinkling fountains. Instead we emerged from the harbor into a bewildering maze of fetid streets with people pushing rudely past cursing us in a Latin dialect hard to understand.

We paid a stonemason carting huge slabs of stone to take us to Rome, for we did not have means to hire a fast mule-drawn carriage. A barrel-chested man dressed in a one-sleeve workman's tunic with his belly spilling over his tightly cinched belt by the name of Fulvius, he told us we were lucky. He had intended to load his stone onto a flat-bottomed barge and sail it up the Tiber, but when he arrived that morning at the appointed time and place, the barge was not there and he could find no other boat. As his cargo had been paid for by Rome's City Works—mostly fine quality marble for decorative work, that being his specialty, he told us—he dared not delay its delivery. But he was more than happy to take our coin as it would offset what he had lost to the bargeman.

We left Ostia heading east along the Via Ostiense, the great paved road that connected Rome and the port, the Tiber on our left.

"It's only nineteen miles," Fulvius informed us, "but the rate these sluggards move it'll take us all day."

Augustine and Adeodatus jumped down from the cart and walked, in no danger of falling behind as we traveled so slowly.

After a while I joined them and it was a joy to stretch my legs after the confined quarters of the ship. Shortly after setting out, the rain stopped, the clouds parted, and the sun came out. The marshy ground along the banks of the Tiber steamed and the reed beds stretching out toward the sea were alive with birds, many of which I had never seen before, and long-legged herons and waders stepping fastidiously on stilted legs.

Adeodatus ran beside the cart like an overgrown puppy sometimes going up the road so far ahead I had to call him back for fear he would turn a corner and be run over by a cart or trampled by slaves carrying a litter. I was astonished at the volume of traffic on the road as if the whole world were either going to or coming from Rome.

"It's true what they say," I said to Augustine.

"What is?"

"That all roads lead to Rome."

"I hope so," Augustine said. "For it is here I mean to come to the notice of important men." He was silent for a time. "The trouble is," he said, "I cannot help but feel I am here under false pretenses."

I glanced at him and saw he looked troubled. "Because you are no longer a Manichee," I said.

He nodded. "My patron is a Manichee and so is our host in Rome. I have not told them I have broken with the sect."

"But you will be a teacher, not a spokesman for the Manichees," I said.

"Yes. That is the only thing that comforts me."

We were walking hand in hand behind the cart but sufficiently far back and to the side so we were not splattered by the mud the ironbound wheels threw up. Augustine squeezed my hand.

"Don't worry," he said. "I haven't dragged you all this way for nothing. I'm not going to resign the post before I've even taken it up."

The sun was sinking at our backs when Fulvius pointed straight ahead. "See those trees upon the hill," he said. "The city is beyond."

I glanced at Adeodatus who was curled up behind me in the cart, worn out by the day's events. I touched his head.

"We are almost there," I said, softly.

He nodded sleepily and rested his head against my back.

Because night had fallen, Fulvius explained he could drive through the streets once we entered the city. There was a law against wheeled traffic in the daytime. Augustine told Fulvius the address of our destination. We would stay at a house on the Palatine owned by a rich Manichee until we found an apartment of our own. This we would do as soon as Augustine received his first fees. He clicked his oxen on, their hooves clopping hollowly on the slab-paved streets that twisted and turned. Eventually he drew up at a door, torches burning in cressets on either side, a door-slave squatting on the step, his chin sunk on his breast, fast asleep. When we pulled up, he opened bleary eyes and, reluctantly getting to his feet, stepped forward to help us with our baggage.

Augustine jumped down, lifted Adeodatus over the side of the cart, and then gave me his hand. I clambered down and Augustine paid Fulvius.

"Welcome to Rome," he said. He nodded shyly to me. "Mistress."

The slave, a youth from the Northern tribes with straw-colored hair and startling blue eyes, piercing even in torchlight, admitted us to the house, and we stood waiting awkwardly in the atrium until the steward arrived, a man with a shriveled monkey face and stiff, haughty manners.

"The master and mistress are in bed," he informed us, "but all is prepared. Come this way."

We followed him down what seemed a labyrinth of corridors until he led us into a small room—a bedchamber and tiny courtyard looking out onto what I could just make out was a row of huts, which I later learned were storage sheds. The steward lit a lamp, the flame guttering. There was no brazier to warm the room. Shielded from the sun by the courtyard and a high wall at the back and the sides that blocked out the sky, the room was cold and damp.

"I will send food," the steward said and left.

When he had gone I sat on the bed and looked around. The plaster on the walls was bubbling and peeling from the damp and parts of a decaying fresco of merry woodland nymphs and satyrs did nothing to enliven the meanness of the room. In a corner a pile of pottery shards and dried lentils were swept into a heap as if the room had once been used for storage and had been carelessly cleaned. Adeodatus had collapsed on a sagging couch pushed against the wall and immediately fallen asleep, the bags he was carrying still clutched in his arms.

Augustine sat down on the bed and put his arm around me. "Don't worry," he said. "We won't be here long. In a few days I will have my fees, and we can find rooms of our own."

I leaned my head against him and closed my eyes, shutting out the squalor of the room. We were in Rome at last. That was all that mattered.

CHAPTER 22

Despite Augustine's promise, we spent those first weeks entombed in our dingy room. Augustine's students endlessly delayed paying him, making up all manner of excuses.

I did not complain about our situation as I saw that the hope he had had of teaching a better class of students here in Rome was beginning to dwindle.

"The fecklessness of youth is the same the world over," he said sadly one evening after waiting all day in the classroom for his students to show up. Eventually, two had straggled in just before sunset, both looking seedy and the worse for drink. He should have had twenty students in his classroom that day.

He was lying on the bed with his arm over his eyes. I sat down beside him and placed my hand on his chest. I had never seen him so despondent, so defeated.

"Have patience, my love," I told him. "It's early days yet."

"I wonder sometimes," Augustine said, "if I have mistaken my calling. Surely a teacher should love his students, whereas all I feel is contempt for their stupidity." He removed his arm from his eyes and looked at me but I had no answer to give him.

When Adeodatus was not with his father, he and I would explore Rome, the city that had brought the entire world to heel. One day Augustine said he would join us. We decided to go to the Forum Romanum.

"After that," he said, "we can wander about and visit the Temple of Vesta if you want."

"Can we see the place where Caesar was killed, Papa?" Adeodatus asked with a young boy's ghoulish relish.

"He was killed in the Theatre of Pompey where the Senate was meeting at the time," Augustine said. Seeing Adeodatus's disappointment, he added, "The Senate House is the place where Cicero gave his most famous speeches."

But Adeodatus wasn't interested in Cicero. His head was filled with the martial exploits of Caesar and Mark Antony and Caesar's betrayal by Brutus. He skipped on ahead of us. Augustine and I were walking arm in arm behind him making sure he didn't vanish from sight amongst the crowds.

I had never seen so many people from foreign lands as I saw in Rome, people of all different kinds of ethnic dress, the most astonishing variation of skin, eye, and hair color: ebony-skinned Nubians wearing brilliant orange, blue, or pink robes, towering over the native Romans and walking with such straight-backed dignity and grace of movement they seemed to float above the ground; Parthians with pointed beards glistening with oil and dark, clever eyes and wearing baggy trousers cinched with gold-embossed belts with great curved knives on their hips—"scimitars" Augustine told Adeodatus when he came running back to ask; Northern men like the door slave at the house with blond or red hair, beards braided into plaits and adorned with beads and tiny bird skulls, a barbaric sight that made me shudder. These men were huge, towering above us, their limbs as wide as tree trunks, their faces tattooed with intricate swirling patterns of blue.

"Celts," Augustine said. "They are said to worship trees."

"They are certainly as tall as trees," I replied. Augustine laughed and we emerged into the Forum hard by the Curia.

First we walked to the Comitia, the hollow in front of the Curia where senators had given speeches to the mob and where the original tribes had voted back when the Republic was founded before Rome grew too huge to accommodate them. Here Mark Antony made his famous speech after the murder of Caesar. Before we could stop him, Adeodatus scrambled up to the Rostra and stood there, posing, flinging the end of his short cloak over his shoulder as if it were a toga. He grinned at me and ran toward the Curia, skidding to a stop in front of it and waiting for us to catch up.

"It's called the Curia Julia and replaced the old Curia Hostilia. You can see the site of the old one there," Augustine said, pointing to the one on the left as we were facing it.

"So Caesar built this one?" Adeodatus asked.

"Well, not exactly," Augustine replied, walking over to him and putting a hand on his shoulder.

I stopped a little way behind them. Father and son framed by the symbol of Rome's might, both dark-haired, Augustine's hand straying as it always did when they were together to his son's head to caress it, Adeodatus looking earnestly up into his father's face.

"The one Caesar built burned down during the time of the Emperor Carinus and was replaced by Diocletian," Augustine was saying. "So what you see is a copy."

"Oh," Adeodatus said, clearly disappointed. "So no blood."

"Blood?"

"Caesar's blood."

"Remember I explained he was killed in the Theatre of Pompey?"

When Adeodatus looked confused, Augustine sighed. "Even if this had been the original building," he said, "there would be no blood after all this time. I imagine someone cleaned it up, don't you?"

"I suppose so."

I caught up with them as they entered the Curia.

Soon, Augustine finally earned enough fees that we moved into our own apartment on the Aventine, two rooms divided by a curtain in a six-story tenement alive with shouts and the sound of children playing. It was paradise after our squalid room and dank courtyard in the Manichee house. The constant noise and activity of lives going on around us reminded me of our rooms in the insula on the street of the silversmiths.

At last, I thought, I will have women to chat with and my son will have playmates.

Our lives soon settled into a routine much like our life in Carthage. Augustine taught in classrooms near the Circus Maximus at the foot of the Great Aventine Hill on which we lived, so close that he would often come home for a midday meal of bread, cheese, and olives washed down by a cup of wine.

We enrolled Adeodatus in the neighborhood school, the schoolmaster a young Greek named Hiero who charged reasonable fees but, more importantly, seemed gentle and not the type to beat his students. Augustine had terrible memories of his own boyhood beatings at the hands of a cruel schoolmaster. He had been sent away to school in Madaura at Adeodatus's age and had hated it.

"The man was a Greek," he told me. "And to this day, I cannot hear or read Greek without a shudder of loathing at that man's cruelty."

"What did Monica say?" I asked. I could not imagine her allowing such a thing to happen. The very thought of someone laying violent hands on my son made me sick to my stomach.

"I never told her," he replied.

Sometimes Augustine would take Adeodatus to his classroom with him where he would sit quietly at the back, or so his father reported to me, a stylus poised above his tablet, eyes fixed on his father's face as if committing every word to memory.

And Augustine, seeing his rapt attention, the way he was trying so hard to understand, began to speak only to him as if his other students were not present.

"Adeodatus may be only nine but he could teach my students a thing or two about respect," Augustine told me, proudly.

In the evening when the lamps were lit my son would come to me and, kneeling, lay his head in my lap with his arms about my waist the way he used to do in Carthage. I would stroke his hair, no word between us spoken, none needed. Then he would rise and kiss my cheek and gather up his books and go silently to bed, and I would watch him draw back from the little pool of light around my chair and melt into the shadows before he entered the door of his bedchamber and was gone. This, I knew, was the fate of every mother: that she must watch her son go from her world to his father's as if she gave him birth again and watched them cut the cord that bound them. I knew that he would soon grow to be a man, that the years of childhood passed swiftly even though the days seemed to pass so slowly, so I treasured these moments of unutterable sweetness to store up in my heart in the years to come like a thrifty housewife preparing her storeroom for winter.

In the autumn of the same year, Augustine heard of an opening in Milan for the prestigious position of orator, and best of all the post and all the traveling expenses would be paid for by public funds, freeing us from dependence on his pupils. Lividus, the rich Manichee in whose house we had stayed when we first arrived in Rome, had recommended Augustine to Symmachus, the Prefect of Milan and a secret Manichee but also a cousin of the influential bishop of Milan, Ambrose. Milan was the seat of the Imperial Court, the place where Constantine had issued an edict almost seventy years before, granting freedom of religion to Christians after the terrible persecutions of previous emperors. Monica, I knew, considered Milan the beating heart of Christendom, although many pagans and followers of other religious sects called the city home.

When Augustine put himself forward for the job, he was chosen almost immediately. And so, once again, we packed our meager belongings and began the long overland journey to Milan before winter set in and the roads grew muddy and impassable.

That winter Adeodatus fell gravely ill. Returning one day from his lessons at the neighborhood grammar school, his eyes were bright with fever, the skin of his forehead when I laid my cheek against it, fiery hot. He was vigorous and healthy in all his parts and ever impatient of stillness, but when I told him to go lie down upon his bed, he did so without a murmur, and I was greatly troubled. Checking on him from time to time during the afternoon, I noted he was still hot. Worried, I left him to sleep, hoping that he was merely overtired and would wake restored and ravenous for supper.

In the early evening when I went in to rouse him and light the lamps I spoke his name, but he did not recognize me and lay moving his head from side to side and speaking words I could not understand, his breath laboring in ragged gusts, his eyes half open and rolling backwards in his head. In terror, I ran to Augustine and bade him fetch Vindicianus, former proconsul and a doctor. Then I returned, stripped Adeodatus naked, and began to bathe his body with cooling water. But the fever did not abate.

When Vindicianus arrived he had me hold Adeodatus still while he leaned his ear against his chest and listened.

"There is something moving in his lungs," he said at last. "Black bile. You must cool him when he is hot and warm him when he is cold. And give him tiny pellets of moldy bread to bring the fever down."

When I looked revolted he said, "I learned this from the Jews, who are skilled healers and I have seen it work. More I cannot do."

My eyes implored him.

"He is strong and healthy," he said, patting my hand. "Take heart."

For days I watched in anguish as Adeodatus tossed and turned, his flesh melting off his bones until he had the aged look I have seen in children who are starved. When not writing speeches for the court, Augustine spent every moment at his bedside and did not bathe or shave or eat.

"You must rest a little," I told him late one night.

"I will not leave," he said, and sat on, his eyes sometimes closing then flickering open as if he made a supreme effort of the will to stay awake.

I was worried that he, too, would take sick and told him so.

He looked at me across our son's bed, his eyes dark. "And what of you, my love?" he said. "What if you take sick?"

"I am his mother," I replied.

"And I his father."

So we took it in turns to stay awake so that our son would see someone who loved him should he open his eyes and recognize us.

One night when I sat awake, Augustine dozing in a chair, exhausted by his vigil, I prayed to the Christian God with all the anguish of a mother's heart and offered him my body and my soul to do with as he wished, only let my son live.

The next night I knew the crisis of our son's sickness had come upon him and this night would see him either dead or recovered. All day he had thrown his wasted body about, his eyes open but unseeing, his lips cracked, blistered from the fire that raged within him, the words he spoke in his delirium a harsh raven's caw. As darkness fell he became still, subsiding slowly into a sleep so profound I thought he was dead save for the barest motion of the sheet that covered his breast. My heart was numb, my tears all wept, my prayers lay stillborn on my lips. Only my hand mechanically dipped a cloth in water to wipe his face, that face that lay so still and waxen in the lamplight, the sweet face of my little son, to squeeze a few drops between dry lips that had not spoken to me or his father for ten days or more.

"Mama?" My son's eyes flickered open.

"I'm here," I said. And when I placed my hand upon his forehead and felt his body cool at last and looked into his eyes and saw them clear, his soul looking back at me calm and sane, I knew that he would live. I crawled upon the bed and took his ravaged body in my arms and lay there, rocking him and stroking his hair and face and murmuring in his ear that he was my treasure, my only love, my joy, while tears of joy poured down my face.

Augustine awoke and seeing us, climbed onto the bed on the other side and we held him between us as we used to do when he was little.

CHAPTER 23

When we feared Adeodatus would die, we had sent a message to Monica during her grandson's illness. Now she arrived, accompanied by Nebridius who, faithful friend that he was, insisted on escorting her on the voyage and long overland journey from Ostia to Milan, even though she insisted she could travel only accompanied by Marta, her maid.

It was a great comfort to me to have them with us during those early weeks of my son's convalescence, especially Monica, for she was skilled in all manner of medicine and knew just which herbs to brew to clear the lungs and which foodstuffs gave strength to wasted muscles and restored the blood. Cybele, who had died shortly after our visit to Thagaste, had taught her well.

When she first arrived and went into Adeodatus, who was still too weak to rise from his bed, I saw her eyes fill with tears when she saw him. He was skeletal and hardly had the strength to lift his arm and clasp her hand.

"Avia," he whispered. "You came."

"Of course I came, silly boy," she said, laying her cheek against his forehead the way mothers do to check for fever. She smoothed back the hair from his face. "What's this I hear about you giving so much trouble to your poor mother and father?"

In this way, she made him smile and hid her grief behind a façade of bustle and mock scolding. But when Adeodatus fell asleep, she took my hand and kissed it.

"I thank you for saving him," she said in a low voice. "If it had not been for you . . ." Here she could not go on. "Well," she said. "Enough of that." She rose and drew me up from the bed. "Now it is your turn to be taken care of. You must get some rest, my dear, for you are almost as thin and worn out as your son. I am here now. Go and sleep. I will rouse you if he calls for you."

And so I did. For the first time in more than a month, I undressed and lay down in my own bed and that was all I knew until I awoke and it was the morning of the next day though I had fallen asleep in the afternoon when the sun was high.

It was not until summer that Adeodatus recovered all his strength and could resume his lessons and his normal life. But his illness had changed him and he was quieter now, more serious, as if he had crossed a threshold between worlds and returned with the imprint of their mystery stamped forever on his soul.

I mourned this too soon passing of his boyhood and missed the uproar of his former games when he would chase around the house and get underfoot until I told him, "*Pax*." Now he sat for hours in the courtyard reading or talking with Nebridius, and when it grew hot and I told him to shift his chair into the shade, he would answer that he was always cold and tilt his face toward the sun and close his eyes, basking catlike in its rays. Monica said this was but a passing phase, a weakness left over from his sickness, but he did not grow out of it. The perpetual coldness he seemed to always feel was like the mantle of snow that lies on the distant mountaintops even in full summer when the lowlands are baking in the heat.

A week before Adeodatus's tenth birthday, I asked him what he would like to do to celebrate. His answer surprised me.

"I would like you to give a dinner, Mama," he said. "So I can listen to Papa's friends talk. They interest me."

"What do you think?" I asked Augustine when we were alone in our room that night. "Don't you think it's a bit odd for a boy so young to want to be with adults on his birthday?" I rolled my head to look at him. We were lying side by side, my head resting in the crook of his arm.

"Perhaps," Augustine said. "But his understanding is far beyond that of boys his own age."

"Even so," I said. "It's as if he is growing up twice as fast as other boys."

"He's an only child," Augustine murmured, rolling onto his side so he was looking down at me. "All he's ever known are adults. It's quite normal. Now," he said. "Whom shall we invite? Symmachus, Prefect of Milan. We can hardly exclude him as he was the one who got me my post, after all." He kissed a corner of my mouth. "Ambrose, his cousin, the great Bishop of Milan." He kissed the other side of my mouth. "Vindicianus is in Rome so we can't invite him. Who else?"

But I put my hands on either side of his face and drew his mouth down to mine and all talk of the guest list was forgotten.

On the night of the dinner party, I was nervous, greatly aware of how small our house was and how plain the fare for the dinner.

"Country food" was how Monica put it. She and Marta had done most of the cooking, had insisted when she caught me sitting in despair at the kitchen table a week before disconsolately turning the panels of my wax tablet where I had jotted down a few recipes from memory, none of them complete.

"I'm used to cooking for more people," she said. "Besides, my cook and steward at home are both wonders and have taught me everything I know."

Together we decided on a simple meal of several courses but not too many.

"Those imperial feasts would choke an elephant," Monica said when I asked if our guests would be disappointed at only three courses and think us stingy if we didn't serve ten. "Besides, it's bad for the digestion."

Boiled eggs and anchovies to begin with a simple garnish of summer greens, bowls of olives to accompany them, an African stew of lamb and apricots and barley for the main course, fresh grapes and spiced wine to follow. And, of course, a birthday cake for Adeodatus. This I was determined to make.

"The bishop is a man of great simplicity," Monica assured me. "He will be more than satisfied, trust me. His cousin, Symmachus, is another matter. He's a wealthy senator and we all know what lushes they are. Pah!"

I smiled to myself. Monica had no patience for overindulgence of which the senatorial class was legendary but her view of Roman senators was also colored by the history of the persecution of Christians. She mistrusted the senatorial class and thought them ready to have her thrown to the lions at a moment's notice.

"He would have to throw his own cousin, Ambrose, to the lions too," Augustine teased her one day. "I hardly think he's going to do that. And don't forget the emperor. He's a Christian too."

The evening of the dinner arrived. We had had a quiet celebration of Adeodatus's birthday earlier, Augustine, myself, Monica, and Nebridius, and had given him our gifts then. *The Odyssey* from his father, an expensive gift as Augustine had commissioned it to be copied; a new wax tablet from me as well as a new tunic I had made for him while he lay sick, perhaps to convince myself that he would one day wear it, that he would not die. Every stitch was a tiny prayer of hope for his life.

"Thank you, Mama," he said, hugging me. "I'll wear it at dinner."

From Monica he received a new leather belt with a sheath on it, and when Nebridius gave him a knife, I knew they had planned their gifts together.

"Thank you," I mouthed silently at them over Adeodatus's head.

Augustine laughed when, later, he found his book discarded on a table. "See," he said, catching me round the waist as I made to walk past carrying a stack of clean table napkins. "I told you he was a normal boy. He's run over to Julius's house to show off his new knife."

I dressed carefully. I was a little nervous lest the bishop and his kinsman disapprove of me as Augustine's concubine and not his wife. Most of all, I was anxious the evening go well for Adeodatus's sake.

I had briefly met Symmachus before when we arrived in Milan but never Ambrose. As I walked into the dining room and saw him standing there talking to Adeodatus, bending down and listening to him intently, I was struck by how much he looked like a soldier rather than a man of the Church. Deep lines scored his brow and around the eyes, showing white when his face was at rest, so sun-darkened was his skin. He was of medium height and blocky and when he straightened, laughing at something my son had said, his movements were fluid and precise as if he had schooled his body to do the bidding of his mind and not vice versa as with most men. His voice was gruff but the expression in his eyes was tender and faintly amused as he looked at Adeodatus.

"This is my mama," Adeodatus said, catching sight of me in the doorway and running up. He took hold of my hand and tugged me toward Ambrose.

I felt a surge of pride at how courteous he was, how quick to make an introduction. The warmth of his hand gave me courage.

"Bishop," I said, inclining my head.

"You're supposed to kiss his ring," Adeodatus said in a loud whisper, suddenly the little boy.

Ambrose smiled. "Not today," he said, taking my hand and bowing over it. "And call me Ambrose, do."

I recalled then that he had been a courtier and moved in the highest circles of the Imperial court.

During the dinner we talked of light things. Ambrose asked Monica how her voyage had been and the state of Carthage on her departure. She and he talked amiably about crop prices and the recent droughts. Nebridius and Symmachus and Augustine talked of the court and which posts were highly sought after. I mostly listened as did Adeodatus. Augustine and I were seated on a dining couch side by side; Monica shared hers with Ambrose; then came Nebridius and Symmachus. Adeodatus started between his father and me but during the course of the meal drifted around to perch on the other couches. Sometimes, Ambrose turned to him and asked his opinion about this or that, especially interested in his voyage on the ship that had brought us to Italy. Adeodatus breathlessly related all the tales he had heard from the sailors.

The grave attention Ambrose gave my son deeply endeared him to me. Symmachus ignored him, and I thought him shallow though he could be charming when he wanted to be and he was an attractive man in his prime. I saw him glance at me from time to time as if fascinated by the relationship between Augustine and me. I reminded myself that he was, at heart, a politician, and, although grateful to him for sponsoring Augustine for his present position, I did not much care for him. He laughed too loudly and seemed to hold Augustine in such high regard that he treated him almost as an oracle. I knew that such excessive admiration of one man for another could easily turn to envy and I mistrusted it.

When the meal was cleared away and only the wine remained, the conversation turned to more serious matters. I could see that Symmachus was surprised Monica and I did not leave the men to their talk but instead remained at the table.

Augustine, catching his disapproval, took my feet and placed them in his lap, something he often did when we were sitting on the same couch. He then refilled my goblet, offered more wine to Monica, which she refused, and set down the ewer.

I saw Ambrose hide a grin.

Adeodatus, the birthday boy, had fallen asleep beside me, his face pushed into my side, one arm draped carelessly over my waist. I stroked his head but he did not stir.

Ambrose took his cloak off the back of his couch and, getting up, walked over to me and draped it lengthwise over my sleeping son.

"He has been ill, I hear," he said. "We don't want him catching cold." Then he bowed to me. "I must congratulate you on your son. Seldom have I seen such a bright and loving boy. Truly he lives up to his name."

It was gallantly said and I blushed a little and then squirmed as Augustine tickled the soles of my feet. A great glow of contentment bloomed in my chest then and it was not because of the wine I had drunk but because of my sleeping son at my side and Augustine caressing my feet.

The men talked late into the night and I listened half-dozing. After an hour or so Monica excused herself and went to bed. When Augustine would have carried Adeodatus to bed, I prevented him.

"Leave him a while," I said. "He is so peaceful."

It was a joy to feel the even rise and fall of his chest beneath my hand, the way he lay so still, his limbs so relaxed. After the terror of his illness and his delirium, I could not get enough of his healthful sleep.

Nebridius was asking Ambrose what he made of the language

of the Bible, if he thought it untutored, almost childish, in its simplicity and confusion of metaphors and parables.

"If it were as eloquent and subtle as Cicero or Plotinus," Nebridius said, "it would make more sense to me."

Symmachus nodded.

"I agree," Augustine said. "Especially the Old Testament. Take, for instance, the story of Adam and Eve. How can we believe that a woman who ate an apple could bring ruin to the world?"

Here he grinned at me then quickly grew serious again.

"How can we believe in a man who built an ark or a sea that parted to give dry passage to the Israelites. It is against all reason. They sound like fairytales for the unlearned and the credulous, not the literal word of God."

Ambrose smiled. "Yes," he said. "They can seem childish, I agree. Consider this: the Scriptures, both Old and New, but especially the Old, are parables, stories that hold a spiritual meaning deep inside like a nut once cracked reveals the meat therein and so sustains the soul. Christ himself spoke in parables."

In response to Ambrose's comment Augustine fell silent, almost brooding. After a while, he said: "Let's say that you are right, that the Bible is, somehow, true. Why would God and his Son speak in riddles? Why not be plain?"

Ambrose choked on his wine and began to cough. Symmachus pounded him on the back. I looked at Augustine, worried that he had offended the bishop, but when the coughing fit passed I saw it had been brought on by his laughter.

"Excellent question, my friend. How I wish more people asked questions like that."

Ambrose sat a while in silence, and I was reminded of the way Augustine ordered his thoughts in his mind before opening his mouth—a trait I did not share.

"'Therefore I speak to them in parables,'" Ambrose quoted, "'because they seeing do not see: and hearing do not hear, neither do they understand.' And again, 'Except you are converted and become as little children, you shall not enter into the kingdom of heaven.' The gospel of Matthew."

"That's exactly what I'm talking about," Augustine said. "Riddles. And we are children no longer with neither will nor reason and require more than childish stories. We require something that is according to reason and not merely blind faith."

This time Ambrose did not laugh but looked at Augustine intently as if weighing him in a scale. "Paradox," he said, "is the space God gives us for the exercise of the will. And our attraction to beauty is what He gives us to draw the will. We desire what is beautiful and restlessly seek it out. When we find it, we find God."

Augustine stared at him as if thunderstruck, but I could not see what had amazed him. An awkward silence fell, one in which I saw Ambrose continue to regard Augustine although Augustine did not notice, so absorbed he seemed in his own thoughts.

Symmachus coughed. "I must thank you, Augustine," he said, raising his goblet in a toast. "Your panegyric for my friend, Bauto, was the most brilliant thing. He is a Frankish general of great repute and you hit the mark exactly."

Augustine acknowledged this compliment with a slight nod of his head. As official Orator of Milan, he was called upon to write such things, but I knew his heart was not really in it. He much preferred to study the philosophers and poets rather than write laudatory pieces for political types.

"The high road to public office," Symmachus went on, still addressing Augustine, "is laid by literary success. You have a bright future ahead of you, my friend. Does he not?" Symmachus said turning to his cousin.

I glanced at Ambrose, who had been looking at Augustine pensively all this while.

"He does indeed," he said at last. "He does indeed."

"In fact," Symmachus said, addressing Augustine again, "the proconsul has taken an interest in you and would like to meet. He believes he may have a position for you at court."

I glanced at Augustine. He looked startled then uneasy. We had only been in Milan a short while and already he had come to the attention of the highest-ranking officials. It was what he had always wanted, and I was puzzled why he did not seem more pleased. I opened my mouth to say something and then caught Nebridius's eye across the room. He shook his head slightly so I left my words unsaid.

As if rousing himself with great effort from his thoughts, Ambrose got to his feet.

"Come cousin, we must go and let these good people have their rest. Thank you," he said, taking my hand and bowing over it. "I have seldom had a pleasanter evening. The food was delightful, the company even more so." He briefly touched Adeodatus's head. "Gift from God," he murmured.

I carefully peeled his cloak off Adeodatus and gave it back to him. "Thank you," I said, "for being so kind to my son."

Symmachus got unsteadily to his feet. He was a little drunk. "Charmed," he said to me, bowing, and headed for the door. Augustine glanced at me and shrugged.

Perhaps feeling chilled without the cloak, Adeodatus stirred so Augustine said his good-byes and picked him up in his arms and carried him to bed. Nebridius also said his farewells.

As the hostess, I saw our guests out.

I stood on the step and watched as Ambrose and Symmachus walked down to the end of the street where Symmachus's litter bearers had been waiting for their master all night. Earlier I had sent Marta out to them with food and drink. Ambrose had walked, he told us on his arrival at the house when Augustine had expressed surprise he was alone. Something he seldom got the chance to do anymore, he said, without being trailed by a train of servants. He loved the peace and freedom of walking at night.

"A brilliant man, Augustine," I heard Symmachus say, his slightly slurred voice carrying clear on the still night air. "Shame about his unfortunate liaison with that woman, though I can see the attraction, believe me. She's a beauty and no mistake. He'd go far if he could only make a suitable marriage to someone of his own class. The proconsul's already expressed his concern. Apparently the emperor frowns on such relationships."

"Be silent, man!" I heard Ambrose say angrily. "She will hear you."

As I turned to go in, I saw Nebridius standing in the atrium behind me, his face in shadow. I shut and bolted the door slowly so that I could erase the effect of Symmachus's words from my face. I felt sick to my stomach, the joy of the evening, the foundation of my whole life, changed in an instant. Then I turned to face him.

"You heard," I said.

"Yes."

I moved past him into the dining room and began to dowse the lamps. When only one remained lit, the flickering shadows providing a kind of refuge, I sat down on the couch where only a short while before I had reclined with Augustine and my son. Nebridius sat down next to me.

"Is it true what Symmachus said? That the emperor is against unions such as ours?"

Nebridius looked down a moment and then turned to face me. "It is true," he said.

"And Augustine knows this." Now I understood the look on Augustine's face when Symmachus had mentioned the proconsul's interest in him.

"He does. It was communicated to him in no uncertain terms when he arrived in Milan. He was told that if he wanted to rise at court he would have to . . ."

"Put me away," I finished for him.

He sighed. "Yes."

I surveyed the room. On the low tables between the dining couches was the detritus of our meal: wine cups not quite empty, a half-eaten round of cheese, the bare stalks of a bunch of grapes. The cushion where my son's head had lain, once warm, was now cold. The brazier had burned low and gave off little heat so the room was growing cold. The house lay silent.

I looked back at Nebridius and asked the question I dreaded to ask. "Is that what Augustine plans to do?" I said. "Put me away?"

"No!" Nebridius's voice was loud and seemed to echo through

the sleeping house. Lowering it he said: "No. He has never said such a thing, not even hinted at it." He took my hand and pressed it. "He loves you, Naiad. You know that."

"Yes," I said sadly. "But like Aeneas, his love for Dido and her love for him made no difference in the end. They were still parted."

We sat in silence for what seemed like a long time. Symmachus's words rang in my head: "unfortunate liaison . . . suitable marriage." I had forgotten what Monica—what even my aunt—had tried to tell me all those years ago. Seduced by time, I had thought as the years wore on, as our love matured and grew stronger day by day, as together we watched our son grow from infancy to boyhood and thence to manhood that Augustine and I would always be thus. I had imagined us in old age, grandparents, Augustine famed throughout the world for the wit and passion and eloquence of his words. But however famous he became he would always, always be my Augustine, my only love, still that shy seventeen-year-old standing on my aunt's doorstep with the shell, that perfect gift, concealed in his hand.

In our youth, we had set out on the same road but now, in our maturity, the road had forked and we must take a different path, one to the right, one to the left. And it seemed to me that all along we had possessed a map that had foretold this but in the passion of our first love we had ignored it. I did not ask Nebridius what could be done. I knew the answer: either Augustine would be forever stalled in his career or he would have to marry and I would return to Africa.

"I have a farm outside of Carthage." Nebridius's voice was low, almost a whisper.

I looked at him uncomprehendingly. Then slowly I understood. "You mean a place where I could live?"

He had not let go of my hand from before and now he squeezed it hard. "It is only so you know you will not be friendless and alone if . . ."

Again, he paused.

"If I return to Africa." I could not say "leave" Augustine or my son nor even think it.

I got up and, bending down, kissed Nebridius good night.

"Take the lamp," he said.

When I left the room he was still sitting in the dark. The house was silent, the only sound a faint splashing from the fountain in our tiny atrium and the lone trill of a night bird far off. I looked into Adeodatus's room and listened a moment to his quiet breathing.

Augustine was sleeping. He had left a lamp lit for me beside the bed. My eyes filled with tears when I saw its tiny flame burning bravely in the darkness, making shadows dance on his face, his closed eyes, a lock of hair fallen untidily across his brow.

He needs a haircut, I thought and smiled a little at my wifely concern. Then all at once I was weeping, tears running silently down my face.

CHAPTER 24

Weeks passed. Monica remained with us, as the shipping lanes had closed for the winter. I found myself watching Augustine for some sign that he had decided to send me away, interpreting each word he spoke, each gesture he made to mean the worst. I became withdrawn, easily startled, more impatient with Adeodatus, whose hurt look when I snapped at him increased my misery. Everyone noticed this change in me, not least Augustine, but when he asked me what was wrong, I said I was fine. Only Nebridius knew what ailed me and he kept his peace.

It was no comfort to me at all that Augustine had never lied to me, had never falsely promised what he could not give. It was I who had lied to myself, told myself that he would not be thwarted by our union. Never in all our years together had he shown me that he regretted his decision to take me to him though many another man would have done so. But I knew that he felt trapped and while my heart pitied him, I also felt an anger borne of helplessness.

Symmachus's words lay lodged in my heart, an arrowhead breaking off when the surgeon tries to remove it, festering there, making me sleepless. At night I demanded Augustine's caresses like a wild animal that gorges itself while it can before the starvation of the winter. I grew so thin and pale he fretted I had taken a secret malady like a lump that sometimes grows in women's breasts until it kills them. He told Monica of his fears, and she questioned me closely about my health, insisting I allow her to examine me.

"I can feel nothing untoward," she said as I was getting dressed again. "As far as I can tell, your body is healthy." She looked closely at my face. "But your heart is sick. What is troubling you?"

Perhaps it was the kindness of her words that broke my silence, perhaps the memory of when she reached inside to turn my child so he could be born. The time had come to do what I knew I must do but could not bring myself to do, like a soldier who must tell the surgeon to amputate his sword arm if his life is to be saved.

And so I told her of Symmachus's words and the sorrow I had been harboring burst out and I laid my head on her breast and wept.

Augustine must have heard me for he came running. "What have you found?" he said. "Tell me. What is it?"

I felt his arms about me but I would not look at him. Monica released her hold on me and sat up straighter. I raised my head and looked at her. She nodded.

And so I told Augustine what I had overheard after the dinner and of what Nebridius had said.

He sat down heavily on the bed. "I did not tell you because I knew it would only have caused you grief."

"Hearing it from that man's lips has caused me more," I replied. Then when he did not answer, I said in a calmer voice: "What are we going to do?"

"I will resign my post and resume teaching." As he spoke his shoulders slumped forward, his arms dangling loosely between his legs. I had seen him look that way in Carthage and Rome after a day of teaching. It reminded me how elated he was when we heard he was to become Orator of Milan, ending the teaching work he had grown to loathe.

When he turned to me he was smiling but in his eyes I saw a kind of hunted look, a despair that reminded me of how he had likened a man to a mule forced to carry a heavy burden against his will.

That he would give up all he had striven to attain and return to the teaching he hated, I had no doubt. But I was equally determined that he should not cripple himself for my sake. His own gift for language—his powers of eloquence and expression—had remained pent up too long. I knew he also hated using his eloquence for the purpose of flattering those in power, but it seemed to me that if he had no outlet for his passion he would go mad.

And so we reached a kind of impasse, Augustine determined to resign his post and I equally determined to prevent him though I dreaded what would follow if I prevailed.

In my memory, that last winter in Milan passed like night when dawn seems impossibly far off. Only once did the clouds part and a shaft of pure moonlight illuminate the darkness.

One morning in deepest winter, we awoke to a strange and eerie light, the morning muffled as if our house lay linen-wrapped like some rare and delicate glass. When we looked outside we saw the world had overnight become a thing of white, soft-swaddled with all its edges gentled by an endless feathered falling from the sky. It was my first snowfall.

Adeodatus was instantly transformed into a four-year-old boy again and went whooping and sliding barefoot in the courtyard until I called him in and bade him dress and put on sandals and warm socks. Then Augustine and I and Nebridius, arms linked to steady us, followed him outside where children played, their faces ruddy with the cold, eyelashes filigreed with white, as if it were a holiday. Monica watched us from the front steps, calling that she would heat wine, for we would be freezing when we returned. All the unsightliness of mud and refuse, the broken ruts that carts had scored in the spongy ground, the charcoal-streaked roofs, was smoothed away as if a kindly god had expunged the ugliness of the world to start afresh. The trees' stark bones, even the smallest twig, each bore a perfectly heaped molding of itself as if its opposite, a tree of snow, had grown there overnight. In the still and frozen air, the smoke from braziers hung motionless. And lettered on the snowy ground a crazy rune of birds' feet soon smoothed, then renewed, then smoothed again as still the snow fell.

That morning of all mornings remains imprinted on the landscape of my mind—my son running, his breath pluming in the frosty air, the warmth of Augustine's arm, his solid bulk on which I leant.

None of us had ever touched snow before though we had seen it on high mountaintops. Lifting my face to the sky, I felt it settle on my skin like duck down loosed from a pillow. Bending, I scooped it in my hands and offered it to Augustine who licked it from my palms. Adeodatus threw a snowball at Nebridius and Nebridius chased him down the street. We were laughing, Augustine and I, and for a brief moment, I forgot the sorrow lodged deep inside my heart. Augustine kissed me and his lips were cold but his breath was warm in my mouth.

Then a hail of snowballs rained down on us and we spied Adeodatus and Nebridius crouching behind a nearby wall. Ducking behind the columns of the porch, we fought back, Augustine yelling mock imprecations, I shrieking when snow slithered down the neck of my cloak, my hair and dress now completely soaked, all four of us helpless with laughter. Monica was smiling in the doorway. At last I gave up and sat down on the ground, breathless, freezing in my wet shoes and clothes. Yet I knew this moment, this day, would remain with me forever, perfect as new fallen snow is perfect, as pure as the sound of my son's and lover's and friend's laughter on a snowy day in deepest winter in Milan.

CHAPTER 25

When early spring arrived, I knew the shipping lanes between Italy and Africa would soon reopen. Augustine had recently been given an important speech to write for the emperor and was told by Symmachus that if it found favor, Augustine would be strongly considered for the post of imperial orator, a position that would effectively make him the mouthpiece of the emperor himself. As a woman with child knows her time approaches by the heaviness of the baby within, its stillness where before it was all restlessness, I knew Augustine and I could delay a decision no further.

Nebridius, Monica, and Adeodatus had left the house at dawn, gone for the day to visit an aged kinsman of Nebridius's who was ailing. Several days before, Monica had overheard Nebridius telling Augustine and had volunteered to accompany him.

"I will make him some strengthening broths and herbal remedies," she said. "And Adeodatus can come too."

She glanced at me and I knew she was clearing a path for me to be alone with Augustine.

As they were leaving, Nebridius drew me aside. "Do you mean to talk with Augustine?"

I nodded, my heart too full to speak.

"Then remember what I told you. The farm is yours if you should need it. I have only to draw up the papers. Augustine knows of it."

Before I could reply, he was walking to the door. "We will be home by dusk," he said.

When the house was empty I sought out Augustine in his study, a tiny windowless room, formerly a storeroom at the back of the house. Standing silently at the door I watched him writing the speech for the emperor. He had his back to me, bent over his desk, papers and books strewn about the floor, for there was nowhere else to put them. I could hear the rhythmic scratching of his pen and feel his concentration like a vibration in the air.

"Augustine."

He finished writing a sentence and then twisted round to look at me, the remnant of a thought still shadowing his face.

"I need to speak with you."

He saw at once that what I had to say was serious, for I would never interrupt him for a trivial household matter when he was working. Immediately he laid down his pen and getting up, stretched his arms above his head, bending from side to side. I knew his back had been giving him pain since he began working in this cramped and cluttered space.

"What is it, love?" he asked, taking my hand as we walked into the small living area off the atrium. It was still too cold to sit outside and I had asked one of the servants to bring a brazier in earlier so the room would be warm.

"Sit down," I said, handing him a cup of wine and honey I had set to warm near the brazier. There was a cup for me but I did not touch it.

He sat back and crossed his legs, relaxed, looking up at me for I was standing. He patted the couch beside him but I shook my head. I needed to say what I had brought him here to hear before I sat near him. If I felt his closeness, the heat from his body, I would not have the courage.

He was frowning now, tense. He put his cup down on a table and uncrossed his legs. "If you are pregnant, Little Bird, you have no need to fear telling me. I am delighted. I have always wanted a daughter, if you recall." He smiled but his voice was brittle underneath the lightness.

"I am not with child," I said. If only I had been, I thought, with a sudden stab of longing. A child I could carry away with me to Africa, a piece of him, a daughter, a piece of my son, a sister, that I could hold warm and tiny and alive in my arms like a newborn kitten.

"We can delay a decision no longer," I said.

He frowned. "I thought we had settled that," he said.

"Nothing has been settled." I began to pace. "You are even now writing a speech for the emperor."

"What is it you think I should do?" His voice had risen, not so much in anger as in frustration. "I must make a living."

I stopped pacing and once more stood before him. "Marry," I said.

I did not mean for it to come out so bluntly, but the word was spoken and could not be recalled.

"What?"

"Marry."

"We cannot." He stood and came toward me but when he tried to take my hand, I stepped back. The look of hurt and bewilderment on his face almost finished me. I turned my back on him so I would not see his pain.

"I am not speaking of myself," I said. "I am speaking of a proper wife for you, someone of your own class. Someone Symmachus and the emperor would approve of." This last I regretted as soon as it was spoken, the reminder that I was but a poor, journeyman's daughter from the provinces with no dowry, no legal status, not even Roman citizenship whereas he was a patrician's son, known and admired at the imperial court.

He took my arm and swung me around so I was facing him. I tried to twist away but he held me there. "What are you talking about?" he said. "I have never wanted any but you. You *know* this." He was shaking me, but out of fear not anger.

"You have wanted many things," I said. "And always when you have them it is not enough."

He turned away from me then.

"Listen to me, Augustine," I said, grasping at his sleeve. "You are stuck here. You will never be considered for that post if you remain as you are." I gestured at the room, at me, at him. "You will be shut out of the highest positions. Positions which you *deserve.* But it's more than that. You cannot go back to teaching because you must write, you must speak. If you cannot use words to speak the truth you will be miserable."

He gave a despairing laugh. "My God," he said, "I am caught by my own logic. All those years when I complained of my students, when we talked of how I could rise in my profession. And this is your solution?"

"It is not mine nor yours," I said. "It is the world's solution. It is the only solution."

He turned back to me, his face drawn, drained of color. "There must be another way."

"There is no other way. For us to love without measure is not enough. The world has a measure. It has weighed us in the scales and found us light."

He was shaking his head.

"Yes," I said. "You know it is true. That is why you have delayed resigning your post. You know you cannot go back, only forward." I caught hold of his sleeve again, desperate for him to understand. "We are not wanting but the world judges us so. And we must live in the world. *You* must live in the world. Do you see?"

A great calmness had come over me now the words had at last been spoken, the permission to the surgeon given, the sword arm amputated. I knew it was a kind of numbing shock I felt, that the pain would soon return tenfold, worse because it was so useless, a pain so utterly without remedy, the phantom pain of an arm that my mind told me was there although my body knew it was gone. Such I have overheard beggars tell each other in the street, crippled legionaries missing limbs.

Like a sacrificial ox struck between the eyes by the priest's sacred hammer, Augustine was silent now, stunned.

I put my arms about him and rested my forehead against his. "Do not grieve," I whispered. "Oh, my love, do not grieve. I knew what I did when I accepted you. Neither of us could imagine denying our love for an impossibly distant future. But that future is now here. I chose to do it. I would do it again now, this very instant. Never have I regretted it." I shook him slightly. "Do you hear me? *Never*. And never have you given me cause. I said then that I did not care what others think of me. That is true. But I care what others think of you, of our son. They think—Symmachus thinks—you are weak to bind yourself to me."

"I do not care," Augustine said in a low voice.

"Yes," I said. "You do."

"You think I am ashamed of you?"

I smiled, even at that moment I marvel I could smile. "No," I said, "I've never thought that. But you know as well as I that you will rise no higher than orator if you do not marry. And marry *well*." Unconsciously I echoed the words he had said in the church all those years ago.

"And Adeodatus? What of him?"

At our son's name, I flinched. It was as if he had struck me in the face with his clenched fist. "Do you think I do not know?" I cried, releasing him and stepping back. "I would rather be torn to pieces in the arena than to leave my child." I groaned aloud as if, even now, I were in labor. "Do you think I do not know that to him my love will look like hatred?"

Augustine laid his hand on my arm but I shook him off. Like a butterfly alighting on an open wound, his touch—so sweet, so necessary, so finite to me now—was unbearable. I fled the room.

Augustine let me go.

I had thought the hardest part was over but I was wrong. The hardest was yet to come, to tell our son—a task so arduous, so killing to us both, we shrank from it. Yet we could delay no further for when he and Monica and Nebridius returned from their visit to Nebridius's kinsman that night, Adeodatus knew something was terribly wrong. His father was silent and withdrawn, shut up in his study. I kept to my room and let Monica see him to bed. I only went in to kiss him good night.

"Who has died, Mama?" he asked, his eyes wide with fear.

"No one," I said, tucking him in. "Everything will be all right. Now go to sleep." I kissed him then bent to blow out the lamp.

"Can you leave it burning?"

"All right."

Adeodatus had not feared the dark in years.

The morning after Augustine and I spoke together, Nebridius was quiet and Monica's eyes were red with weeping. It was as if we were a house of mourning, which indeed we were.

The day dawned bright and warm as if to mock our sorrow.

"Let's go for a walk," I said to Adeodatus at breakfast. "You, me, and Papa. It is such a beautiful day."

When Adeodatus ran off to fetch his cloak, Monica laid a brief hand on my arm. Nebridius got up abruptly and left the room.

"Are we going to the market?" Adeodatus asked as we walked hand in hand down the street, my son on one side, Augustine on the other.

"I thought we would go to the wood," I said, "to see if the bluebells are out."

That seemed to satisfy him and he let go of my hand and raced ahead, doubling back when we lagged too far behind. I watched him run, his strength now fully returned after his illness though he was still too thin, and marveled at how much he had grown over the winter. Soon he would be eleven and his limbs were already beginning to lengthen out, a prelude to an adolescent's awkward lankiness. The next time I see him, I thought, he will be a child no longer.

"I must be the one to tell him," I told Augustine.

He said nothing but squeezed my hand tightly.

We passed out of the city and came to the wood, an ancient growth of oaks once worshipped by barbarian tribes come down into the plains from the distant Alps before the time of Caesar.

"Look, Mama," Adeodatus called. "You were right."

In a small grassy dell shadowed by a vast canopy of leaves, the ground was blue with flowers, so many it seemed the very air absorbed their hue. Against the roots of a tree, Augustine spread his cloak and we sat down.

Adeodatus began to gather flowers and link them in a chain by splitting the juicy stems with his thumbnail the way I had showed him many years before and threading them through the stalks. He had a look of complete absorption on his face, the way children do at play, and I saw the care with which he strung the flowers making sure not to tear or bruise them, the deftness of his busy hands, the sideways glance when he felt my eyes upon him, his grin.

"I'm making you a crown," he said, thinking me impatient for my gift.

"Thank you," I said.

"I'll make one for Avia after."

"What about me?" Augustine asked, smiling. But when he glanced at me I saw his eyes glittering with unshed tears.

Adeodatus sent him a pitying look. "You're not a queen," he said.

"True."

Watching my son, I wished with all my heart that time would stop and not move on, that forevermore he would be like this, a child making chains of flowers with which to crown me and his grandmother, the two women who loved him best in all the world.

"There," Adeodatus said. "All done." He put the circlet on my head, adjusting it so it was straight. Then he touched my cheek with his finger. "Why are you so sad, Mama? Don't you like it?"

I grabbed him into my arms then and held him fiercely. "I love it," I said. "I love you."

I let him go and sat him down beside us. "We must tell you something," I began. "Something very important. And you must try to understand. Promise?"

He nodded solemnly looking first at me and then at his father.

Even then I knew I could leave my words unspoken, that we could go home and that somehow we would find a way. But once I spoke to my son, there was no going back, no turning from the fork in the road, as once I had known there was no going back when Augustine asked me in the church to be his and I said yes. A terrible temptation came to me to keep silent. His face so trusting, so full of love, was looking at me and I told myself that for me to speak the words I had brought him here to speak would be no less than murder.

Without thinking, I put my hand up to touch the flowers but Adeodatus stopped me. "It is best not to," he said. "They are already wilting."

A bird began to sing in the branches above our heads, a blackbird's song so sweet and singular it was like a shaft of light.

"I must go away," I said. "Back to Africa."

At first he cried and then he grew angry, hitting out at me with his fists and pushing me away when I would hold him. Then he grew quiet. That was the worst.

"So you see," I said, "it is not because I do not love you that I must go away." Even to my own ears, this sounded like a cruel riddle with which to confuse a child, the kind adults make when they rationalize their actions yet know them to be wrong.

I tilted up his chin. "Do you understand?"

He raised his eyes to mine. They were his father's eyes.

"I am your father's concubine not his wife. Under the law I have no rights. Even as a wife I would have no legal right to take you with me."

"It is not fair," he said, tearing up great fistfuls of grass and letting them blow through his fingers.

"No," I said. "It is not."

He turned to his father. "It is your fault," he said. "I hate you."

Suddenly he tore himself away from me and got up. "I am going home," he said and walked away. Never had he done such a thing before. Hastily, we gathered up the cloak, shaking the bluebells from it, and silently followed.

He looked back from time to time to see if we were behind him but he did not walk beside us. By the time we entered the house, he had shut himself in his room.

CHAPTER 26

It was high summer when I took a ship for Africa but my heart lay deep in winter. The preparations for my departure took but a few days so little did I own in my own right—clothes and remembrances of Adeodatus chiefly, a broken wax tablet upon which he had traced his first letters; the sandals Tazin had made him, the leather dry and cracked with age, one strap broken; the earrings my father had given me long ago. And all the books and clothes—the green cloak that was my first birthday gift—and jewelry Augustine had given me, the tokens of his love over the years, as well as Neith's little figurine, which since her death had always rested by my bed. The shell Augustine had given me that day at my aunt's house—his first gift to me—I could not find.

Neither Augustine nor Adeodatus could bear to see me pack. Only Monica helped, moving silently about the room folding clothes and handing them to me.

We were almost done when Nebridius knocked and came in.

"I would speak to you alone," he said.

Monica nodded and left the room.

"Naiad," Nebridius said crossing the room and taking both my hands. "I have not involved myself in what you and Augustine have decided to do because I felt it was not my place."

I opened my mouth to tell him that he was my brother, my family, and had every right, but he squeezed my hands hard in his and I remained silent. I knew he needed to get out what he had resolved to say, that he was in great anguish of heart and I would not prolong his suffering for the world. A vision of him waving to me at the gate, when my father and I left his father's country estate all those years ago, flashed into my mind.

"I will return," I had shouted.

He did not reply but watched, a small still figure standing in the road, until I passed out of sight. His face was, as now, stricken.

"I have deeded you the farm outside Carthage with slaves to run it and a yearly pension plus whatever profit you can make on it," he told me. "Since my father's death, it is my right to dispose of all properties the way I see fit as I am now the *paterfamilias*."

The legal terms seemed out of place coming from his mouth. For the first time, I realized Nebridius was a landowner of considerable wealth, that he had many responsibilities and burdens. Always I had thought of him as the boy who had spilled water on me, who was my companion as a child, my friend as a young woman in Carthage. Now I saw that threads of gray had appeared in his hair, that his face was prematurely lined and careworn as if some inner fire had eaten up his youth.

"I have the papers here." He took a rolled piece of parchment from his belt and handed it to me. I recognized the imprint of his seal on the outside—a water nymph with long wavy hair. We had laughed at that, Augustine and I, when we first glimpsed it on his ring finger in Carthage many years ago, Augustine asking him if it was his girlfriend, but he had closed his fist to hide it and refused to answer. Abashed and obscurely aware that we had offended him, we quickly held our peace. Since then I have never seen Nebridius without the ring.

"This is an instruction to my lawyer in Carthage," he was saying. "You must give it to Anaxis, the steward, who will meet you at the harbor and take you to the farm. He will make sure it is delivered." He handed me another piece of parchment. "This is for Anaxis. It informs him of my wishes and that all authority, both legal and moral, is now ceded to you in your own right. You are provided for," he said. "You shall want for nothing for the rest of your life."

"I cannot accept such a gift," I said, tears coming to my eyes. It had been arranged that I would stay at Nebridius's Carthage home in the city until I could rent a small apartment of my own. I had even wondered if the insula in which we had lived in the street of the silversmiths might have a vacancy, but then I discarded that idea for it would be unbearable to be reminded of Augustine and Adeodatus there even if the memory of Neith would sustain me.

"You must accept it," he said. "It is mine to give."

I put my arms around him, and, after a moment's hesitation, I felt his arms encircle me and crush me to him.

"Oh, Nereus," I said. "I will miss you."

"And I you, Naiad," he whispered. "I will miss you more than you will ever know."

I stepped back then and looked up at him. For a brief moment it was as if a door opened and through it I glimpsed an anguish as great as my own. Then the door closed and I did not know if I had imagined it or not.

"You are not responsible for me." My words sounded cold to my ears, but intuitively I knew he needed me to create a distance between us now, to move back a pace from what I saw, or thought I saw, in his eyes.

"Maybe not under the law . . ." he said.

I waited for him to finish but he did not.

Under the law Augustine was not obliged to support me even if he had had the means, which he did not. I was not his wife and had brought no dowry to our union. All I had were the clothes on my back and a few possessions.

I realized that he and Nebridius had taken counsel of what to do to provide for me. I had thought that when I heard them talking in low voices in Augustine's study, it was of Augustine's pain at losing me.

As ever, Nebridius was the means of our rescue. Such he had ever been and suddenly I was filled with shame at the way we had used him, had always counted on his generosity and friendship.

"Forgive us," I cried, flinging my arms about him again. "Forgive *me*."

"Hush," he said, stroking my hair. "There is nothing to forgive. It is little enough I can give. I would do more if I could."

At the time, I thought he was speaking of the farm.

On the day of my departure, I left before dawn. I had said farewell to Monica the night before. She had come into my bedroom where she found me sitting on my bed, numb that the time had now come, that only a few hours remained. I was trying to steel myself to go to Adeodatus and kiss him good night for the last time.

"It is not right that I intrude when you say good-bye to Augustine and my grandson in the morning," she said, sitting down beside me. "But know, my dearest daughter, that my heart will always be with you." She shook her head and the tears that shone there fell like rain onto my hands. "Know that never, in all my long life, have I known nor will ever know such courage, such love. We are not worthy of such love."

I looked down. I did not feel courageous; I felt like a coward running from a battlefield, abandoning his brothers in arms.

She put her hand under my chin and tilted up my head, the same as I had done with my son in the wood. "What you have done, my child, what you are doing, has taught me more about love than any sermon I have ever heard. 'No greater love hath a man than to lay down his life for another.'" She smiled as I flinched a little. "Forgive an old woman for quoting scripture at you again. But it is true nonetheless. I will never forget you and what you have done. If God grants it, I will see you again."

She kissed me with great ceremony and deliberation on each cheek then once on the mouth, tenderly as a mother kisses her child. Then she made the sign of the cross on my forehead. "Go with God," she said and left.

My bags were loaded into a mule-drawn gig Augustine had hired; he had also hired the man to see me safely to the ship as I had refused to have anyone go with me. This was expensive but the fastest and safest way to travel overland from Milan to Ostia where I would take ship back to Carthage. When Nebridius had offered to pay for it, Augustine had reacted with anger and despair.

"Must I always be beholden to you?" he cried. Then putting out his hands to Nebridius, "Forgive me, my friend. I did not mean that."

Nebridius clasped his arms. "Forget it," he said.

I knelt before Adeodatus. Since I had told him of my leaving he had been aloof and cold with me. It broke my heart but I understood. His eyes glittered with unshed tears; I saw a muscle in his jaw working as he fought not to cry. My heart was torn as I saw that he had become a little man.

I lifted the iron citizen's ring Augustine had given me, as a pledge of his love, from around my neck where I wore it on a chain and looped it over Adeodatus's head.

"Wear this for me," I told him.

"I will never take it off, Mother," he said. Since that day in the wood, he had refused to call me Mama, preferring now the correct and cold formality of *Mater.*

The ring I gave him, I have now. It was returned to me later and it lies hidden against the breast that once gave him suck, against the heart that beat with love for him, still beats though his heart is stilled. This piece of metal was once warmed by his living flesh, an endless circle with no beginning and no end, the hollowness at its center a space in which my love for him is contained. The silver ring Augustine gave me is still on my finger.

I took Adeodatus in my arms and held him fiercely as if I could press his body back into my own as when I carried him inside me.

He held his body stiff and resisting but made no attempt to pull away.

At last I released him and stood.

Now I turned to Augustine.

"I will never love another," I told him. He took me in his arms and the feel of him was as familiar as my own body, our flesh one flesh, our hearts one heart.

"I love you," he said. "I will always love you." His fingers dug into my flesh, his whole body shook as if with a fever. "You must believe me."

"I do," I said.

When he released me it was as if my very self was torn in two, one part remaining with Augustine and my son, the other, I know not where.

I remember nothing of my journey to Ostia, nothing of where we put in for the night, of what I ate, what I wore, what I thought. I moved as a shade not yet passed over the river Styx to the Underworld for lack of a coin to pay the ferryman. I remained on the earth but I was no longer tethered to it.

At Ostia, the crash of cargo, the shouts of stevedores, and gulls screaming overhead and then flashing down to feast on offal and bicker at my feet returned me briefly to the world of the living. I thanked the driver and paid him off. Then I boarded the ship.

CHAPTER 27

On the second day out of port, a storm arose, its coming heralded by a blackening sky and a shrieking wind, the waves rising and curling like mountains to engulf the ship. The captain shouted for me to take refuge in the cabin on the deck but I refused. He looked at me as if I were mad then ran to save his ship.

A day and a night the storm raged and my spirit exulted in its elemental howling. After so many months of silence, of keeping my sorrow locked tight inside me, it was as if the lid of Pandora's box had been lifted, as if all my pain were released into the world.

The Christian sailors crossed themselves and called me a Jonah, the pagans made the sign to avert the Evil Eye. When the sky cleared and the sea became quiescent once more, none would come near me but cast me sidelong glances. I did not care nor did I rejoice that we were saved. With the storm's passing a huge lassitude had come upon me as if its violence had drained me of my spirit and left me a shell. When I disembarked at Carthage I was fevered and weak; I, who had nursed my son through his near mortal sickness and survived, was now gravely ill.

Later I learned that Anaxis, the steward, carried me delirious from the ship and laid me in the cart. Then he drove to the farm outside Carthage and I was put to bed. All this was like a dream to me, fragments of sky above my head, the branches of trees in full leaf, a strange jolting motion so I sometimes thought I was still on board the ship and the storm raged on.

I lay near death for weeks, sometimes floating in a void as if I journeyed yet on a flat misty sea without form or delineation or end, sometimes on a swell that lifted and bore me down, the great indrawing and exhalation of the world's breath the only sound I heard. Other times I was assailed by faces that loomed out of the fog and spoke to me: My father saying, "Sleep, Little Bird"; my aunt telling me to take the box, open it; my infant son babbling his first "Mama"; Monica's "I dreamed of a young man" and Nebridius's "Naiad."

Augustine saying, "I will always love you."

I regained my wits only after summer had passed and the grapes were purpling on the vine, the wheat cut and shaken onto the threshing floor and gathered into the barns. I awoke to a world of plenty under a sun that dripped amber over fields and orchards, a final sweet blessing before the pinch of winter. It was the time of year my father always returned from his travels, and as I lay looking through a window at the beauty of a world divesting itself of its gorgeous apparel before its long sleep, it came to me that I had willfully done to my son what my father, against his will, had done to me.

That first winter at the farm I remember as a monochrome of gray and black, a charcoal drawing of lines and empty space—the white square of my room, the window that, on warmer days, darkly framed the outline of a yet darker tree; on colder days, wooden shutters blocked out the light and left me in perpetual dusk, the red eye of a brazier in the corner of the room a sun forever sinking. I lay in half-light in a half-world, the sounds of life beyond my door of footsteps, hushed voices, the clatter of wooden bowls, and, once, the snuffle of a dog before a sharp command drew it away as alien to me as words spoken in a foreign tongue.

During the worst of my illness, a woman tended me and often, when I opened my eyes, she was sitting by my bed. She smiled and called me Domina, but I turned my head away confused, not knowing to whom she spoke. She lifted me, bathed me, fed me, and sometimes I thought I was a child again, that she was my aunt, and all that I remembered as the past but a dream of things to come.

One morning when I was strong enough to sit up and eat, the woman who was tending me put a rolled piece of parchment in my hand.

"This came by messenger when you were sick," she said. "It has been waiting for you to read."

She smiled at me as she picked up the tray lying on the bed. "My name is Tanit, Domina," she said. "I am the housekeeper."

I stared at her, not fully comprehending. For a moment, I did not understand, then comprehension slowly dawned. The voices I had heard beyond my door were the people of my household. I was their mistress. And it came to me that the time had come when I could no longer be a child, that I could no longer hide in my room while the life of the household, the farm, continued without me. I must rise from my bed and be a woman, a true domina like

Monica, not a pampered, enervated thing like Nebridius's mother, waited on by servants.

"Thank you, Tanit," I said. "I think I will get up today."

She was a tall, strongly built woman of about my own age and of my own race with hair that shone like polished onyx. Named after the consort of Ba'al Hammon, the Punic sky god, she reminded me of Neith.

She looked surprised. "Are you sure, mistress?" she asked. "Are you strong enough?"

I drew back the covers and swung my legs to the side of the bed. They looked pale and sticklike. I drew down my shift to cover them.

"I am quite sure," I said, although now that I was standing I was not. I felt as weak as a newborn kitten.

Tanit put down the tray and quickly came to me, throwing a warm robe about my shoulders. With an arm around my waist, the way Augustine had held me when I was recovering from childbirth, she helped me to a wicker chair under the window. When I was safely seated, she drew up a footstool, placed my bare feet on it, and covered me with heavy sheepskin rugs.

"There," she said, putting her hands on her hips and looking down at me. "That should do." She placed a beaker of honey water on a table beside me and a small bronze bell. "Ring if you need anything," she said.

"Thank you."

She smiled at me again. "It is good to see you up," she said shyly. "There were times we thought we would lose you."

"I am well now," I said.

"Yes," she replied. "I can see that you are."

"And Tanit?"

She stopped in the doorway.

"Thank you for nursing me through my sickness."

A look of surprise briefly flickered over her face and then she nodded quickly and left the room.

When she had gone I sat looking at the parchment in my hand. Then with fingers that shook, I unfurled it and read:

Dearest Love,

What can I say? I have no words. This great Orator of Milan, this eloquent wordsmith, has no words. For you left so I would rise in my profession, to make possible what my restlessness craved, yet now I am struck dumb. All that I wanted before—position, fame, the praise of influential men—is so much chaff in the wind. A marriage to advance my career? The very thought appalls.

Yes, my love; it was my ambition that drove you away.

Forgive me: I should have done more to persuade you to stay; I should have prevented you from leaving.

I know now that my mother was right when she said I seduced you on a path that would bring your ruin. For I made you leave your child and so your heart also bleeds from a wound that may never heal. Your courage overwhelms me, humbles me, shames and rebukes me. Compared to you, I am nothing. Less than nothing.

You told me I never lied to you but that is not true: I lied to myself and so I lied to you. In my pride, I thought I could have whatever I desired. The first moment I saw you in the church with the light enveloping you like a gorgeous mantle, I knew you were the one. And I determined to have you. Like the pears, I stretched out my hand and you, in your innocence and trust, took it. But not content with having you, I despoiled the tree, the source of life itself. My restless heart has destroyed all that is good and true and beautiful. It was not Eve that plucked the fruit, but Adam.

My heart is cut and wounded, a trail of blood stretching between us from Italy to Africa.

I can write no more. Forgive me if you can.

Always,

Augustine.

I traced his name with my fingers. The same extravagant flourish of the *A* and *g* compared to the neatness of the other letters, the thousand times I had seen him make this mark, as familiar to me as the color of his eyes, the feel of his body against mine. And I could hear his voice in his words as clearly as if he were standing there.

Smoothing out the parchment I saw a postscript at the bottom. Instantly, I recognized the hand:

p.s. Papa is sad. I am too. We miss you. I am sorry I did not hug you when you left. I was angry then but am not angry now. Just sad. I love you.

Your son,

Adeodatus

p.p.s. Papa says I can come and visit soon.

CHAPTER 28

In early March I was strong enough to sit outside and turn my face toward the soft African sun, and as the earth revived so did my body but my spirit remained stricken. I longed for the sight of Augustine and my son more than I longed for the warmth and light of summer, more than for life itself. During the winter, the shipping lanes were closed and I received no more letters. The one I had was so worn with reading and rereading that I feared it would disintegrate in my hands.

As my health returned so did an interest in the farm. Despite my travels with my father, I had been a city child and knew little of country ways. The house itself was of moderate size and comprised a single story set around a courtyard in the Roman fashion: a small entrance hall led into a modest-sized atrium with a rectangular pool and fountain open to the sky; to the right under a pillared walkway lay three bedroom cubicles with only the master bedroom large enough for windows set in two adjoining walls at the corner of the house. My bed was beside one window and a wicker basket-chair and footstool stood before the other, a table and chest the only other furniture. A reception room was situated to the left of the atrium opposite the bedrooms with a kitchen and small vegetable garden at the back of the house.

Compared to the cramped apartments in which I had lived most of my life until we moved to Milan, this house was more spacious than I could have hoped. Best of all, set a little way from the main house but joined to it by a trellised walkway was a tiny bathhouse. During my long convalescence I spent many hours sitting in the steam room as if the sweat that ran from my body could purge me of the poison in my soul.

With the house came slaves who I learned, when I was strong enough to go to Carthage to consult Nebridius's lawyer, were now transferred to my ownership. This was the first time in my life I had owned property, and I recalled the estates my father and I had visited, the slaves we saw there, some happy and well-fed, many starved and beaten, and the strange feeling, almost of guilt, that I was freeborn. I wondered then, as I wonder now, what makes the gods decide who shall be free and who a slave, who will conquer and who will be overthrown. It seemed a cruelty beyond all cruelties that when I was poor I was free and now I had means I was a nothing. Gradually, my shame of ownership grew to love, especially when I recalled my servants had saved my life when I lay sick, performing all those intimate tasks while I lay helpless as a newborn.

More than anything else, it was the life of the farm that revived me, the life of its people. Tanit I began to know during my illness, the other members of my household during my convalescence: Anaxis, the steward who had fetched me from the ship and brought me here; Anzar, the foreman of the farm, a man most skilled with his hands who could fashion a new pump for the well just by looking at the broken one. Often I would see him crouching down before something he had disassembled and spread out on the ground before him, turning over this piece or that in his hands and then squinting at the sky for long moments.

"He tells me he is thinking when he does that," Tanit said when she caught me watching him. "He says Ba'al Hammon inspires him. Me? I just think he's puzzled." And she laughed and when she saw me smile she nodded to herself as if she had accomplished what she set out to do.

Anzar and Tanit, I soon saw, loved each other although they thought I did not notice. I would see them looking at one another across the kitchen table, hot, hungry looks, and once, when I had gone for a walk along the road at sunset, I saw them outlined against the red of the sky holding hands, their heads bent close as if they talked. As I walked back to the house, I felt a kind of happiness, the first since leaving Italy, and I determined to do all in my power to help them. From that moment a plan began to form in my mind.

A few weeks later I summoned them to me. I had had my bed moved to the far wall and a table and a straight-backed chair placed under the window. It was the exact placement of Augustine's desk in our apartment in the street of the silversmiths, and sitting at it with the afternoon sun falling on my books, I felt close to him, would often sit gazing out of the window, unseeing, wondering what he did, what he felt, if he had forgiven himself. Seeing my son. It was here at the desk that I wrote to him and Adeodatus every week, saving up the letters until the trade routes opened in the spring.

Tanit arrived wiping her hands on her apron, Anzar with a streak of dirt across his forehead from repairing a wall in the lower pasture. They stood a little apart, and aside from the briefest glance at one another, there was no indication they were a couple. I smiled a little to myself at that and thought that Augustine and I must have been just as transparent.

"Tanit, Anzar," I said. "Do you love each other?" I had decided the direct approach was the best.

Then they did look at each other and their glance was so full of longing that the brisk demeanor I had decided to adopt almost failed me.

"We do, mistress," Tanit said.

Anzar nodded.

"Is it your intention to marry?"

Again they looked at each other. Again, Tanit spoke for them both. "We cannot," she said.

"If you were free, would you marry?"

"Yes," they said together. They moved a little closer to each other.

From the desk, I picked up the two pieces of paper I had prepared. Handing one to each, I said: "These are your manumission papers. If you make your mark beside my signature they will be legal." I dipped a pen in ink and gave it to each of them in turn. As if in a dream, glancing repeatedly up at me as if they thought I was playing a cruel trick or making a strange out of season Saturnalian joke, they each put a cross next to my name.

"Good." I blew on the ink to dry it and then rolled up the papers. "I will keep these safe and when I go into Carthage I will deposit them in my strongbox at the bank."

I went to Tanit and took her hands in mine, those strong brown work-hands that had ministered to me in my illness.

"Congratulations," I said, kissing her formally on each cheek. I turned to Anzar and shook his hand.

"We don't understand, mistress," Anzar said. "We are free to marry? We are no longer slaves?"

I smiled at their bewilderment, their dawning hope. "That is so. You are free to stay or go as you see fit. If you stay, I will employ you in your current positions. What I can pay will depend on the annual profits from the farm but I can put a roof over your head and food in your belly. This will always be your home."

"What of the others?" Tanit asked.

"I intend to free them as well."

After that I called the others into my study one by one. Anaxis, the oldest of my household and the most experienced, calm and kind and a confirmed bachelor, Tanit told me.

"I would like to stay, Domina," he said. "If that is pleasing to you. I have lived here since I was a young man and know no other home."

"I was hoping you would," I replied. "And you need not call me Domina."

He smiled at me, not a servant's smile but as one adult to another, the sort of smile one gives a friend when they are being unusually dense.

"You will always be the Domina," he said.

Likewise I freed Rusticus, Anzar's right-hand man responsible for all livestock; Maia, the housemaid and Tanit's kitchen helper, who was little more than a child; Marcellinus, a half-grown youth, supposedly Anzar and Rusticus's apprentice though they told me he was bone idle and spent all his time chatting up Maia in the kitchen when he should be working.

"He's young yet," I told them. "But keep an eye on him around Maia. She's only twelve and too young to fall with child. I will speak to Tanit also."

In the end, they all decided to remain on the farm. They took counsel amongst themselves and informed me, shyly, that they would continue to call me Domina.

The acreage of the farm was small but of sufficient size to feed us and have enough left over to barter or sell for the things we lacked like tools and grain and dyes for our wool. We grew no wheat, but grapes and figs, apples, pears, beans, and olives. The grapes and olives we pressed at a neighbor's oil-press and stored in long-necked amphorae bedded down in straw or sold for wheat so we could make bread; the fruit not eaten in season we dried and put up in honey syrup to give a taste of summer when winter came.

For live things we had bees and sheep and poultry, goats, mules, two oxen for the heavy work, and a cow. Anaxis told me that in Gaul where cattle are more numerous than goats, they made cheese, and so he showed me how to make it from the whey and told me his people drank the milk warm from the cow. But this I could not do, preferring wine, teas brewed from borage or mint, and water from our spring, so clear and cold from the mountain snow it made my teeth ache.

With the wool we sheared each spring, Tanit showed me the art of making thread, and I bought a loom so I could weave it into cloth. In the kitchen garden Tanit, Maia, and I planted herbs for medicines, onions, radishes, and green stuff for our salads and grew raspberries against the southern wall. We boiled endless vats of fruit and poured them into earthen jars, plucked ducks and chickens for the table, and stuffed pillows from their feathers. I helped Rusticus birth a mastiff bitch's pups and lay them blind and mewling on her teats to suck.

In pots in the atrium I planted pomegranate trees, their scent more intoxicating than spikenard, their flowers a heaven for my bees, their fruit so numerous Tanit showed me how to make the surplus into a jam, which she used as a garnish for lamb and chicken throughout the winter. I had planted the trees in memory of when I was with child with Adeodatus and craved pomegranates and Perpetua had found them for me, an unexpected grace and one that sealed our friendship. Over the years, as the trees grew from seedlings to saplings to mature trees, as lambs and goats and dogs and calves and foals were born and grew and engendered their own young, this and a thousand, thousand other things of country life, endlessly ripening, dying, renewing, rubbed away the sharp edges of my grief like waves on rock until only the weight of it remained.

CHAPTER 29

One day in high summer of my first year at the farm, the year my son turned twelve, a cloud of dust appeared on the road leading to the house. I set out toward it, my heart lurching between hope and terror. As the rider drew nearer I recognized his shape, the manner of his riding, before his features at last resolved themselves out of the haze.

"Nereus," I shouted and began to run.

He reined up at the sight of me and flung himself from the saddle. "All is well," he said, for he had known my haste to greet him was out of fear that he brought calamitous news and not only the joy of seeing him.

In two strides I was in his arms, laughing and crying at once, until that moment unaware of how fearful I had been, how famished for touch, for the sight of a beloved face.

To my silent question he said, "I have brought letters." Briefly touching my cheek with one finger as one would touch a robin's egg, he said, "You have changed."

"I have been ill."

He frowned.

"I am better now," I said. "Come."

He caught up the reins of the horse and we walked side by side toward the house as if we were children again returning from our day's play, tired and hungry and too content to speak.

"How is Adeodatus?" I asked. His name on my lips was sweet but painful. The guilt I felt at leaving him an ever-present torment.

"He is well," he replied, glancing at me. "He misses you."

"And Augustine?"

"He is well too."

As we approached the house, Anzar came to take the horse and stable it.

Anaxis was waiting on the doorstep peering out into the yard as he was shortsighted. "Domine!" he cried when Nebridius got nearer. Tanit was standing back in the shadows behind him, drawn from the kitchen at the back by the commotion.

"Old friend," Nebridius cried, striding toward him and taking his outstretched hand. "It is good to see you again."

Then I remembered that all my household knew him, for, since his father's death, he had been their master, and some, Anaxis certainly, must have known him from a boy. He did not yet know that I had freed them, and for the first time, I worried that Nebridius might think I slighted his gift. Anzar returned followed by the others. Maia hung shyly at the back, for she was the youngest and did not remember Nebridius.

"Anzar," Nebridius replied, clasping him forearm to forearm the way comrades do, the way Augustine had greeted Cyrus when first we arrived at his childhood home in Thagaste. "How are you?"

"Well, Domine," Anzar replied and then drew Tanit forward out of the doorway by the hand. "We are married."

If Nebridius was surprised he did not show it but congratulated them both and kissed Tanit's cheek.

Then each of the household came out to greet him one by one, and I watched as he chatted with them, asking after their aches and pains, their concerns about the farm, whether the last harvest had been plentiful and had the neighbors to the west made any trouble this year over the meadow beneath the spring. I smiled at Rusticus idly scratching his chest as he spoke of the livestock under his charge, the number of lambs born that spring, the need, perhaps, for more oxen if this year's harvest was as good as last year's, whether it was more profitable to buy or lease them out from the farm across the way.

Tanit told him the kitchen garden had been overrun with pests but, for all that, she did not despair of salvaging the raspberries and putting them up in syrup for the winter.

At last everyone drifted off to their tasks and Nebridius and I went in to the coolness of the atrium beside the fountain. I saw that Anaxis had left a tray with wine and goblets on it; Tanit, a huge platter of bread and cheese.

From a leather pouch at his side, Nebridius retrieved some letters. These he handed me.

I eyed them hungrily but put them down on a table.

"Aren't you going to open them?" he asked.

"Later," I said. "You are my guest here and you must be tired from your journey."

He looked at me while I poured wine. "You remind me of Monica," he said. "That's just the type of thing she would say."

I handed him the cup and he emptied it. "Ah, that's better," he said. "I must have breathed in the entire African coast on the way here. The roads are tinder dry."

"It has not rained since spring," I said, pouring again and adding a generous measure of water. He saw what I was doing and grinned.

"Don't want to get me drunk before I tell you all the news?"

"Something like that," I said, smiling. "But then again, I know how much you love water, Nereus."

"Hah," he said and drank again. "Trust you to remind me of that. Actually," he said, "the idea of you throwing water at me is quite a pleasant one. I feel as dry as an old boot." Then he leaned his head back on the chair a moment and closed his eyes.

And as worn out, I thought. His clothes were covered in the thick yellow dirt of Africa and around his mouth and eyes exhaustion lines were deeply etched. He must have ridden straight from Carthage without spending a single night at his house in the city. He half-opened his eyes. "Speaking of Monica. She sends her love."

"No message?" I was disappointed. I knew Monica could not write but I had expected her to give a verbal message.

"She has not been well," he said, sitting up.

In all the years I had known Monica she had never fallen sick. "What is wrong?" I asked, sitting down beside him.

He shrugged. "She says it is nothing."

"She would," I replied. I thought of Monica; she was not so old, perhaps in her early fifties now. Although a slight woman she had ever been strong, moving with the suppleness of a much younger woman until, quite recently, her joints had begun to pain her. She walked a little stiffly now but when I had last seen her in

Milan she was as fit as ever. I could not imagine her an invalid, too weak to get out of bed during the day.

"Is it a fever?" I asked, fearing the worst.

Nebridius shook his head. "Just a weakness that will not go away. She gets angry when we fuss."

I smiled at this.

"She promises to send a message before the end of summer."

"I will put up some dried herbs for you to take back to her," I said. "I grow them myself and I know she will not be able to get them in Italy. It will comfort her to have something from home."

Feeling a little better about Monica, I put a hand on Nebridius's arm and leaned forward.

"Now," I said. "You must tell me everything."

Nebridius took another long draught of wine as if to fortify himself, then began: "Right after you left Milan, Monica arranged a marriage for Augustine with a girl from a prominent family." He glanced at me to see how I would take this but I sat quietly, outwardly calm though inwardly I felt the world spinning.

"Go on," I told Nebridius for he had fallen silent. "Are they . . . ?" I could not say the word "wed."

Nebridius shook his head. "They were betrothed."

I had not realized that I was holding my breath. Carefully, I let it out. "So she is still young," I said. I did not ask how young; I did not want to know. I was almost thirty now, considered well past my prime although my body was whole and healthy now I had recovered from my illness and there was still no gray in my hair. Nevertheless, a surge of jealousy rose in my breast, an image of her young, perfect body in Augustine's arms. I beat it down. "Go on," I said again.

"Last winter Augustine broke off the betrothal."

I stared at him. "Why?"

Nebridius paused. I saw him gathering himself to tell me something, and, again, my heart beat with fear.

"You told me he and Adeodatus were well," I said, gripping his arm hard. "They are well, are they not?"

Nebridius smiled then and placed his hand on mine. "They are well," he said. "In body and in soul. Augustine and Adeodatus are baptized. As am I."

"You are Christians?"

"We are," Nebridius replied calmly.

I thought back to the dinner we gave for Adeodatus's birthday, of how Ambrose had challenged Augustine when he said the gospels were crude stories written for the unlettered by simple fishermen. Ambrose had called them parables and spoken of paradox. At the time, I could see that his words had deeply troubled Augustine and knew that in the months leading up to my departure, he had talked with Ambrose again.

Part of me had always known he was on this path. I remembered our many conversations about the body and the soul, my metaphors of birds in cages and yeast in bread, his reading of the Neo-Platonist Plotinus, of Cicero.

Seeing the comprehension on my face, Nebridius laughed, a beautiful carefree sound such as he had used to laugh when he was a boy, such a laugh, I realized suddenly, that I had not heard him give for many years. "Augustine told Ambrose you were his best teacher, better than all the poets and philosophers and so-called theologians combined. And Ambrose said: 'I believe it! Women are much wiser than men.'"

I turned to him. "And what of you, Nereus? A Christian? I thought you were a happy pagan."

"Not always so happy," he replied.

"You are my dearest friend, Nereus," I said, lifting his hand and laying my cheek against it. And we sat that way until the shadows grew long and night fell.

CHAPTER 30

Nebridius would not talk more of Augustine or my son, saying that their letters would tell me better than he could, and so we talked of other things. I told him I had freed the slaves and they had chosen to stay on.

He looked at me but I could not make out his expression in the growing dusk, for we had not yet lit the lamps. "Yes," he said. "I can see you doing that."

"You don't mind?"

He smiled. "Of course not." He spread his arms indicating the house and the farm. "All this is yours now."

After dinner we walked around the property. I was eager to show him how well tended the farm was, how thriving, for I considered it only mine in trust rather than in ownership although I did not tell him this. I questioned him closely on all that pertained to the farm and was amazed at how knowledgeable he was, for aside from that summer in our childhood at his country estate, I had only ever known him in the city.

This was another side of Nebridius I had been blind to and I bitterly reproached myself for it. It was as if as long as I had

Augustine I had neglected my oldest friend, had failed to see him as he truly was, a kind and patient man, a man who carried his loneliness deep inside him, hidden from those closest to him for fear it would make them unhappy or cause them to pity him. But I should have seen it, I told myself, as we wandered back in the fast falling darkness. I should have known. And I did not feel pity so much as a kind of awe at his fidelity and bravery.

In the atrium, I kissed him on both cheeks. "Thank you," I said.

He looked embarrassed. "For what?"

"For everything."

"I am glad you are happy here on the farm," he said. "Good night."

Standing in the atrium alone, I thought: *I was not speaking of the farm.*

Alone in my room, I sat down in the wicker chair and broke open the letters Nebridius had brought. The first was from my son:

> Dearest Mama,
>
> I miss you every moment of every day but now I understand why you left. Papa explained it to me, but it wasn't until Avia told me how terrible it was for you that I forgave you. I am sorry I was so mean to you at the end, when you told me in the wood, when we came home. On the day you left I did not want to cry so I did not hug you properly. I wish I had. Oh, Mama, I wish I had.

If you are reading this then Nebridius is with you and I am glad. He has been very kind to me; he and I go for long walks together and we talk of you. He is like my uncle.

Speaking of uncles: Uncle Navigius is visiting. But Aunt Perpetua is at home in Thagaste. I wish I could come back to Africa and see you. Papa says I can come soon.

Papa and I were baptized by Bishop Ambrose—the nice man who came to my birthday dinner. We had to take off all our clothes—it was cold in the room in the back of the church where the font is—and then walk down some steps into a deep octagonal pool; then we ducked down under the water three times as the bishop said prayers. When we came up the third time, we were made new in Christ. Afterwards, we dressed in white robes and processed into the church. Avia was crying. I don't think I have ever seen her cry before. She told me they were happy tears, which I thought was an odd thing.

The ceremony was exciting but I don't feel any different inside, which surprised me. I thought I would feel holy, clean somehow. But I am happier now, Mama, although it is painful not seeing you every day, not feeling your arms about me . . .

Here, I had to lay the letter down, for tears blurred my eyes and I could not read on. After a while, I resumed:

. . . not hearing your voice or your laugh. The hardest time of the day is when I go to bed, for then everything is quiet and it is as if there is a big hole in the world. How I long for you to come in and say good night as you used to. Avia said that this is the time I should think of you especially and say a prayer for you, that your broken heart will soon mend, that you are well and happy, that I will see you soon. So I do.

Papa has some good news to tell you so I will not say anything but let him tell you himself but only say, I am happy about it. I was very angry with him at first; I blamed him for sending you away. Then Avia told me that you and he were forced to do it for Papa and his career. Then I was angry at the world for being the way it is. I think I will always hate the world but I can never hate you and Papa.

Avia says that she has never seen such great love as yours in all her life. I think so too. It reminds me of Jesus's mother giving her son for the salvation of the world and watching him die on the cross. I think it must have been a kind of death for you to leave us. I know it felt like death to me and Papa. I keep seeing you alone on the ship taking you back to Africa and it makes me cry. I am sorry I did not understand it then but I do now.

Avia has been a little sick but she says she is over that now. I think she still feels a bit poorly but she won't admit it. She is funny that way. I try to help her as much as I can around the house, and we go to market together and I carry her basket.

My studies are going well; Papa and I are reading the Scriptures together. I like the stories a lot, especially the one about the Prodigal Son.

Avia is calling so I must go. I love you Mama. I miss you. Write soon and tell me all about the farm. Nebridius has described it, but I want to hear about it from your own lips.

May God bless you and keep you safe. Avia sends her love. So does Uncle Navigius.

Always, always your dearest son,
Adeodatus xxx

Now it was my turn to cry tears of joy. *Yes, my son,* I thought. *It is a strange thing that happiness makes us cry.* As if at the heart of every joy there is a loss but somehow this makes it all the sweeter.

It was as if Adeodatus had been speaking to me in my room so clearly did I hear his voice. I marveled at the wisdom of his heart, the depth of his understanding, could see how much he had matured, how much the boy was growing into a man. In a few weeks he would turn twelve. I kissed his name and the three little crosses he had made over and over, careful not to wet them with my tears and smudge the ink. Then I sat perfectly still, loath to break the spell, the sense that he was a living presence in the room with me. A night bird sent its piercing song into the darkness and the tree outside my window rustled, a faint breeze stirring its leaves. The sweet scent of jasmine came to me on the air.

After a long time, I laid the letter down and picked up the one from Augustine.

Dearest Love:

If you are reading this then Nebridius will have told you that I am betrothed. And Adeodatus will have told you that I have something important to tell you, for I know that your mother's heart will read his letter first.

Know that I have broken off the betrothal.

I broke off the betrothal, for it was nothing but a stepping stone to higher preferment at court and utterly abhorrent to me for a woman to be sold so I could rise in the world, although her father was eager to do it. I have informed Symmachus that I am resigning from my post as orator. He is disappointed in me, but Ambrose says I am doing the right thing.

Once I had rid myself of the burden of my ambition, I began to ponder the meaning of my life, of how I had come to be in the place I found myself, losing everything I held dear. For my profession I found I did not care a straw.

Slowly I began to understand what you taught me by loving me. When I spoke of beauty and love before, they were just ideas, but you taught me to know them as experiences. The beauty of you is indistinguishable from your love. Or, to put it another way: love is the beauty of the soul. This you have always known; this I have come to understand late.

But who can map the various forces at play in our souls? Man is a great depth; the hairs of his head are easier by far to count than his feelings, the secret movements of his heart.

I was hidden from myself but I was not hidden from you. And in the mirror of your loving gaze I saw myself. And I am not hidden from God. And in the mirror of His loving gaze I now see myself.

But even then I held back from accepting a higher truth—Love itself—for I was afraid of another fall, another loss. And in this condition of suspense I felt myself dying inside.

In the months before you left me—that terrible winter—I know now that God was calling and shouting and trying to break down my defenses, the pride in my own reason, in my cleverness, in my soul. He flashed, shone, and scattered my blindness. He touched me and I burned.

In your sacrifice I saw the sacrifice of Christ, a love so perfect He was prepared to die on a cross to save a wretched sinner such as myself.

Your going was a great evil to me—the greatest I have ever known—but good has come out of it. At least, I begin to feel the good although I am often wracked by fear and doubt and longing. Such longing for you I sometimes fear I will go mad.

Forgive my rambling. Nebridius is even now booted and cloaked for his journey to you, so I must finish this long letter more hastily than I intended.

What the future holds I cannot tell. I only know that I will trust in God's mercy and grace.

When Nebridius returns to Milan we will go—Adeodatus, Nebridius, Navigius, my mother, and I—to a friend's villa near Lake Como in Cassiciacum. There I hope to make a retreat so I can more clearly see my way.

I do not ask you to forgive me. I only pray that you may find happiness.

Augustine

Blindly, I put down the letter. If to love another is to desire their happiness above all things no matter what the cost, then my soul rejoiced that Augustine had found a kind of peace. But my heart was sorrowful unto death. He had broken his betrothal only to make another more indissoluble than the first: He had betrothed himself to God.

CHAPTER 31

Nebridius stayed at the farm for two weeks. We did not speak of the letters, and I was glad, for my heart was still heavy with sorrow and I could not find the words. Instead, each day we walked the property lines of the farm with Anzar. Five winters older than me, he and Tanit had been born into servitude on another property owned by Nebridius's family. Tanit looked on this as their good fortune, for, she told me, the master was kind and just, never beat or starved them, and they had never known another life. She spoke of Nebridius's family as if it were her own, with pride at their accomplishments and wealth.

"They love you," Nebridius said.

We were sitting outside on the last night of his visit, both loath to go to bed but with hearts too heavy for conversation knowing that, in a few hours, we must part. A full moon cast a light like early dawn, pale, tentative, and ghostly, only the silence of the birds a sign it was full night and not the beginning of a new day, so quiet I could hear the hollow clack of the cattle bells in the far pasture and, nearer, the soft whinny of a horse in the paddock.

"This is my home now," I said. "I will never leave."

I heard Nebridius turn toward me but kept my eyes on the road which, like a silver arrow, pointed due north toward the sea and to Italy.

"You know Augustine loves you," he said. "Will always love you."

"I know."

"But he is set on a different path now."

"I know."

He touched my shoulder.

"I must to bed," he said, getting up and stretching. "I have a long ride in the morning." He was returning to his country estate and from thence to Carthage to see his lawyer about redrawing his will. "For you never know," he said.

I shivered and drew my shawl more closely around me although the night was warm.

"Do not talk of dying," I said.

He laughed. We embraced.

"Dear Nereus," I said. "Take care."

"And you, my Naiad."

My son turned twelve in midsummer, and I celebrated by reading his letters and began to make him a new tunic from wool I had woven, dyed a brilliant shade of crimson, although I feared it would be too small. Tanit found me sitting with it in my lap in tears.

"I do not know his size," I said.

She put her arms around me. "Don't fret, Domina," she said.

"Boys that age grow like weeds. No mother can keep up. When he visits you can adjust it."

Comforted by her words, I resumed stitching.

Late summer began its slow slide into autumn, the days shorter but still hot, the nights cool. I had now been at the farm a year and still had not set eyes on my son. I dreaded the turning of the seasons, for then the seas would close to ships and I would neither see nor hear from my son until spring. I would be like Proserpina in the underworld, longing for the touch of sunlight on her face.

One afternoon I was in the orchard gathering windfalls, a basket propped against my hip, my skirts twisted up through my girdle so my legs were free, feet bare so I must tread carefully amongst the wasps. Tanit had injured her back lifting a heavy cauldron off the fire and she could not lift the baskets. I had made her sit in a cane chair with her feet propped up as once I had done at Monica's house long ago. She protested, saying it was not right that I, the mistress, should work and she, a mere servant, should take her ease, but I told her that gathering fruit on a golden day in fall was not hard labor, and besides, she could sort the apples into those we would keep for drying from those too bruised and wormy. Mollified, she consented to sit, and, glancing at her soon after, I saw she had fallen into a doze, the apples she had been sorting fallen off her lap onto the grass.

The day was warm, the air heady with the scent of fomenting fruit, Anzar's voice sounding now and then behind the house as he directed Rusticus and Marcellinus. After freeing my household, I had ordered new dwellings to be built—a small house with two bedchambers for Anzar and Tanit and for Maia—Tanit insisted Maia live with them as she did not trust Marcellinus to keep his lustful hands off her. A long, low building divided into individual rooms and a central living space and kitchen was for the single men. We would all, I announced, use the bathhouse, mornings for the women, afternoons for the men as it was done in Carthage and Rome. They gaped at me and I did not know whether it was because of the luxury of hot water instead of the icy water from the well or the prospect of daily bathing that astonished them the most.

Soon after I had manumitted them, Marcellinus took it in his head to see the world. I gave him a purse of money, Tanit gave him food, and Anzar gave him an earful of advice, which I could see Marcellinus ignored. He returned a month later, his money all spent on wine and games of dice, sheepishly asking to be taken on again. Anzar winked at me over his head as the youth stood looking at his feet, a picture of dejection.

"I think we can find you something, lad," he said. "How does cleaning out the pigs sound?"

I was smiling to myself as I remembered this and thinking that Marcellinus was like the Prodigal Son, Adeodatus's favorite parable, when Tanit awoke and cried: "Domina! Someone is coming."

I heard the sound of hooves. Dropping my basket, I ran to the road and saw a mule-drawn gig approaching. There were two people in it. As it drew nearer I felt a joy so fierce I could not breathe. "Adeodatus," I whispered. Then a great cry: "Adeodatus!"

And his aunt was seated next to him. "Perpetua!"

Adeodatus drew up the mules so suddenly they sat back on their hind legs, their front hooves pawing the air, eyes rolling white.

"Steady, nephew," Perpetua said. "You'll kill us both and we have only just arrived." Then she, too, was scrambling down.

Adeodatus threw himself off the gig and, running to me, gathered me in a fierce embrace that drove all the air out of my lungs.

"Mama," he said, his face buried in my chest. "Oh, Mama."

I was laughing and crying. I could barely speak. "My son, my son." I could not believe I had the feel of him again, more solid than when I held him last, his shoulders broader, his head on a level with my own. I kissed him over and over again, my tears wetting his face so I did not know if he wept or if it was only I.

"I am come to visit," he said and then laughed at the obviousness of his words.

"Your father?"

"He is still in Milan," Adeodatus said. "He has chosen another path. I will tell you about it by and by."

I marveled at the firmness of his tone, an assuredness that had not been there before. His eyes, brown and serious, studied mine.

"All will be well," he said. "I promise."

Perpetua was standing back a little. Over Adeodatus's shoulder I saw her smiling with tears flowing down her cheeks. At last I released my son and embraced my friend.

"Perpetua," I said. "How I have missed you."

"And I you, dear sister." Then she held me away from her and looked at me with her head on one side, pretending to be critical. "Humph," she said. "We must fatten you up. I will give you some of my flesh. I have enough."

She was now a mature matron, her waist thickening a little as she grew into middle age.

"You are beautiful," I said. "Blooming."

"You are too," she said. "I am so glad."

"How many children now?" I asked as we walked back to the house, Adeodatus on one side and Perpetua on the other, our arms linked. I didn't think I could ever let go.

"Five," she replied. "And, God help me, they are a handful. A bunch of savages."

"I know exactly what you mean." I jerked my head at Adeodatus. "This one drove me near mad at times."

And we all burst out laughing and went into the house where Tanit, bless her, was already laying out food and wine in the atrium.

CHAPTER 32

Never have I known time to pass so quickly as those weeks I spent with Adeodatus and Perpetua. As I look back, it seems as if each day was haloed by a light more golden than the sun, the heat of it the love that wrapped us round and illumined everything we touched. We were not to be parted, my son and I, nor indeed with Perpetua, although she would sometimes go off by herself to give us time alone. We spent the days sitting side by side in the orchard or walking the lanes and fields about the farm, talking, always talking, the days too short to tell of all we felt.

Adeodatus had changed greatly in the year we were apart, not just in outward appearance, but in his inmost self. The boy I said good-bye to at Ostia was gone, even the boy who wrote me that letter saying how much he missed his mother; a young man stood in his place. I mourned the death of his childish ways, his guileless need of me, but more I felt a pride in him, an enormous thankfulness that I could now depend on him for strength when my courage failed. The only blight upon our time was its brevity, the fact that we knew it must end.

He told me he was present in the garden when Augustine heard a child singing, "Take it and read, take it and read," although my son heard nothing.

"Opening up the Bible, Mother," he recounted, "Father read: 'Not in quarrels and rivalries. Rather, arm yourselves with the Lord Jesus Christ.'"

"Monica must have been happy," I said, thinking of the dream she had related all those years before. The young man starving for food she could not give him. My mother's heart was glad for her, for what mother can watch the suffering of her child?

"She was," Adeodatus replied simply. "She said it was a miracle that as St. Paul was freed of his chains by an angel while the guards stood amazed, so too her son had been freed from the chains of his doubt. Afterwards," he went on, "Father, Nebridius, and I were baptized. We are to go to Cassiciacum on my return to Italy."

At the mention of his departure, I grew quiet. He put his arm about my shoulders. "Do not grieve, Mama," he said. "I will come back. Papa says he will return to Africa, that his future is here and not in Italy."

Then he made me laugh by turning cartwheels on the grass, his wise heart knowing that to act the boy would be my greatest comfort.

Perpetua was interested in every aspect of the farm. She and Tanit spent hours in the kitchen discussing recipes, how best to braise lamb with apples, how to cure a ham whether with applewood or other. She wrote down the recipe for Tanit's pomegranate preserve.

"I should squeeze the juice from these," I said, indicating the pomegranates on the trees in the atrium. "I owe you."

She laughed. "Tanit's recipe is sufficient recompense, my dear."

I had given Adeodatus the tunic I made for his birthday. It was a little short but it fit him in the shoulders.

"That's the main thing," Perpetua said. "I see you wisely left a good hem."

I smiled at Tanit, for that had been her suggestion.

"It can be easily let down," Perpetua said. "Turn around, nephew."

We had made Adeodatus get up on a chair in the middle of the atrium, and Perpetua, Tanit, and I were walking around him, pulling on the material and measuring it critically with a piece of yarn. I especially wanted to be sure to get the right fit and jotted down his measurements on the silver-framed wax tablet Monica had given me all those years ago in Thagaste. Come winter, instead of pining for the spring, I intended to make him a full set of new clothes, which I would present to him on his next visit. I was already anticipating his delight.

Adeodatus was a little embarrassed at being the center of all this female attention but he endured it stoically, obediently turning and straightening his shoulders when we told him he was slouching. But at last, even his patience wore thin.

"Mama," he said, "can I get down? Rusticus wants to show me the new foal."

And so we had pity on him and let him go. He ran outside and I could hear him shouting for Rusticus. The sound was so sweet to my ears that I suddenly felt dizzy and had to sit down.

"Are you all right?" Perpetua asked, concerned.

I nodded.

"It's because your blood is still thin after your illness," Tanit said and she went to fetch the apple cider she had made from last year's crop.

At mealtimes I loved to watch Adeodatus eat, his appetite insatiable, Tanit nodding with approval as he cleaned his food bowl twice and asked for more. When at last his hunger was sated and the lamps lit, we would sit in the atrium, me in a chair, my son at my feet, his head laid sleepily against my knees as he was wont to do when a boy, Perpetua sewing quietly in a corner. Tanit, Anzar, and the others would sometimes join us but not often for they knew how precious my time was with my son. This was just one of many loving courtesies they showed me and Adeodatus and my heart was filled with gratitude.

My son spoke of his father, hesitantly at first because he knew it gave me pain, then with more assurance when I reassured him that I loved to hear his father's name on his lips, that the pictures he drew for me would be my solace in the years ahead.

He told me how much happier Augustine was, how filled with faith, how the doubts that had plagued him were quite gone.

Listening in the darkness with the lamps guttering and the shadows flickering on the walls as if we sat, secretive, in the center of my heart, he conjured Augustine to me, and I could even believe that at any moment he would walk in from his study where he had been writing and bend to kiss me and ruffle his son's hair.

I sat quietly and let Adeodatus talk, grateful just to have him with me and make believe we were three together again.

"Mama," he said, as if the past and present, boy and man, could mingle in this hushed and half-lit space. "He loves you, misses you every moment, but has found a happiness he did not know before. I can see it on his face. No longer does he strive for something out of reach, like Tantalus, but now holds fast to something real."

The purity of his love, of his desire to make things right, his young man's ardor I had known and loved in Augustine when first we met, pierced my heart. Adeodatus lifted his head to look at me.

"Losing you broke him," he said. "But it was needful for him to come to God. He had to lose the thing he loved the most to find what he had been seeking all his life. Do you understand?"

"Yes, my son," I said, stroking his head. "I do."

Before I was prepared to part with him, the time of Adeodatus and Perpetua's departure came. Perpetua was to see him to the ship in Carthage and then return to Thagaste and her children.

"Navigius is still in Milan with Augustine," she said. "Oh to be a man and travel the world." For a moment she looked sad and I realized that the life she led in Thagaste must sometimes be dull for her.

We embraced with many tears. "I will visit again soon," she said. "If I don't fall pregnant again, that is."

"Not much chance if Navigius is in Italy," I joked.

"There's a thought," she said, suddenly brightening. "I must admit I am a bit sick of always being with child."

Adeodatus helped his aunt into the gig and then turned to me.

We embraced. Holding him I did not think I would ever have the strength to let him go but, after a long time, I did. I held him at arm's length so I could look him in the eyes, so tall he had grown.

"I love you more than I love the world," I said. "More than I love myself. Remember that I love you, my son."

"I love you always," Adeodatus replied.

A final kiss, a hand lifted in farewell, and they were gone.

CHAPTER 33

After Adeodatus and Perpetua's visit I was filled with a contentment I had not known since I left Italy. The shortening days of fall, the crops harvested, the fruit picked, the grapes pressed and stored, all this seemed a benediction, a promise that the harvest of my life's labors was full. I heard there was plague in Carthage but here in the country we passed unscathed. Neither did I fear for my son as he was in Italy, even more removed from the city than I.

The winter came and, with it, very cold days such as we had seldom known. But Tanit said it was a good sign, that the cold would kill the plague in the city and stop it spreading to the countryside.

It was at this time that I realized Tanit was with child. I noticed a rounding of her belly when she was stretching to reach a bowl off a high shelf in the kitchen. I should have known before, I chided myself. She had been more tired of late and once I caught her retching in the yard behind the house.

"You are with child," I said. "That is wonderful."

She smiled shyly. "Yes, Domina. If the gods will it."

"How far along?"

"Four moons," she replied and I was reminded of Cybele asking me that exact question long ago.

I determined that nothing would go wrong. I would watch over her like a hawk. With Neith, I had been so ignorant, so inexperienced, I had failed to see the signs that all was not well, at least I had told myself this over the years. Tanit and her baby, I vowed, would live.

After supper one evening in late spring I was walking along the road, the sun sinking in swathes of crimson in the west, the coolness of the coming night soft against my skin, when I heard a horse approaching. I called out, afraid I would be trampled. A letter, I thought, although I had not hoped to get one so soon. The horse reined in, blowing hard, feet skittering in a shower of stones that stung my ankles.

"Augustine?" He was just a faint outline against the darkening sky, but I would know him even in pitch blackness.

He threw himself down from the horse and in the next instant was holding me. I could not believe he was alive and in my arms. Then I drew back. There was something different about him, something dark and terrible in the feel of him.

Gripping my shoulders hard, he said: "Our son is dead."

I did not, could not, understand him. "No," I said. "The plague was here. It was not in Italy."

"We returned to Thagaste two months ago."

"No," I said again, shaking my head. "No."

Ever after, whatever he told me that night about my son's last days, how the fever had come upon him all at once, one day healthy, the next hot and feverish, how he lay in a delirium for days and then woke one morning serene and lucid with a great thirst, his only thought to be forgiven by God, his last words to me: "Tell Mama I will always love her," then slipping softly away, as the lamps were lit against the night as if he were a child falling asleep—these images returned always, like the ocean beating on the shore, to the first words I heard: "Our son is dead."

The fact of it, those dreadful, final words, was like a mountain rearing in my path, huge, immovable, impossible to climb or circumvent, a dark mass against which I was stopped.

"It cannot be," I said, over and over. "It cannot, cannot be."

"We buried him," Augustine told me, "five days ago beside his grandfather in Thagaste. A priest said prayers at his gravesite with incense and the sprinkling of water, all that was proper."

I would have climbed down into the grave and held him to my breast, for he was always fearful of being confined, would cry out at night if he became entangled in his sheets. I saw him lying there, gravecloths covering his face, his body wrapped in shrouds, that quickening body I held against me so little time ago, had always held in my heart's embrace, and now would hold no more, the dark earth falling till he was hidden forever in the ground and me above it.

I also learned that Monica had died the previous year at Ostia. I bowed my head at this, but my heart was so stunned with grief over my son that I did not know what I felt. My only thought: at least she was spared the sorrow of her beloved grandson's death.

We had walked to the house and were standing in the atrium

in darkness, our arms around each other, Augustine's voice, the voice I had longed to hear, now speaking words that were the end of everything. "Our son is dead."

We clutched each other as shipwrecked sailors clutch at flotsam in a roaring sea and when they look for land see only a vast emptiness.

At last we could stand no longer and sank down onto the floor still holding onto each other. We stayed like that all night. I cannot remember if I wept; I cannot remember if Augustine wept. What I can remember is that I knew this was the end, that I had reached the utmost limit of everything I thought I knew or was. All was darkness.

I must have slept, for when I awoke on the floor of the atrium it was dawn and I was alone. Augustine had covered me with a cloak and laid a pillow under my head. On the floor beside me was a piece of parchment folded into a square. When I opened it, Adeodatus's ring, the one I had given him when I left Milan, his father's citizen ring, fell out and rolled across the tiles. I watched it go. It came to rest beneath a table, but I did not stoop to pick it up. Opening my hand, I let the note fall unread. Then I went into my room and closed the door.

I kept to my room and neither ate nor slept nor did I weep. It was as if time had ceased to flow, as if my son had taken the world with him when he died and left a blankness in which I could not measure my proximity to any living thing nor navigate which direction to go. My body was a nothing, a mere shell, its needs irrelevant, unheeded. I did not even long for death, for if consciousness there was beyond the grave, I was already dead and did not fear it.

I do not know how the soul survives such things, how the heart still beats, the nerves and sinews obey the mind's commands and move the limbs though the will is dead. When Tanit came to tend me, I said, "My son is dead," as if I could explain the whole of it, could make her understand that nothing mattered any longer, that this time my sickness would not depart.

A year ago my body had revived, grown stronger with the passing of the seasons, linked as it was to the life of all that was, hidden in winter, coming forth in spring when the sleeping earth awoke. Now I was forever invulnerable, cut off from humankind, a thing immortal which neither time nor death could touch. In this way, my son's death freed me from all fear, for while he was living I had care for him, was fearful of harm from accident, sickness, and the evil of men. Now I felt myself indifferent to life's sorrows, its vicissitudes, the cruel games it played on men.

Time passed. In my mind's eye I saw my son as he had been the last time I saw him, an agony so great I groaned aloud as if I were once again in labor. I saw him running in the fields, his arms held wide as if he were a bird, crying, "Catch me, Mama." I felt the weight of his head against my knee on those summer nights we talked and then, sometimes, at my breast as if he were a babe again and I were nursing him, his tiny fingers playing with my hair. I heard his laughter, his chatter when a boy telling of a bird's nest he had found with eggs so blue they looked made of summer sky. I kissed his scrapes and tied his little sandals, watched him fall asleep while my story was yet half-told, one hand curled in mine, the other flung wide across the covers. A thousand images played before my eyes more true than those I saw in the theater at Carthage where I laughed and wept to see the tragedies and comedies of men upon a stage, knowing them for make-believe.

CHAPTER 34

I do not know how many weeks passed only that I might have crouched there forever in my room had a piercing cry not shattered the night and tore the bindings from my shrouded heart. It was an animal's cry, long drawn out, utterly wild until suddenly cut off. Then it came again and, after it, the frenzied barking and howling of the dogs. Throwing on a cloak I ran out into the night toward the house where Tanit and Anzar lived.

The scene was utter confusion, the air choking with incense, someone's muttered incantation, a crowding of bodies around the bed and on it Tanit, half lying, half sitting, knees drawn up, her face a tragic mask, her hair like Medusa's, her mouth a black hole out of which that inhuman keening started up again.

"Mistress, mistress," someone implored.

"Anaxis," I said. "Silence those dogs." I pushed Anzar down on a stool by the head of the bed. "Hold her hand," I commanded. "Speak to her."

His lips moved but no sound came out, his face ashen. Then, as if awakening from a trance, he took his wife's hand and leaned in towards her. "My love," I heard him whisper. "My strong goddess."

An image of Neith laboring in vain with Tanzar praying beside her came to me.

"Maia," I said, "run to the main house and heat water; take the sheets from my bed and tear them into squares."

Her eyes were fixed with horror on Tanit, her hand covering her mouth as if to stifle a scream. Barely out of girlhood, she had shrunk into the smallest spaces of her mind the way a woodland creature will crouch motionless in the hollow of a tree when a predator is near.

"Go," I said, pushing her. "And bring a sharp knife. Make sure you boil it first."

I leaned over Tanit, waiting for her pains to ease, speaking softly. "I am going to feel inside you to see if the baby is stuck. It will hurt and I am sorry for it but it must be done."

Her eyelids flickered for a moment and I thought I saw her nod. Then she was gone again into that red vortex, swept down against her will, her head rolling from side to side, that awful feral sound issuing again from her lips.

I waited until Maia returned carrying a bowl of hot water and towels then washed my hands, dried them, and took a flask of olive oil and poured it over my hands until they glistened in the lamplight.

Tanit lay still.

"Now," I said and gently felt between her legs, the flesh taut and hot, impossibly stretched and, at the opening, a round hard lump, the baby's head. She groaned as I probed deeper, blindly feeling for the face, downwards to the neck then my fingers touched something ropelike. I sat back and wiped my hands.

Anzar's eyes were pleading with me but he did not speak. I motioned for Maia to take her place by Tanit's side then drew him to the door and spoke in a low voice. "The cord is wound around the baby's neck," I said. "That is why she cannot push it forth."

"You will save them," he said. "I know you will."

"I will try," I replied. "Stay with her a moment."

I left the house and went to find Rusticus. He was standing by the barn; I could hear the dogs whining and scratching at the door behind him but, mercifully, they had ceased to howl.

I explained the position of the baby. "You must help me," I said.

"Domina," he replied, panic in his voice. "I know only animals."

"Please," I said, placing my hand on his arm.

"The gods help us," he muttered. Then, as if gathering himself: "You must slip the cord over the young one's head before it chokes," he said. "Leastways, that is the way of it with calving."

"Show me."

When we reentered the house I saw Tanit had used up all her strength. Her cries had sunk to moans, her eyes when they flickered open were vacant and unseeing. She was retreating to that place that is the antechamber of death, her body with us still, her soul already on the wing. Anzar's face in the lamplight, a rictus of despair, but he did not cease his litany of love, a murmured plea for her to rally and to live.

"You must do it," Rusticus said. "My hands are too big."

Once again I washed my hands and bathed them in oil then, heedless of the pain I would cause, slid them inside Tanit on either side of the baby's head. Slowly, carefully, with the tips of my fingers groping for purchase, I began to ease the cord toward me over the child's head. Many times it slipped from my grasp and I had to begin again. Tanit had ceased to move; Maia was crying quietly in the corner. The others clustered silent in the doorway.

"A little farther," I heard Rusticus say.

And then the cord slipped suddenly over the baby's head so that, with my hands cupped on either side of it, I could gently draw the head and then the body forth. A tiny girl-child, her face empurpled, her body a skinned rabbit's, the life-giving cord that had encircled her neck like the iron ring of a shackle spiraled darkly from her navel. She lay quite motionless on the bed.

Rusticus quickly reached over and, taking the baby by the heels with one hand, hung her upside down. Fluid poured from her nose and mouth. Then he struck her lightly on the buttocks, once, twice, and she gave a tiny gasp. Then she drew in a great rasping breath and when she let it out it was as a cry, a thin wavering sound like the bleating of a newborn lamb.

I saw a smile appear on Tanit's waxlike face; Anzar laid his forehead on the bed and wept.

The child was named Ifru after Tanit's mother. For weeks after her birth Tanit lay gravely ill, sometimes raving, sometimes sane, no strength to hold her child still less to give her suck. Anzar was no use to us at all so frantic was he his wife would die; day and night he sat at her bedside cradling his daughter in his arms while Tanit slept. When her bed needed changing he would lift her tenderly as he lifted his child and it was all we could do to take her from him again and lay her down when the bed was made. His tools lay forgotten in the yard, his face remained unshaved until, one day, seeing him hollow-eyed, his face quite sunken, I ordered him to quit his vigil and sleep.

"What use will you be to Tanit if you die?" I said to him but he refused to leave, remaining hunched upon his stool, his face set, his hands gripping his knees so tightly his knuckles shone white. So I had him carry Tanit to the main house while I walked behind holding the baby. I installed them in my bedchamber, for it was the largest, with a pallet on the floor for Anzar and a basket for Ifru bedded snugly down with sheepskins.

"Now rest," I ordered.

I tended Tanit and the child while Maia took over the running of the house. It was the first time I had held a babe since I cared for Neith's children, but I found my arm curving just so, her tiny head resting sweetly in the crook of my elbow, my hips swaying from side to side to lull the child to sleep, as if all those intervening years had never been and I was young again, a new mother, as if my body were wiser than my mind. I spent long hours walking her, for she was colicky and would not thrive, seeming always to be hungry yet unable to keep much down. I was determined she and her mother would live, for I had had a bellyful of death and grieving and fought for their lives with a kind of dogged rage.

I found a wet nurse from a neighboring farm, a woman whose own child had died at birth, and then later, when it looked as if Ifru would live, I fed her cream to put some flesh on her tiny, stick-like limbs. In deep winter when the earth lay sunken into its dreamless sleep of waiting, the ebbing of the tide of Tanit's and

Ifru's lives turned and began to run swift and full again and, with it, my own.

Once Ifru was born, time—frozen since my son died—began to flow again. Each milestone of her little life, the day she lifted up her head unsupported, the day her wavering hand closed round her foot when I was changing her, her eyes opening wide in amazement to feel it was her own, the way she would creep along the floor like a little worm, reaching what she sought and grasping it with triumph, these little markers of her growth were drops of time accumulating in a bowl that grew to fullness.

When she began to walk, we drained the pool in the atrium and used it as her play place knowing she could not climb out. In the evening Anzar carved bits of wood into animals for a miniature farm while Tanit, Maia, and I sewed her clothes, for she was growing fast. We made dolls from linen scraps, inked in the faces, and fashioned hair from wool. Now that the danger to her life was passed, she grew robust and strong with sturdy limbs still chubby from her babyhood, black eyes filled with mischief, dark silky curls I tied up in a ribbon, just enough to curl once around my finger even as her tiny fist had curled when she was born and we despaired of her. Sometimes she would lapse into a dreamy state and sit, unmoving, her eyes wide open and unblinking as if she saw things hidden from other's eyes. Tanit believed she possessed the Sight, but I thought it was a weakness left over from the manner of her birth, the cutting off of air, though I never said so out loud.

I have heard Christians speak of grace as if it were something without substance, something which falls on them from the heavens like light or air. Grace, for me, is flesh and blood, bones and sinew, someone whom my mouth can name: Father, Augustine, Adeodatus, Nebridius. And now, when I thought I had lost all grace: Ifru. And it was not as if she replaced my own son, her birth coming so soon after Adeodatus's death; rather her small life fell like a drop of water on the stone of my heart, in itself so tiny, so ineffectual, but oft repeated over time, with the power to wear it smooth.

Years later, when I looked for the last time on the farm I loved, the faces of those I loved more, I understood what Nebridius's gentle heart had known: that this small plot of land, of all the places on the earth, could raise a crop of love from the stony soil of my heart.

Even the news of Nebridius's death of the same fever that took my son's life soon after Ifru was born did not break me, so accustomed I had become to loss. The legacy of his kindness has sustained me these forty years and I will bless his name forever. I lived longer in this place than in any other and, most wondrous thing of all, came to call it home, a place where I found, if not peace, a kind of deep contentment when I could say: This is the harvest of my life and it is good.

CHAPTER 35

When I was a child each day passed as if it were a year; as I have grown older I have found that a year can pass as quickly as a single month. And so ten years passed. I did not see Augustine again. I heard he had been ordained a priest and then a bishop. Recently he had written a book called *Confessions*, a memory of his life before he was a priest, a chronicle of the journey he had taken to God. He sent me a copy and wrote on the front these words:

"For love who showed me Love itself."

That is all he wrote; there was no letter, not even his name.

About this time an imperial edict banning pagan worship and ordering the closing of pagan shrines sparked rioting in Carthage. The religious unrest spilled out into the countryside where bands of men and youths, emboldened by the emperor's edicts against heresy and pagan rites, set upon innocent laborers working in the fields or people gathered at gravesites to hold feasting for their dead as was the African custom, one that even Monica had observed until Ambrose told her it was unseemly. A neighbor who was known to be a worshipper of Baal was murdered, his house and barn burned. One evening Rusticus came home from the fields, his face bloody from a fight.

"It was this that saved me," he said, showing me a wooden cross he wore on a leather cord around his neck.

After that he made me nail a simple wooden cross above the lintel of the door to show that we were Christian. I did it to protect my people though I felt apostate, as if I had recanted a faith I did not have. Although I did not worship the Punic gods as Tanit and Anzar did, as Neith and my father had done, yet I also did not worship the Christian God. He had taken too much from me. The next day when I was weeding in the kitchen garden, a hawk swooped down and snatched a snake up in its talons. Tanit, who was with me, straightened, one fist pushed into the small of her back, the other hand shading her eyes as she watched the bird's flight.

"It is a sign from the gods, Domina," she said, though of what she never explained.

Old age approaches slowly step by step, at first so distant as to be unseen, unheard then, one day, it is there. Thus did my old age come upon me, the sudden pains in my limbs when I awoke each morning, the silver strands appearing in my hair until the dark turned wholly gray, then white. My hands so used to hard work, the wringing out of clothes in the icy stream behind the house, the beating of the olives from the trees at harvest, the punching down of dough upon the kitchen board, grew stiff and gnarled like the branches of an ancient apple tree long since barren. At first I was angry my body would not obey my mind, thinking it a recalcitrant child who refused to do his share of labors, but I grew more tolerant and mild, preferring more and more to sit in the shade of the orchard and watch the chickens pecking at my feet, watch the swelling of a pear upon the branch until—nature's amphora, brimful with juice and sweetness—it was ready to be plucked. The rhythmic chanting of the laborers at harvest would pulse across the fields, reminding me of my childhood with my father, our solitary travels, their singing a signal it was time to return to Carthage for the winter.

In these quieter years I spent many hours reading, my only luxury a library I had collected scroll by scroll and now filling a closet in my room. Ovid's stories of the gods, the tales of Cupid—Amor—and the women he ruined, held me spellbound. Daphne, in her desperation to escape, changed into a tree; Europa, Leda, Arachne, Philomela, all pursued by love and forever changed from one nature into another.

Like these women from the ancient stories, I, too, had changed. I was no longer the young girl who thought a man's desire was love, his caresses proof of his devotion, nor even the young matron proudly carrying his child on my hip who now believed our son would ratify his fidelity. I was now an old but still living tree, tough, resilient, able to bend to winter winds, bare branches awaiting the coming of spring with patience and a longing to hear birdsong once again.

The pain of my son's death had dulled with the passing of

time, lodged now like the broken tip of a knife in a wound encased by scar tissue, a foreign object I would carry to my grave.

As I grew older, sleep became elusive and so I would arise and light the lamps and sit in my chair and look deep into my memories and see again Adeodatus and Augustine and it was as if I was young again and we were together.

One event stands out in my memory during those long, quiet years when season followed season in an unvarying round and religious unrest died down. Half a day's journey from Carthage, we would often receive news of the world outside our tiny sphere of life. One morning, I heard the sound of wheels and saw a neighbor, a farmer called Linus, draw his mule-drawn rig up before the house.

"Have you heard?" he said. "Rome has been sacked by Alaric and his army."

It seemed a thing incredible that Rome, the ancient center of the world, should fall. It was as if the earth had shaken, the seas had risen to overwhelm the land, all nature turned upside down. I remembered the streets of Rome, dirty, teeming with people from all the corners of the earth, its temples rising huge and white against an azure sky, the amphitheater that Vespasian built, the largest in the world, beside the ancient forum of the Caesars.

Though born on a different continent, a child of a conquered race, I had lived my whole life in the shadow of the Romans, their culture my culture, their ways my ways, like the water that flowed from their aqueducts to the city fountains from which we drank and thought little of it except that our thirst was sated. Linus, a devout Christian, weeping told me of the sacrilege committed by the Goths, how they raped holy nuns, slaughtered priests, pulled down statues, and stabled their beasts in churches fouling the beautiful mosaic floors with ordure. We felt, Linus and I, citizens of Africa Province and all the Roman world, as if the whole world perished in that one city.

One day, during my seventy-fourth year, news came that the Vandals had landed on the African shore east of the city of Hippo Regius and had begun to lay waste the countryside, burning farms and villages, killing and enslaving the inhabitants.

I had also heard some months previously that Augustine was ill, had left Hippo in the winter for his health but had returned still ailing. It was rumored the barbarians had their eyes on Hippo Regius, a rich and ancient coastal city, that if it would not surrender they intended to sack it and put it to the torch.

The next morning I awoke before dawn, knotted a few belongings inside a cloak, including Neith's statue, placed the scroll containing my will leaving everything to Ifru on my bed, and left the house. I saddled the old mule, Hannibal, in the barn, a hard task to lift the heavy saddle and buckle it around his fat girth, then led him out into the orchard and tied him to a tree to graze. A faint light was showing in the sky, a pearlescent sheen above a stilled landscape, the only sound the sleepy sounds of birds as they awoke. The dogs came and nosed my hand, whining and looking up at me with their great innocent eyes as if they knew what I intended. I murmured their names—Torch, Orion, Tecla, Nimrod, and Sisyphus—the great-great-great-grandchildren of the dogs that bared their teeth at me when I first came to the farm, a stranger to their sires. Torch butted his great head under my hand, his feathery tail sweeping back and forth in placid greeting. I stroked his wiry muzzle, grizzled now, remembering how, when he was born the runt of the litter, I had had to guide him to his mother's teat and protect him from his stronger brothers and sisters. He had outlived them all.

I knew I must leave before the rooster crowed and woke the farm but I lingered, walking the paths about the house, seeing it as I did a lifetime ago when I was a woman bruised almost to death.

A figure appeared in the doorway, no longer lithe and girlish but thickened now with the bearing of her five children. In her hand she held the scroll I had left her. Long ago I had taught Ifru to read, so she knew very well what it meant.

"Mina," Ifru said, the infant name she first used when she had been unable to pronounce *Domina* now as familiar to me as *Mama*. "Where are you going?"

I came toward her and took her by the shoulders so I could see her face and look into her eyes, the eyes of her mother, Tanit.

"It is time," I said, "for me to make one final journey. I go to Hippo Regius."

"No," she wailed, tears starting in her eyes. "It is too dangerous; you are too old."

I smiled at this and patted her cheek as I used to when she was a child and needed comfort.

"That is why I will be safe," I said. "Who is going to notice an old woman like me?"

"They will rob and murder you," she said.

"I have nothing that they want. All I have is yours, Little Bird. Take what you can and flee, for the Vandals will not be content with Hippo Regius but will sweep west consuming all before them until they reach Carthage. If you love me you will go."

I embraced her then, astonished to feel her woman's bulk when it seemed to me she was still a girl.

She helped me on my mule, weeping, and that is how I saw her for the last time, standing in the lane, her hand uplifted in farewell like my son all those years ago, except it was I who was leaving and she, like me, was left behind to grieve. I clicked my tongue at Hannibal and he set off.

At the rise of the hill I drew up and looked back over the coastal plain where my farm sat, miniature as a picture in my father's mosaics, a thin tendril of smoke now rising from the oven as Ifru baked the day's bread as if this day were like any other.

To see it down below, knowing how the morning light was slanting into the atrium, a band of gold illuminating the mosaics I had put down in memory of my father, the clash of pots from the kitchen, the distant call of voices as the household awoke to the smell of baking bread. All this was as familiar to me as the sound of my own breathing, yet it was removed from me, too, as if I gazed upon a living picture of my life long distant from my present. It came to me then that all my life had been a journey from one place to another, each time thinking, this, surely, is the last.

I did not have a premonition of my death except to know this body that had carried me faithfully through life, even as Hannibal plodded placidly on with me upon his back, would soon be no more.

"I am coming," I said aloud. Hannibal's ears twitched at the sound of my voice.

"Not you," I said, patting him. "Another. Though equally mule-like."

I took the inland route reasoning that the coastal road would be swarming with the Vandal army, for they never liked to be far from the sea. It was high summer and the fields were filled with laborers, the lanes with farmers taking their produce to market, their oxen slow and ponderous, snatching mouthfuls from the hedgerows as they went, the farmers' children running behind the cart, their bare feet caked in dust, their tunics dirty from their play, staring to see one so ancient as me until their parents bade them sharply to mind their manners.

Many a stranger stopped to ask me how I did, if I was lost, and could they point the way, addressing me as Mother and Grandmother.

"No, thank you," I told them. "But if you have news of Hippo Regius I would be glad."

None had news but some said they had seen black smoke rising in the east, too early in the year for it to be the burning of the harvest stubble. As I drew closer to my journey's end, the farmers and the travelers were replaced by refugees fleeing the environs of Hippo, an endless train of carts piled with belongings deemed too precious to be left behind: a feather bolster, a crate of squabbling chickens, a baby's cradle filled with pots, an oven, chairs, tables. Small children sitting on the laps of grandparents or ancient slaves, those too young, too old, to walk, stunned by their misfortune. It seemed the whole world was on the move.

At night I camped in the fields beside a stream if I could find one now the heat of summer had shrunk the watercourses to a trickle, its cheerful music an accompaniment as I lay and watched the stars wheel in living arcs above my head.

Each morning I rose and filled the water-skin I carried and was on my way before the sun had risen. This journey, my last, contained all my journeys, a contraction of time, a pressing of my life till it ran pure and clear, ready for storage in time's vast vessel.

These same roads I traveled now, Augustine had surely trod, for he was known throughout the diocese for his frequent visits to villages and towns, determined to know the people of his parish, that recalcitrant flock of adulterers, drunkards, heretics, thieves, and graspers after wealth, all whom he cajoled, harangued, rebuked, and comforted with his tongue and pen until it wore him out.

Now he was dying while a barbarian horde massed at the city gates, their only desire to destroy what he had built up these forty years or more. Our lives were joined in some mysterious way, as if we were as identical twins who, when one dies, the other dies not long after.

He was the last remaining witness of my life, the only one who knew me from my youth, and when his eyes beheld me once again it would be as if a stamp were placed upon a document to verify its legality, that it had the force of law. My life was that document, drawn up over time, each clause, each paragraph painstakingly inscribed so there would be no loopholes, no way to wriggle out. I had come to present him with the bill of my life and demand payment, even to the smallest coin, each jot and tittle.

My journey was also a last tribute to my father whom I had accompanied on these same roads in my childhood, whose body lay unburied and long since turned to dust in some ditch, some distant field beside a stream, his last sight the same stars that filled my nights and made me weep to behold their splendor, their vast indifference.

Did he think of me as he lay dying, my face the last thing he saw and reached out to, as the darkness came upon him? Or did he die in his sleep, his dreams the mosaics he would make tomorrow, the swirls and patterns, trees and flowers, birds and beasts, slowly resolving into depth, a living color, until he knew he was in Elysium, no dream of art but art itself. I spoke his name out loud—Kothar, "the skilled"—my eyes dimming with tears, and asked him, if afterlife there was, to wait for me with my son, the grandson he never knew, for I would see him soon.

CHAPTER 36

As I drew closer to Hippo it became too dangerous to travel by day and so I traveled by night, the distant beacon of a thousand campfires guiding me. In a wood behind the city facing the eastern gate, I unsaddled Hannibal and placed my hand on his soft muzzle, his lustrous eyes regarding me with intelligence, even love.

"Good-bye, old friend," I told him. "I thank you for your faithfulness." And slapping his rump I drove him off amongst the trees, for I was anxious lest he be taken by the enemy and butchered. Once he turned back, bewildered by that strange place, until I drove him off with stones. He gave me a last reproachful look and then trotted off, and I sat down and wept the tears I had not shed when I parted from Ifru and my home.

Wiping my face and clutching my bundle to my chest, a stout stick in my right hand, I set off for the city before me, its buildings standing white and tall against the great openness of the western sky where the land gave way to the ocean, around its walls a desolation of filth, animal bones, the stinking corpses of the dead blackened by flies that rose in swarming clouds as I passed by. It was as if the City of Man in all its squalor had sought admittance to the City of God and been denied, forever to remain encamped outside its shining walls.

Mumbling to myself as if I were senile, I made my way toward the gate, passing soldiers squatting by their campfires gambling with dice or sharpening weapons, some calling out to me in their strange tongue as if I reminded them of their own great-grandmothers across the sea, some making a sign with their hands as if they feared I was a witch, but none molested me.

One young man, blond hair long and braided, outlandish trousers covering his legs such I had seen Germans wearing in Rome, strange tattoos on his arms, steadied me when I stumbled over the thigh bone of an ox. Looking in his eyes, a rain-cloud gray with amber flecks, his lashes golden, I thought: *You are only a little older than my son when he died.*

I had been as far west as Hippo once before with my father when we owned a mule and cart until he gambled them away when he was in his cups. Thereafter we had to walk, lugging his tools, keeping to the countryside around Carthage, the villas set along the coast, the estates of the rich on the inland plain beneath the mountains to the south.

I passed under the gateway, jostled in a crowd of refugees who sought protection within the city walls, rich landowners by the quality of their clothes, who had seen their villas burned, their crops and livestock destroyed, their vines and olive trees hacked down, all their wealth taken in the blink of an eye. I could have told them that wisdom lies in knowing happiness is a fleeting dream, that barns crammed full with oil and grain, gold chains on neck and wrist, costly perfumes to anoint the body cannot sustain the soul when hard times come. The slaves who stumbled along behind their masters knew this—I saw it in their eyes, their disenfranchised lives more weighty than their masters' purses, their loss so great a small thing now to lay down their life. In this knowledge they were rich and their full-fed masters poor.

I remember Hippo as a city that smelled sweet, like Carthage, perched as it was on twin hills above the ocean, scoured by its cleansing winds. I remember how Rome, by comparison, had smelled like a midden, its noxious vapors trapped among its seven hills, its alleys stinking with refuse thrown from windows despite its vaunted sewer, the *Cloaca Maxima*, which emptied into the Tiber and made its licker fish the largest in the world, grown huge on human waste.

But now all that had changed; the streets lay deep in the filth of animals penned up within its walls, the alleys oozing runnels of human waste. The buildings' porticos and pillars, made of marble from its glory days when Hippo was the second port of Africa Province, were streaked with soot from the cooking fires of refugees camped under the shade of their wide roofs, the walls of buildings so many eyeless skulls where wooden doors and shutters had been taken for fuel.

Gone was the prosperous hum of barter and haggling over goods, of children playing in the streets, matrons gossiping out of windows, the calls of stevedores from the wharfs. Now the sound was a continuous lament of hungry babies, frantic parents screaming for their children, men raging at each other for a scrap of bread, a sliver of shade, a cup of water to revive their pregnant wives.

The city's great harbor, formed by a river that flowed down to the sea from the inland plains, was choked with all manner of vessels taking people on board, fortunes in gold and jewels exchanged for a single berth, the jetties of the harbor a heaving mass of bodies clamoring for passage, young children trampled underfoot or abandoned on the wharf, wailing, the old vacant-eyed and lost, all bonds of family obliterated in a conflagration of fear.

I took one such child by the hand, a small boy of three or four, and led him out of the crush.

"Where are your parents?" I asked.

He stared at me huge-eyed, his face tear-streaked, a dirty finger in his mouth. Then I heard a shout and looking up I saw a man push through the crowd. Without a word, he snatched the boy up and plunged back toward the harbor's edge, soon lost to my sight. Abandoning the harbor I made my way back up to the city, resting frequently on the steep steps leading upwards to the forum, keeping to the side so I would not be swept away by people hurrying down, a vast river of humanity flowing to the sea, and I, the only one going up.

The forum was wide, with porticoes on three sides containing shops behind the deep shade of their pillars, statues, temples, and small monuments commemorating Roman generals of long ago. To the north of the forum was a public fountain, flowing sluggishly, around which many had set up camp, erecting makeshift awnings of cloaks on poles to shield them from the sun. Nearby a rectangular-covered courtyard I remembered as the place where markets were held was now crammed with refugees taking shelter in the shade. Behind this, to the east, looming above the Christian quarter a large church, beside it a baptistery and other buildings, which I knew must be the bishop's house and private chapel. Toward these I walked and entered a small courtyard in the center of which grew a pear tree. Beneath its shade I sat down, my journey over.

CHAPTER 37

Across from me is a doorway, narrow and dark, out of which the young man comes each morning to fill the water jars. Outside where I sit the world shimmers, mirage-like, a scorching brightness that dazzles the eyes. Beyond the doorway a shadowed world, death's antechamber, through which I must soon pass.

I wait patiently for the sun to set, for the bells to ring out the day's last prayers before the night, the courtyard emptying, growing silent. Now I am alone except for he who lies nearby, all the frenzied world he loved now shrunken to its sounds, the smell of food cooking over the evening fires, the faint flicker of the lamps, the rustling of the pear tree as a wind picks up from the west, the whispers and soft footfalls of the death chamber.

Rising I enter the door. I touch the iron ring on the chain around my neck, my son's last gift to me apart from his love. I take it off and hold it in my fist. In my pocket, the note Augustine left me when he told me of our son's death, a single line: "It is yearning that makes the heart deep."

Before me is a passageway lit by a single oil lamp in a niche, the flame winnowing along its length as I softly close the door. I hear faint voices, the sound of footsteps moving away. Behind a doorway to my right I hear murmuring, a soft chant, like someone praying. I push open the door and step into a room, no light within save that which comes from an open window through which I see the pear tree, its branches black against a blood-red sky.

I see a man on a bed, propped up on pillows, eyes closed, lips moving, the voice familiar but his body unknown to me, his face so gaunt the flesh seems molded to the bones, his arms above the coverlet wasted, wrinkled like old leather, his breathing a harsh and painful susurration, chest shuddering with the effort of each breath. On the walls are sheets of papyrus with words written in bold black letters; they rustle in the breeze from the open window. As I get nearer I see that they are the penitential psalms and Augustine is reciting them from memory:

Amplius lava me ab iniquitate mea; et peccata meo munda: Quoniam iniquitatem meam ego cognosco, et peccatum meum contra me est semper.

"Wash me from my iniquity; and cleanse me from my sin. For I acknowledge my iniquity; and my sin is ever before me."

"It is I," I say.

He smiles but his eyes remain closed. His lips do not cease to move.

I step close beside his bed, take my son's ring, and thread it over the fourth finger of his left hand. His skin feels dry, scaly, so unlike the flesh I knew long ago when we were young, firm and warm and strong, without blemish or taint. Yet the shape of his hand is the same, the bones and sinews, the wrist bones so delicate for a man, almost womanly, the architecture of his body as familiar to me as my own.

He opens his eyes and looks at me. Suddenly Augustine is there, not the broken man upon the bed nor the bishop nor the shadowy figure in the atrium where I did not have the courage to light the lamps and look into his eyes for fear I would see my own suffering figured there, him saying over and over: "Our son is dead."

Here is the youth I once knew, the man into whose keeping I gave my soul and heart and body, the father of my son. Here is he who caused me such sorrow.

And the years fall away and we are young again in the church where we first met, a shaft of sunlight lighting up his eyes, my gaze dazzled by the sight of him and all pain dies away, all bitterness.

He lifts his left hand and looks at the ring then, slowly, turns over his right hand and opens it. Resting on his palm is the shell he once gave me, the shell I thought I lost long ago.

I lay down Neith's statue on the table beside his bed and take the shell. It is warm from his hand.

"I broke my troth with you," he says. "Forgive me."

In answer, I place my lips upon his lips. His flesh is hot with fever but the shape of his mouth is the same, the feel of him the same. I cannot see him for the tears that blind my eyes but I can feel his hand holding mine. I am the living heart of a tree uncovered by the axe, still pliable, still green and full of sap. I stand beside him and hold his hand. Once I lift a cup of water to his lips and he drinks. When the room grows dark I light a lamp so I can look upon his face and he can look upon mine.

In the middle watches of the night Augustine slips into a coma, his eyelids fluttering as if he dreams, his breathing grown intermittent, sometimes stopping then starting up again with long pauses in between. I smooth his hair back from his face murmuring his name.

"I love you," I say, but he does not hear me.

The road he trod these forty years was mine, save he had gone on ahead. Perhaps the disappearance of my father and Augustine on the road of my life was fated, that left alone I could become the woman I was meant to be, a domina of an estate, a mother to my people, not just my son. It was as if the pain of loss had widened me, scooped out my heart so it could hold a greater love outside the circle of my kin.

He does not awake again but dies just as the blackness beyond the window is lightening. I kiss his still warm lips, fold his hands over his chest and remain, keeping watch over the body I have loved, the greatness of his spirit more.

Augustine.

He is the last to hold my shape in the vessel of his heart and with his passing my story dies as if I had never been, like cities fallen in the desert and returned at last to sand. I am become the merest flicker of a shadow, passing fugitive and brief along the edges of another's life.

AUTHOR'S NOTE

I first came across the mysterious figure of Augustine's concubine when I was twelve and a student at Loreto Convent School in Manchester, England. In religion class we read Augustine's *Confessions*. I remember putting up my hand and asking who this woman was, the one Augustine referred to as "*Una*"—the One. Sister Bernadette replied: "No one knows. She is lost to history."

That phrase, "lost to history," stuck with me. I thought: so many great women are lost to history, eclipsed by the lives of the men they loved. So, forty years later, I decided to go looking for the concubine so she could tell her story. Augustine said in the *Confessions*: "Our use of words is often inaccurate and seldom completely correct, but our meaning is recognized nonetheless."

This is a work of fiction. Augustine scholars will see that, in places, I have taken liberties with the historical facts for dramatic purposes. An example of this is in the character of Alypius. I have made him a contemporary of Augustine whereas, in fact, he was several years younger and not a fellow student but a pupil of Augustine's. I also omit him from scenes in Rome and Milan even though he was an important figure in Augustine's life and went on to become a fellow African bishop.

I have altered the chronology of some events. For example, after being kicked out by Monica, Augustine and the concubine and their son lived in Thagaste for three years where he taught before returning to Carthage. I have them return to Carthage immediately. Historically, Adeodatus is thirteen when they go to Rome; in this story he is nine or ten.

The most obvious change is that I have made the concubine's casting off a little more ambiguous than is strictly historical. The conventional interpretation is that Monica arranged a marriage for Augustine and that the concubine was sent away before the betrothal. I retain this sequence of events, but I have rejected the modern notion that this was a coldhearted and cynical act on Augustine's part. In the *Confessions,* Augustine writes: "the woman with whom I had been living was torn from my side as an obstacle to my marriage and this blow crushed my heart to bleeding because I loved her dearly." Nor is Augustine's refusal to name the concubine equally cold-blooded. Along with the great Augustine scholar Peter Brown, I believe that Augustine's refusal to name the woman he loved was in order to protect her anonymity. He knew the *Confessions* was going to be the fifth-century equivalent of a best seller and would draw unwanted attention to himself and to those he loved. If anything, this refusal to name her leads me to suspect she was still living at the time the *Confessions* was published.

A word about concubinage. To our modern ears "concubine" sounds synonymous with "mistress" or even "prostitute." In the ancient world this was not the case. Concubinage involved a monogamous sexual relationship when the man and woman involved were not, or could not be, married for societal reasons. It almost always involved a man of higher social status and a woman of low social status. One of the most famous examples is Caelis, the freedwoman and concubine of the Emperor Vespasian, who was held in high esteem by her contemporaries and had much power at the imperial court. Frequently, concubinage was voluntary on the part of the woman and her family as it involved a means by which she could attain economic security. The resulting union was not unlike common-law marriage today. To be labeled a concubine was not a derogatory term in the ancient world and was often inscribed on tombstones as a title to denote the status of the deceased. Ambrose, the Bishop of Milan and known to be a strict moralist, argued for allowing concubines and their partners to receive the Eucharist. This reveals that he did not consider their union to be sinful so much as irregular.

In the fictional letters I have Augustine send to X, I have freely paraphrased Augustine's own words taken from the *Confessions*, as well as letters and sermons from his life as priest and bishop. The voice that emerges is, therefore, Augustine more as he was to become than as he was at the historical date the events take place.

Recent history has often judged Augustine harshly, portraying him as a kill-joy lecturing primly against sex. He has also been accused of being a hypocrite for having enjoyed an illicit relationship for years and then preaching about chastity. This is due, I believe, to the fact that it is assumed the *Confessions* is the summation of Augustine's thought and life whereas it is only the beginning of his spiritual journey. The Christian Neoplatonism that marked his conversion would over time mature into a deeply sacramental understanding of the flesh and spirit aided, in part, by his campaigns against various gnostic sects during his life, including the Manichees, the Donatists, and the Pelagians.

The mature Augustine would cause rioting in his church when he gave a sermon criticizing men for saying women were weak when they themselves were committing adultery and fornication. The old and sick Augustine would make a final journey to a town on the coast to visit a young girl who had been kidnapped, raped, and then ransomed back to her parents by pirates. It had come to his attention that the townsfolk, and even the parents, regarded the girl as "defiled." He spent more than an hour talking with the girl alone and then emerged to sternly tell the parents and town that the girl was the innocent victim of sin and not the perpetrator. For his time, this was a radical stance to take toward women.

It is worth noting that in the Middle Ages, Augustine was regarded as the Saint of Love and is often depicted in paintings holding a large red heart with flames shooting out of it. Today, we tend to see him puritanically wagging his finger at us. Augustine would have roared with laughter at this. He was a passionate, fiercely intelligent, humorous man with a gift for friendship. It seemed to me that only a similarly remarkable woman would have fallen in love with such a man. For a balanced portrait of this great man, I recommend Peter Brown's magisterial biography, *Augustine of Hippo*, to which I am deeply indebted.

Finally, it is my hope that this novel will bring X, Augustine, Monica, Nebridius, and Adeodatus to life so that you may love them as I have grown to love them.

DISCUSSION QUESTIONS

1. As a woman in the ancient world, X's options are very limited: not only is she a female and, thus, without legal status, but she is poor—and not a Roman citizen. Do you think she makes the right decision in agreeing to become Augustine's concubine or do you think she should have married Paulinus, the man her aunt chose for her? What would you have done?
2. Augustine is obviously a restless soul. As he famously said: "Our hearts are restless until they rest in thee, O, God." Do you find it believable that the concubine could have loved such a man given their differences in social status and education? Do you think she shows great courage in love or great naivete?
3. Does her decision to leave Augustine for the sake of his career shock you or do you admire her for her self-sacrifice?
4. Do you think that X should have been more guarded in her relationship with Monica? Do you think that Monica truly loves her as a daughter or has she only got her own son's interests at heart?
5. Do you think Monica is a good person or is she the proverbial passive/aggressive mother-in-law?
6. In the ancient world, men and women led much more segregated lives than they do today. Did you find this distinction between the public world of men and the

domestic world of women jarring? Do you think the women characters in the novel are diminished because their sphere of influence is limited to that of the home and family? Do the women in the novel have attributes of character that may have been lost or forgotten in our contemporary world?

7. Childbearing and childbirth were the dominant realities for women in the ancient world. Do you think this limits the female characters or reveals a hidden strength that is often overlooked and undervalued in our own time?
8. Does the concubine's decision to leave her son shock you? Do you think she is a bad mother?
9. Do you find it believable that X frees her slaves? What would you have done?
10. One of the recurring themes in the story is the conflict between "flesh" and "spirit." Augustine in particular struggles with the nature of the body. Do you think X helps him to change or grow with regard to these issues?
11. In the forty years that X and Augustine live apart, do you think X still loves him? Do you think Augustine still loves her? Why do you think she goes to Hippo Regius to be at his deathbed? Do you think her decision to go is a sign of weakness or of strength?
12. X states plainly that she neither prays to the Punic gods nor to the Christian God. Her reasoning is that the Christian God "took too much from me." Do you consider this a sign of her integrity or spiritual blindness? When Augustine converts, do you think she should have followed suit? Do you admire or feel critical of this independence?

ACKNOWLEDGMENTS

I want to thank Daisy Blackwell Hutton, fiction publisher at HarperCollins Christian Publishing, who has been a tireless advocate of this book and whose editorial suggestions returned me to the story with renewed vision. I also want to thank Ellen Tarver for her superb line edits and Carol Mann, my agent. I am enormously grateful to Dr. Owen Ewald, C. May Marston Assistant Professor of Classical Languages and Civilizations at Seattle Pacific University, who graciously agreed to read the completed manuscript with an eye to historical inaccuracies and errors. Thanks also to my friend and colleague at Seattle Pacific University, Dr. Christine Chaney, who as former chair of the English department worked on my behalf in a variety of ways.

Many, many thanks to Jim and Bev Ohlman as well as Terry and Corrie Moore who allowed me to live in their beautiful Orcas Island homes for long stretches over the past four years so I could write amidst the tranquility and beauty of the San Juan Islands.

This book has consumed the last eight years of my life, and I could not have accomplished this without the love and support of my husband, Gregory Wolfe, and my children, Magdalen, Helena,

Charles, and Benedict. Gregory is, and always has been, my first reader and editor; his critiques and advice have made this the book I wanted to write. My children have patiently endured their mother's obsessiveness and exhaustion not only without complaint but with great charity. Thanks, guys. I can never repay the debt I owe you.

ABOUT THE AUTHOR

Wolfe-Blevins Photography

Suzanne M. Wolfe grew up in Manchester, England, and read English Literature at Oxford University, where she cofounded the Oxford C.S. Lewis Society. She is Writer in Residence at Seattle Pacific University and has taught literature and creative writing there since 2000. Wolfe is the author of *Unveiling: A Novel* (Paraclete Press, 2004) and co-founder, along with her husband, of *Image*, a journal of the arts and faith. Suzanne and Greg have also co-authored many books on literature and prayer and are the parents of four grown children. They live outside of Seattle.

Visit the author's website at www.suzannemwolfe.com.